"I do not frighten you, Miss Hunter? A brave young lady! I am, according to my own cousin, a scoundrel and a blackguard. Each member of the household has given me some token of their wealth. Since you are determined to be included in this family scene, is there nothing you can contribute to my venality? Nothing I can steal from you?"

Catherine hated the way she knew the color was rising in her cheeks, as Dagonet slowly walked towards her. Yet there was something so magnetic and powerful about him, that she could not even have glanced away.

"A lock of hair, perhaps?" he said smiling, as he reached long fingers to her cheek. He smelt wonderful: of clean masculine soap and the outdoors and very faintly of brandy. With astonishment she saw in his eyes the last expression she would have expected: they were alight with suppressed laughter. "If you have nothing else, I shall have to steal a kiss." As she gasped aloud and before she could turn away, he had bent her head to his and the fine lips closed firmly over hers. His muscular arms held her in a firm grip; but even if they had not, would she have pulled away?

*   *   *

Praise for Jean Ewing's SCANDAL'S REWARD:

"Compelling reading from a rising star in Regency fiction."
—Mary Kingsley

"Jean Ewing writes with true Regency wit and charm. In SCANDAL'S REWARD she creates a delightful novel with an intriguing rascal of a hero who will capture every reader's heart."

—Jo Beverley

ZEBRA'S REGENCY ROMANCES
DAZZLE AND DELIGHT

A BEGUILING INTRIGUE   (4441, $3.99)
by Olivia Sumner

Pretty as a picture Justine Riggs cared nothing for propriety. She dressed as a boy, sat on her horse like a jockey, and pondered the stars like a scientist. But when she tried to best the handsome Quenton Fletcher, Marquess of Devon, by proving that she was the better equestrian, he would try to prove Justine's antics were pure folly. The game he had in mind was seduction—never imagining that he might lose his heart in the process!

AN INCONVENIENT ENGAGEMENT   (4442, $3.99)
by Joy Reed

Rebecca Wentworth was furious when she saw her betrothed waltzing with another. So she decides to make him jealous by flirting with the handsomest man at the ball, John Collinwood, Earl of Stanford. The "wicked" nobleman knew exactly what the enticing miss was up to—and he was only too happy to play along. But as Rebecca gazed into his magnificent eyes, her errant fiancé was soon utterly forgotten!

SCANDAL'S LADY   (4472, $3.99)
by Mary Kingsley

Cassandra was shocked to learn that the new Earl of Lynton was her childhood friend, Nicholas St. John. After years at sea and mixed feelings Nicholas had come home to take the family title. And although Cassandra knew her place as a governess, she could not help the thrill that went through her each time he was near. Nicholas was pleased to find that his old friend Cassandra was his new next door neighbor, but after being near her, he wondered if mere friendship would be enough . . .

HIS LORDSHIP'S REWARD   (4473, $3.99)
by Carola Dunn

As the daughter of a seasoned soldier, Fanny Ingram was accustomed to the vagaries of military life and cared not a whit about matters of rank and social standing. So she certainly never foresaw her *tendre* for handsome Viscount Roworth of Kent with whom she was forced to share lodgings, while he carried out his clandestine activities on behalf of the British Army. And though good sense told Roworth to keep his distance, he couldn't stop from taking Fanny in his arms for a kiss that made all hearts equal!

Scandal's Reward

Jean R. Ewing

ZEBRA BOOKS
KENSINGTON PUBLISHING CORP.

ZEBRA BOOKS are published by

Kensington Publishing Corp.
850 Third Avenue
New York, NY 10022

Zebra and the Z logo Reg. U.S. Pat. & TM Off.

First Printing: August, 1994

Printed in the United States of America

For Gemma and David
with love and appreciation
for the years at Highfields House.

"Reputation is an idle and most false imposition;
oft got without merit, and lost without deserving."
—*William Shakespeare,* Othello

1

"Oh, Cathy, you shall not do it! I could never forgive myself, if I thought that my sister had sacrificed herself for my sake. Mama, say that Cathy shall not do it!"

Mrs. Hunter, who sat with composure at her needle-work beside the small vicarage fire, cast a shrewd glance at her two eldest daughters. Catherine was calmly folding and putting away her harpsichord music; while Amelia, who had been helping her, now stood hem-deep in the pages that had just dropped from her fingers.

"Pray, do not be such a pea goose, Amelia," answered Catherine Hunter, with just a hint of a smile lurking at the corners of her generous mouth. "I am not, like Iphigenia, about to be immolated! On the contrary, Lady Montagu has the most beautiful pianoforte, and I am to be treated quite as one of the family. I intend to enjoy the post, and if the alternative is marriage with Mr. Crucible, then I assure you that my mind is quite made up."

"But to become a paid companion! If Captain Morris had not come to speak to Papa for my hand, I know you would not have done it."

Neither of the girls was dressed in the first stare of fashion, but Amelia's ivory muslin set off her golden beauty, and Catherine had so much natural grace, she looked elegant even in her simple green jaconet. Their mother's glance was full of affection for them both. Of course, it would have been preferable for Catherine, as the eldest, to marry first, but Mrs. Hunter was afraid her bold sense of independence was not what the eligible young men of the neighborhood usually found attractive. When Catherine, in spite of a complete lack of encouragement on her part, had mysteriously gained the attentions of the impossible Mr. Crucible and that gentleman had insisted on making her an offer, the entire family had found it a wonderful joke. She wondered now, however, if Catherine's pride had not been rather wounded after all: that she could elicit no better offer, when Amelia had been able to win the heart of someone as eligible as Captain Morris. If taking a post as companion to Lady Montagu would help her to forget the humiliation, then it was all to the good.

"You display an excess of sensibility, Amelia." Mrs. Hunter's motherly voice was as calm and rational as always. "Catherine knows perfectly well that she was under no obligation to accept either this post or Mr. Crucible's offer, and may stay quietly at home here with us. It is all her own idea to leave before your wedding, but the Reverend Hunter and I have no objection. Lion Court is, after all, the most prominent place in this part of Exmoor. It is still the property of Lady Montagu's father, Percival, Lord Blythe, even though he lives in Bath, and he *is* the Marquis of Somerdale. For Miss Hunter to take a post with Lady Montagu, now that she is widowed, is quite unexceptionable."

"Come, Amelia," said Catherine, linking her arm affectionately with her sister's, her eyes alight with laughter. "It isn't a three-act tragedy! As daughters of a country parson, none of us may be independent, you know. Unfortunately, we have not all been endowed with your ravishing blond curls and blue eyes, so that we may attract the attention of such handsome young gentlemen as your Captain Morris. I know you would rather I was married first, but if Mr. Crucible represents the kind of offer I am likely to receive, David Morris would pine away to a shadow waiting for the nuptials. I am two and twenty, Amy, positively on the shelf! I do not, however, intend to age sadly in my father's parlor like some worn-out overstuffed cushion; there for occasional support, but neither really decorative nor useful."

"How can you speak such fustian? I know you are teasing me!" persisted Amelia, for whom life could hold no other possible attractions at the present than immediate matrimony. "Mr. Crucible is not what anyone would wish, of course, but there are other gentlemen. You have the finest eyes in the world, and Nurse always said you had the best bone structure of any of us, the kind that would last."

"So I shall become a handsome old lady!" laughed Catherine, entirely without rancor. "I also have the dullest brown hair, not a single rosebud in my cheek, and am quite three inches too tall. I shall make a most seemly lady's companion, and Lion Court will suit me very well. Lady Montagu may even go to London, and you know how I have longed to travel. So your concerns are entirely misplaced, and even with both of us gone, Mama will still have four daughters on her hands."

Amelia was not to be so easily persuaded. She turned her limpid blue eyes on her father, who sat opposite his wife at the modest basket fireplace. He had already lifted his gaze from the book which lay in his lap. "Can you truly like it, Papa? Was there not some dreadful scandal at Lion Court some years ago?"

"Catherine shall do as she thinks best, pet. Nothing that occurred then at Lion Court can possibly affect her taking a post as companion to Lady Montagu."

And that was too much for twelve-year-old Annabella Hunter, who had been sitting in a concentrated silence throughout the previous conversation. It was an unusual state for Annie, but she had noticed that the evening was drawing in to that point where, unless she remained unnoticed, she would be sent upstairs to join her three little sisters, who were presumably snugly abed and long since asleep. She didn't mean to listen where it was none of her business, but if both Catherine and Amelia were to leave home, then she might be able to have their bedroom, and not have to share with the little ones in the nursery any longer. She had also been trying quite hard to remember who Iphigenia was—she was sure it had something to do with the Trojan War and Agamemnon, and that a goddess had rescued her before she was actually sacrificed—when she heard reference to the old scandal. Her eyes opened wide. "It was about Devil Dagonet, wasn't it?" she squealed, her plan of silence forgotten, and then blushed painfully as four pairs of eyes turned in her direction.

"Charles de Dagonet has been gone from Lion Court for seven years," said her father sternly, "at which time you were five years old. Pray, miss, what can you know of the matter?"

Annabella was scarlet, but she defiantly stuck out her chin. "I heard Cook and Polly talking one day. They said he was wilder than Beelzebub, and could kill a man with his sword, and played sailors' songs on the organ, and he jumped his horse through the church lych-gate for a wager. But his grandfather cut him off without a penny, because he drowned a maidservant in the Lion Court Lake and held her under until she turned blue. And Polly said that still he was an awful dashing young gentleman, and had tons of lovers!"

"Miss Annabella Hunter! You will apologize to your mother and sisters. Go to bed this instant!"

Annie, her face a flag of embarrassment, mumbled something inaudible and charged from the room. Mrs. Hunter tried to swallow her smile and look serious. "I shall have to talk to Cook, Reverend Hunter. How could she be so careless in front of the child? Of course, the circumstances of the drowning were the *on dit* of the time, but to think that the servants should still talk of it, and fill Annie's head with such nonsense!"

Catherine laughed and moved from the harpsichord where she had earlier been playing, to sit beside her father. "Devil Dagonet! To think that I am to live in the household which produced such a famous reprobate! Of course, neither Amy nor I ever met him, but I do remember some infamous tales of his exploits!"

"It was very shocking," began her mother. Mrs. Hunter had seen enough of the ways of the world in her time as a country parson's wife to take a great deal in her stride. "He became quite the black sheep of the family! He was half French, of course, even if he was born and raised at Lion Court." Her tone implied a certain disapproval of anyone with a French father, however blue the blood on both sides. Every red-blooded English citizen knew that the French were an outlandish lot. "Yet it seemed to me that there was no real harm in him, just high spirits; and he was, after all, an orphan. Let me see now, he must have been about ten years old when his parents were killed, and the Marquis had Sir Henry

Montagu move in and become his guardian. Lady Montagu and Dagonet's mother were sisters, you see; the Marquis had no sons. They called him Devil Dagonet: he had a ruthless charm even as a boy. It must have been very hard for him to have his uncle's family take over Lion Court, and feel displaced in his own home by his cousin. Yet I'm afraid Dagonet would always put Sir Henry's own son George in the shade. The boys were the same age; but Charles was his grandfather's favorite. It was always expected that Lord Blythe would deed Lion Court to him when he came of age. Not surprisingly, I believe Sir Henry was rather rough on the lad. At any rate, Charles de Dagonet ran wild."

"He did jump a horse through the lych-gate, didn't he?" exclaimed Amelia.

The lych-gate at the Fernbridge church was a famous historic landmark. It was a funny little structure with a low thatched roof supported by four carved pillars at the entry to the churchyard. The pillars were surrounded by a stone wall with a wooden gate at the front and back. Inside the enclosed space were two benches, one on each side. How anyone could jump a horse through such a tight space, Catherine had no idea.

"Yes, and it set the parish all by the ears!" Mrs. Hunter gave a wry smile. "It was two years after Trafalgar. You must have been fifteen years old, Catherine, which, now I come to think about it, was the same age as poor Millicent Trumble, the girl that was drowned. Charles de Dagonet and his cousin George Montagu were both down from Oxford for the summer. I believe that George's sister Charlotte and her husband, Mr. Clay, were also staying at Lion Court earlier that year. Devil Dagonet was a fearless horseman. I think he would have taken any wager. His father was the Comte de Dagonet, you know. No doubt Dagonet shared the usual faults of his class!"

"No wonder," commented Catherine dryly. "With Sir Henry Montagu as his guardian. Don't you recall, Amy, how Sir Henry caught us trespassing in Rye Water as little girls? I thought he would take his horse whip to us!"

"That's as may be," continued their mother. "Sir Henry was a hard man, and young Dagonet seemed to take delight in defying him. It went too far when one of the maidservants was involved in his adventures, and she was found drowned."

"And he was thought to have killed her?" asked Catherine.

"Nothing could be proved," replied the Reverend. "The circumstances of the drowning were rather a mystery, you see. But there was a great deal of talk, and either way Dagonet was seen to be responsible for Millicent Trumble's death. There was the most dreadful family scene. Lord Blythe came down from Bath, and young Dagonet was shown the door. The Marquis changed his will, then and there, in favor of George Montagu, and Charles was completely disinherited. He couldn't stay in England after that, and he went for a soldier."

"How responsible? Perhaps she drowned herself in a fit of remorse," said Amelia, her blue eyes shining. "Did the dashing Dagonet entice her into holding up carriages after dark, or into stealing the family silver?"

"Oh no, she was an honest girl in that way, I'm sure. That was not the kind of trouble laid at Dagonet's door. No, poor Millicent was with child."

At which point Catherine wondered how on earth that interesting fact could have been kept from her all these years. Even though she and Amy had been away at the Young Ladies' Seminary in Exeter, she remembered the time of the drowning quite clearly. Her father had insisted on burying the girl in hallowed ground, which he should never have done if she had been a suicide. Surprisingly the Montagus had agreed, though in the eyes of the parish it was almost as good as admitting that they thought their own nephew had committed murder, as well as ravishment. She remembered Sir Henry Montagu as an unpleasant, florid-faced man with a loud voice. It had been seen as a great act of charity when he had moved his family into Lion Court and taken care of the orphaned Charles de Dagonet, even though, thanks to old Montagu's gaming debts, they had arrived penniless. The revenues of the Lion Court estates had saved them from Queer Street. The ancient grandfather, Lord Percival Blythe, owner of Lion Court and responsible for the arrival of the Montagus, was supposedly an irascible old man who had never approved of either daughter's marriage: the younger to a financially ruined, but otherwise impeccable sprig of the Montagu family, and the elder to a French count who lost everything in the Revolution, when his son Charles was a small boy, and then managed to kill both himself and his wife in a carriage accident some years later. The entire family, she supposed, had thus always been dependent on the old Marquis's good will, and it was Charles, his favorite, who had been the one to irrevocably destroy it. He may have turned out to be the black sheep, but still Catherine did not envy the wicked and fearless Charles de Dagonet his relations.

Well, she didn't see how any of it could possibly affect her. Devil Dagonet was not expected to show his face in Exmoor again. His cousin George Montagu now lived in London, as did the widowed sister, Charlotte—Mr. Clay had died soon after Dagonet had left England—and their father, Sir Henry Montagu, had collapsed of the apoplexy just the previous winter, leaving Lady Montagu a widow, alone at Lion Court. She had approached Catherine one Sunday after church, and then offered her the post of companion. Lady Montagu was certainly a little pathetic, but only lonely and vulnerable. The arrangement seemed acceptable—and as Catherine had never tried to hide—very preferable to Mr. Crucible's absurd and unwelcome attentions. But as she had not admitted to Amelia, it was indeed her sister's impending marriage to Capt. David Morris that had led her finally to accept. Her pride alone forbade her from staying on at home. Besides, Annabella was growing up, the vicarage was small; at twenty-two the eldest should move out and make room for her little sisters.

Mrs. Hunter had risen to her feet. "Well, I shall go up to poor Annie; she has probably cried enough by now."

"Then I shall come up with you, Mama," said Amelia, kissing her father on his balding pate, "and go to bed. Captain Morris is to take me out in his curricle tomorrow, and I must look my best. I have a new poke bonnet to wear; it's the very latest twig!"

When they had gone, Catherine turned to her father. He seemed lost in thought. "Sir Henry Montagu believed Millicent Trumble's death was Dagonet's fault, didn't he? And the Marquis? No wonder they flew up into the boughs, and he was cast off by the family! I remember, when I was quite a little girl, you used to go up to Lion Court and tutor the cousins in their Latin and Greek. What manner of boy was this Charles de Dagonet? Did you think he would grow up to be capable of ruining a girl and then drowning her?"

The Reverend Hunter looked up and smiled at her. Catherine did not quite realize that he hadn't really answered her, when he said: "It was a great tragedy, my dear. Charles de Dagonet was a remarkable young man. He was capable of anything."

Ten minutes later, Catherine was brushing out her hair; which, while certainly a deep russet brown, was by no means dull. Her sister watched her across the little bedchamber that they shared. Amelia's perfect dimpled chin was resting on her folded arms, supported by her knees beneath the quilted cover of her bed. Her golden hair lay around her shoulders like a halo. "I wish I could have met him," she said to her sister.

"Who?" Catherine was not thinking about the conversation they had exchanged downstairs, but about her father. Six daughters were a dreadful burden for a country vicar. She had definitely made the right decision. Indeed, she should have acted before, instead of waiting at home in the vain hope that a Prince Charming would turn up for her, as he had for Amelia.

"Devil Dagonet, of course."

"Amy! He sounds like a complete renegade. He was said to be quite ruthless!"

"But don't you think it's really the most romantic thing? That our own neighbor should grow up to be so profligate, and be disinherited? Suppose he should come back and fight Sir George Montagu for Lion Court!"

Catherine laughed aloud. "Amy, we are living in the nineteenth century, and this is England. I should not imagine that Devil Dagonet will ever come back to Exmoor. Anyway, it's not in the least romantic. He must have been dreadful to earn such a name."

"No, just the opposite, according to Polly." Amelia's blush wasn't that different from her little sister Annie's. "I asked her when I came up to bed. The country people and the servants all liked him. It was only because of his reputation with the ladies that they called him Devil Dagonet."

"Well, it can hardly matter now what kind of a libertine he turned out to be." Catherine slipped between her covers and blew out the candles. Her next remark was made to the sweet summer darkness, that filled the air like a fluid. "I think we can be certain that none of us will ever have the misfortune to meet him."

Some days later, Catherine tied the strings of her chip bonnet firmly under her chin, and, climbing up out of Fernbridge, headed for the moor. The morning sky shone bright and clear, and the heather-scented heights beckoned. It was the last day of August and her final day of freedom, before she began what she firmly expected to be an extremely uneventful time at Lion Court. Within a couple of hours, she had reached the slopes of Stag Hill, overlooking the entire Rye Water valley and the Lion Court estates. There was one better vantage point, on Eagle Beacon itself; but it was a steep scramble from where she was standing, through the swamps at the head of Rye Water. The track that led there was extremely hazardous unless you knew it well, which was why Catherine was so surprised to see that a horseman was cantering that way with careless abandon. He wore a serviceable dark coat over plain buckskin breeches; leather saddlebags and a sword case were strapped behind him. Since she had never seen such a magnificent gray thoroughbred before, she knew that it must be a stranger. Unless he slowed his pace, he was putting both himself and his mount in considerable danger. Casting caution to the wind, she called out and began to run down the rock-strewn slope towards him. "Sir! Sir! Pray stop! You will be into the bog!"

She tore off her bonnet and waved it wildly in one hand as she ran: he must notice her! With an extra burst of effort, she managed to reach the track just as the gray spun around a bend towards her. There was a little slope of short damp grass just above the muddy path, and as the heel of her boot struck it, her feet went from under her, so that she sprawled onto the track at the very feet of the horse. The thoroughbred reared, giving her an uncomfortable view of his iron-shod hooves, but the rider expertly spun him away and pulled him to a halt just three feet from her shoulder.

"Good God, you little idiot! Whatever do you think you're doing?"

Catherine sat up, and tried to regain some sense of dignity. She was displaying an unconscionable length of white petticoat and silk stocking, now splattered with mud. She had never felt herself to be at such an awkward disadvantage. "You are a stranger here, sir. This track is dangerous, and I thought to warn you."

"The only danger is caused by your impetuous and unnecessary interference! You could have been killed." The tanned face that looked down at her was carved as if from stone. Brilliant green eyes under straight black brows gazed directly into her face, but he made no move to help her.

"I think you might dismount and offer me some assistance!" She stared back up at him. Really, he had the longest black eyelashes she had ever seen on a man.

His face was instantly transformed by a charming smile. "You seem to be unhurt and able to regain your feet by yourself," he said lightly. "My close proximity is usually considered perilous to unchaperoned young ladies."

"What?" she shot back without thinking. "Do you make a habit of ravishing any female that crosses your path?" She struggled to her feet. She had entirely smashed her straw bonnet in her hand when she fell, so she was unable to put it back on. Instead she thrust it behind her. There was a smear of green stain right down the back of her muslin skirt, and one of the flounces was torn.

He raised an eyebrow, and the emerald gaze swept over her in the most insolent manner. "Only those who are capable of displaying some feminine charm, alas; not hoydens who fling themselves at my feet like some screaming dervish."

"I am not a dervish!" Catherine became uncomfortably aware that this was not at all a proper conversation for her to be having with a total stranger. She attempted to return to safer ground. "The moor is full of hidden traps for a horseman. The bogs cannot be seen, until you are in them. You might thank me for my efforts."

"Cassandra also received no thanks for her warnings of Doom."

"Like Cassandra, I am only trying to save you from disaster!"

With a grim laugh he reined his mount away from her. "I may need saving, young lady, but not from the hazards of riding a horse! Good day!"

And with that, he touched his horse with his leg and the gray bounded away, leaving Catherine standing speechless with anger on the path. What an insufferably rude and arrogant man! Well, he was probably no more than some officer passing through on his return from France. England was full of retired soldiers now that

Napoleon was safely imprisoned on Elba. Nevertheless, he should not get away with the parting shot!

"I hope you drown in Rye Combe Bog!" she shouted at the retreating back.

2

Lion Court was a pleasant, ivy-covered edifice that had been, at the time of Good Queen Bess, the home of a wealthy wool merchant. The house, solidly built of the local stone, enclosed three sides of a courtyard and presided over several topiary box bushes, like a hen with her chicks. The stone lions which had given the house its name had weathered and crumbled, until they had the rounded, toothless look of pug dog puppies, begging.

Catherine loved the place. To the north she could just catch a glimpse of the sea in the Bristol Channel, with the hills of Wales faintly shadowing the horizon. To the south behind her rose the purple tops of Exmoor, home to wild ponies and red deer. Out of sight to the west lay the whitewashed village and church of Fernbridge by its pebbled beach, where her father had his living. And, a little further along the coast, stood small, elegant Stagshead, set back from the road in its ancient grounds; the home of Capt. David Morris who, returning from the Peninsular Campaign when Napoleon was defeated, had come into his inheritance and won her sister's heart.

Up behind Lion Court marched woods of beech and oak, ash and birch, and below and through them, like a slash in a bread loaf, tumbled Rye Water, carrying the rain from the moor to the sea. The stretch of Rye Water which ran past the house had been tamed with plantings and little iron railings. There was an artificial grotto with a marble nymph forever pouring water from an urn, where she and Amelia had been caught trespassing as children. Within half a mile upstream of the curved ornamental bridge and the water lilies, however, the stream coursed wild through its craggy little gorge, full of mosses and light-shading ferns, from the boggy heights of Eagle Beacon. And at one place, below the stables and barns, past the birch spinney, Rye Water emptied into the pleasant, leaf-shaded lake where poor Millicent Trumble had been found drowned seven years before.

Lady Montagu was not elderly, perhaps only fifty-six or seven, but she was bored and fainthearted. Catherine read to her in the evenings, or played hour upon hour at the piano and sang. In the day she would accompany her in little drives in a dog cart, or on sketching expeditions around the estate, or perhaps just fetch and carry, while Lady Montagu worked listlessly at embroidery or drawn-thread work.

The house and grounds entranced her. It was an old-fashioned house, full of interesting nooks and crannies. Over the centuries, various owners had carried out their improvement schemes, so that the withdrawing and dining rooms boasted beautiful Jacobean plaster ceilings, while the great hall downstairs still displayed its massive Tudor beams, curving away into the roof space. There was an eclectic collection of furnishings, representing much of the past two hundred years, but each piece settled in next to its neighbor in complete harmony. It seemed to Catherine that the house had always been loved by its occupants, except perhaps by Sir Henry

Montagu. No one could claim that the atmosphere had been happy, after he had moved in with his family—what?—seventeen years ago. Even now that he was gone, the lovely rooms still seemed forlorn and sad. The house must once have resounded to the laughter of large families and good-fellowship. Even though Sir Henry had been dead for over a year, it was as if the Queen Anne dressers and Persian carpets still couldn't quite shake off his baleful influence.

Catherine had been at Lion Court less than a week, when one afternoon she heard the rattle of a large carriage as it pulled into the courtyard, accompanied by outriders and followed by a baggage cart. She and Lady Montagu had just come in from a walk on the terrace past the glorious display of flowers in the gardens, and she had gone upstairs to remove her bonnet. From the head of the stairs, she heard loud voices and squeals of feminine delight, followed by the gruff tones of a man.

"By the devil, don't take on so, Mama! You'll bring on palpitations. Anyone would think you hadn't seen me in years. Deuced miserable journey, rained all the way from London to Bath. Dashed if I wasn't ready to turn around more than once, but Charlotte wouldn't hear of it."

The widowed Mrs. Clay kissed her mother on the cheek. "George is the most impossible traveling companion, Mama. I declare he takes a delight in discomfort and complaint. Dear Mr. Clay was always so proficient in arranging everything to one's satisfaction when traveling."

"Good God, Charlotte! If I hear one more word about your sainted husband, I shall go mad. Dear Mr. Clay this, beloved Mr. Clay that. It's enough to send a fellow to perdition, and damme if the chap hasn't been dead these seven years, and was a dreadful dull stick when he was alive!"

An attack of the vapors was the only possible response to that, so Catherine decided that it was an opportune moment to make herself known. She moved down the stairs and approached the little group. Charlotte had begun to gasp and clutch at her throat, but at the interruption, she immediately swung around and peered at Catherine through her quizzing glass below heavily plucked brows. "So this is your companion from the vicarage, Mama? How quaint! Of course, I should see hiring a female companion as an affront to the memory of dear Mr. Clay, the only true soul mate I shall have in this life. How do you do, Miss Hunter? I declare you quite tower over Lady Montagu, and that is not a flattering gown. But don't mind me! I believe in plain speaking; Mr. Clay always advised plain speaking." And with another absent peck at her mother's cheek, Charlotte Clay swept away up the stairs to her room.

Charlotte was ten years her brother's senior. They could not expect to be particularly close. She had in fact, to the dismay of her family, run away to be married at the tender age of seventeen, three years before the family had come to live at Lion Court. That Mr. Clay had unexpectedly inherited a great deal of money, however, had done much to soothe the ruffled feelings of Sir Henry and Lady Montagu, and then when he had shown the good grace to die and leave his wife the fortune, the fact that their only daughter had eloped was entirely forgotten. Charlotte Clay had her own establishment in London, where she was able to enjoy the giddy life of the *beau monde* as a respectable, childless widow, past the age, at thirty-seven, of being expected to compete in the marriage mart. George, on the contrary, was still entirely dependent on his grandfather for his allowance. The difference grated.

"Dang me, if it ain't a trial to have an older sister! Charlotte would stop at Bath to visit grandfather. Old Percy must be eighty if he's a day, and he was having the worst attack of the gout. Just about had his manservant throw us out! Been taking the waters, he said, and didn't need a lot of money-grubbing relatives trying to hurry him into his grave. He may be your father, Mama, but he's a damned old curmudgeon!"

Lady Montagu, who had been clinging all this time to her son's arm, was being shaken off, none too gently, so she released him and straightened her cap. "Yes, well, apart from Charlotte, we are all dependent on him for everything. He was very overset about what happened with Dagonet, you know. I'm surprised it didn't kill him, when he struck him from the will. You know Dagonet was always the favorite and Lion Court was always expected to go to him, just as my sister was the favorite when we were girls. But Lord Blythe has left you his fortune now and makes you the most generous allowance; it is only right that you should pay him your respects."

"Well, Charlotte would bore on to grandfather about Mr. Clay, until I thought he would strike me from the will there and then. And she had to indulge in a fit of plain speaking about his drinking too much port. I thought the old miser would have apoplexy! Say, isn't there anywhere a fellow can get a drink in this house?"

Lady Montagu instantly, with a touching solicitation, began to shepherd her son towards the drawing room, and Catherine tactfully began to make her escape, when for no reason she could name, George's next remark made her stop, her pulse suddenly unsteady. "Actually it's because of Devil Dagonet that Charlotte and I decided to come down, Mama. Now that the war's over, he can't make a living as a soldier anymore. I heard he's already been seen in England. Now, don't turn vaporish! I've prepared a suitable reception, should he dare to show his face here at Lion Court."

George and Charlotte were, of course, expected. Catherine had helped prepare for their visit, principally by running up and downstairs with the housekeeper and seeing to everything herself, while her mistress lay prostrate with expectation on the drawing room couch. George was to occupy the room he had used as a child, and Charlotte the best blue guest chamber. They were both handsome rooms in the most modern wing, with large marble fireplaces and sweeping views of the grounds. She was not sure why, when she had been standing with the housekeeper in the gracious hallway before George's bedroom door, she had suddenly said, "Where did Charles de Dagonet have his room? I see no other suitable bedchamber in this wing." It had already struck her that there was not a single portrait of the de Dagonet family on display in the house. Until George's arrival, the name of Devil Dagonet had not been mentioned; nor did Lady Montagu ever talk about her deceased sister. One would think that they had never lived there.

"No, ma'am. After the Montagus moved in, George took his cousin's room, and young Master Charles moved up over there."

And why had she then gone where the housekeeper pointed, up the winding stair and along the balcony that ran around the library into the little chamber that the orphaned boy had been given after the arrival of his relatives at Lion Court, and which he had left, ten years later, in such disgrace? The room was an oddity, tucked in below the roof and above the entrance hall, and Spartan in its furnishings. It commanded views of the drive in three directions, from a bank of ornamental windows. It could not have been intended as a bedchamber, because there was no fireplace, and in winter the little room could only have been damp and cold. Now, however, with the early September sunlight streaming in the south windows, it was positively stuffy instead. Catherine opened a casement. The room was not dusty, nowhere in Lion Court escaped the efficient ministrations of its army of servants, but it couldn't have been used since Dagonet had left. Curious, she ran her finger along the rank of books and papers above the narrow bed. There were titles in Greek and Latin, French and English. She stopped and pulled out several thin volumes. They were musical scores: music for violin, piano, harpsichord, all the great composers and some more obscure. Songs and sonnets were set to music in a flowing creative hand, many she was sure, quite original. Catherine sat down suddenly. Whatever she had expected, it had not been this. It made no sense at all. He had been known as a daredevil and an athlete. "It must have been very hard for him," her mother had said. He had liked music! A misfit in this blunt household with the red-faced Sir Henry. Yet he had casually destroyed poor Milly Trumble. What was the truth about him? How had the country people's hero gained such a dreadful reputation? She had a sudden vision of a ten-year-old boy, waiting at home for the return of his beloved parents. His face must have lit up when he heard a carriage pull into the drive at last. What a terrible blow it must have been when instead his uncle, Sir Henry Montagu, had descended with news of the fatal accident. Had it been broken to him with any

gentleness or understanding at all? From what she knew
of Sir Henry, she doubted it. Catherine replaced everything with care, and went down thoughtfully to rejoin
Lady Montagu and her children.

She was to play for them all after dinner. It had been
a little uncomfortable during the meal, since Lady Montagu insisted over Charlotte's finer sensibilities that her
companion dine with the family. Catherine had tried to
keep the peace by at least dressing plainly, and conduct-
ing herself as meekly as possible. She wore a simple dark
green dress that was cut high to the neck and possessed
only one deep flounce around the hem. As if to empha-
size their difference in social status, Charlotte was ar-
rayed in a dazzle of jewels. Diamond pendants swung
from her ears, and a matching necklace lay around her
short neck above the décolletage of her puce silk. Even
Lady Montagu wore a set of pearls that Catherine had
never seen before, and George's elaborate neckcloth was
pinned with a diamond which matched the small jewel
on the face of his fob.

"The necklace becomes you, Mama," said George, as
they all went into the drawing room and Catherine
folded back the lid of the piano. "I don't know why you
didn't think it right to wear it." He winked at Charlotte.

"That is such a common gesture, George! The pearls
look very well, Mama, but to speak plainly, they would be
better suited to a younger lady. I only wish Mr. Clay
might have seen me in these." She patted the earrings.
"He liked to see me wear fine gems."

"I own I cannot really like it, George," insisted Lady
Montagu. "We really have no right, even at a family
dinner."

"Yes, just a trifle vulgar, wouldn't you say?" said a
strange voice in dulcet tones.

A man stepped from the shadows at the corner of the room. He moved with the power and grace of a tiger. The muscled limbs and broad shoulders were elegantly dressed in immaculate evening clothes, and his dark head was bare. In his right hand, almost casually, he held a pistol which seemed to have an unerring attraction for George's capacious chest. Lady Montagu uttered a small scream and sat down. Catherine quietly put down the music book and stood, her heart thudding, beside the piano.

"What the devil do you mean by this, sir?" sputtered George, his face puce above the folds of his cravat.

The stranger moved a little further into the candle-light. His gaze was a deep green, and fathomless, like the sea. It was the rider of the gray thoroughbred.

"What, no warm welcome for the prodigal returned from the pigsty, Charlotte? And Cousin George? You look as if the ghost had just appeared before you on the battlements: 'How now, Horatio! you tremble and look pale: / Is not this something more than fantasy?' I am not the harbinger of doom, my dears, only cousin Dagonet, come back from Spain. Perfectly harmless, really."

"The servants had instructions to show you the door, sir, as a scoundrel and a blackguard, if you ever showed your face here again!"

"Don't be pompous, George, it doesn't become you. I was, of course, turned away when I humbly presented myself at the front door. Such a lamentable lack of family feeling. But no matter, he who is denied entrance by the door, must needs come in at the window."

"What can you want here?" cried Lady Montagu faintly. "Oh, this is all quite dreadful!"

"Then I am sorry to distress you, my lady," replied Dagonet with perfect courtesy. "But I came among other things for the family jewels. Don't move, George! If I were forced to kill you, there would be no male Montagu anymore, and no one to inherit Lion Court from our grandfather. Charlotte, you really should take a seat and close your mouth."

While George sputtered and the ladies wrung their hands, Devil Dagonet moved smoothly from one to another and divested them of their jewelry. Catherine, forgotten by the piano in her plain unadorned frock, moved as quietly as she might around the sofa and the Sheraton chairs, to the bellpull beside the fireplace. So the insolent stranger on the moor had been the notorious Dagonet. He should not get away with stealing the jewelry, if she could help it! She had the rope in her hand and was about to give it a mighty pull, when the entire length of silk cord, suddenly severed, slithered past her arm and coiled on the floor at her feet. A small knife, expertly thrown, quivered in the cornice above her head. He was looking straight at her, his eyebrows very slightly raised above the emerald eyes.

"I do not believe," said Dagonet with perfect grace, "that I have had the pleasure of making your acquaintance?"

Catherine was steadily meeting his gaze, her color high. Her dark brown hair was drawn back in a simple knot, which only accentuated high cheekbones and magnificent hazel eyes, lashed like a deer's. Her breath, coming rather fast, was making her breast rise and fall rapidly, in a fascinating contrast to her slim elegance.

"My name is Catherine Hunter, sir. I am Lady Montagu's companion. We met, in case you have forgotten, on the moor. It seemed to me to be about time to interrupt this melodramatic little scene, by inviting in some other members of the household. I don't suppose that even you can shoot both Sir George and the butler at the same time? However, you have severed the bellpull, and neatly prevented me from being the heroine of the hour."

"Ah, the servants." He stood for a moment, as if considering. The last thing he wanted was to involve a daughter of the Reverend Hunter, but he could not allow her to interfere. "Unaccountably, it has occurred to no one to scream, Miss Hunter. Perhaps the family do not wish any witnesses? Or," he looked straight at George, "perhaps they do not wish me to meet certain members of the staff?"

Catherine stood her ground. "Perhaps they are simply embarrassed by childish games. It is already distressful enough for Lady Montagu to have a nephew whose name is used to frighten children in the village, without having the pearls removed from around her neck in her own drawing room. Not having any such scruples myself, of course, I could very well cry out for help!"

"And I do not frighten you, Miss Hunter? A brave young lady! I am, according to my own cousin, my companion from childhood, a scoundrel and a blackguard. Each member of the household has given me some token of their wealth. Since you are determined to be included in this family scene, is there nothing you can contribute to my venality? Nothing I can steal from you?"

Catherine hated the way she knew the color was rising in her cheeks, as he slowly walked towards her. The sea-green gaze swept over her simple frock in the most insolent manner. For no good reason Annie's silly words kept running through her mind: "he's had tons of lovers," and Amy stating with such confidence: "It was because of his reputation with the ladies that they called him Devil Dagonet." He shall neither charm nor frighten me, she promised herself. He shall not! I shall scream, if he comes a step closer. Yet there was something so magnetic and powerful about him, that she could not even have glanced away.

"A lock of hair, perhaps?" he said smiling, as he stopped directly in front of her and reached long fingers to her cheek. He smelt wonderful: of clean masculine soap and the outdoors and very faintly of brandy. Defiantly she returned his gaze. With astonishment she saw in his eyes the last expression she would have expected. There was neither anger nor malice in the emerald depths: they were alight with suppressed laughter. "But I must not disappoint our audience. After all, I have my reputation to live up to." His hand brushed her neck. "If you have nothing else, I shall have to steal a kiss." As she gasped aloud and before she could turn away, he had bent her head to his and the fine lips closed firmly over hers. She was helpless with astonishment. Besides, his muscular arms held her in a firm grip; but even if they had not, would she have pulled away? She lost all sense of where she was: the candlelit room, its scandalized occupants, all disappeared from consciousness as unwittingly she gave herself up to his practiced embrace. Moments later he broke away and murmured against her ear, "I apologize for not being sucked down in Rye Combe Bog as you directed. It did display scurrilous manners not to instantly die so, after treating you so cavalierly. Though it is no excuse, I was rather preoccupied, and, of course, I have known the track perfectly well since childhood. I hope you will forgive me, Miss Hunter; but please don't call the servants. I don't want to have to slay any of the footmen."

Then he had pulled away and crossed the room. No one had moved, they stood like pawns awaiting the hand of the chess master. Dagonet laughed aloud. "I thank you all for your contributions." Turning to Catherine, he swept her a bow, then sat on the windowsill, folding the ladies' gems and George's pin and fob watch into his pocket handkerchief.

"Damn you, Dagonet! What do you intend to do with the jewels?" It was George, his face suffused with rage.

"Why, what would you expect me to do with family heirlooms? Sell them and support my dissolute lifestyle, of course."

"Then you can go to the devil!"

Dagonet's eyes opened a little in amused astonishment. "How can I possibly go, George, where I already reside?"

The curtains parted and fell together again, and he was gone. Then Catherine had her hands full with two hysterical women, and a puce-faced man who was throwing back glass after glass of brandy and doing nothing whatever to recover the stolen property. Suddenly, just as Catherine had finished with the burnt feathers and the smelling salts, George turned to the women and said, "What the deuce did he mean by that Horatio stuff? Damn him!"

Catherine was the only one who could answer. "William Shakespeare, Sir George. Hamlet, Act One," said the vicar's daughter. "When the ghost of his father appears to Hamlet. I believe Horatio replies: 'In what particular thought to work I know not; / But, in the gross and scope of my opinion, / This bodes some strange eruption to our state.' I fear we may be in for some disruption to our peace and tranquillity here at Lion Court."

3

Devil Dagonet rode straight along the coast road, through Fernbridge, to Stagshead. He had left his horse—since he had been so unceremoniously turned away from the stables—tied to the railings in the woods at Lion Court. At Stagshead, in contrast, he had no such difficulty, for he put his mount into a loose box and rubbed him down himself. A few minutes later he strode unchallenged into the study, poured himself a glass of brandy, and dropped with the simple ease of the athlete into a chair beside the fire. He propped his booted feet on the fender and leaned back, the firelight playing over the planes of his face. He appeared to be listening, and in a moment, quick footsteps sounded in the corridor, the door was flung open, and Capt. David Morris stood framed on the threshold. Dagonet casually turned his head, and at the look on the newcomer's face, burst out laughing.

"What did you fear? That I should be chained in a dungeon by my cousin, and removed forever from the company of civilized men? Fortunately, Lion Court doesn't possess an oubliette, much to my great regret as a boy. I will freely admit, however, that the meeting was quite unpleasant, and if Cousin George were a medieval baron and not a modern man-about-town, you might now be hearing the echoes of my groans, hollow in the moorland mists."

"But he must have been expecting you? Surely out of common courtesy, he would receive you with good grace? You are first cousins!"

"And blood is thicker than water? But, my honest friend, George Montagu has no blood in his veins, only bile. Of course, he was expecting me! I have written to him at least three times this last month. Any courtesy in our exchange, however, has been entirely on my side. His only response was a damnably rude warning to keep away. He was no more sympathetic in the flesh."

"So he refused you the house?"

"He did more. He had told the servants to set upon me with horsewhips. It was only my insufferable charm that persuaded them to desist, and the skills that we honed together in the Peninsula! So, after escaping from the dubious welcome of the henchmen, I crept in at the window instead, and awaited my loving relations in their own drawing room."

"Charles, you didn't!" Captain Morris poured himself a drink and sat down opposite his guest. His brow was still marred by a slight frown of anxiety.

Dagonet tossed back his brandy. "You should have been there! Not only did I enter the house like a common thief, but then conducted myself in a perfect imitation of Tom Faggus, the famous Exmoor highwayman. Here is my haul." He set down his glass, and the jewels slid from his pocket and lay bright in the candlelight across his lean hands. "Rather pretty, don't you think?"

Captain Morris leaned forward. "May I?" he said,

taking the diamonds. "These must be worth a fortune, Charles."

"Before the French Revolution my father had considerable wealth, and my mother, they say, was a beauty. The diamonds she wore at the court of Marie Antoinette, and sometimes she displayed these pearls entwined in her hair. I remember it. They are all I have left of her."

"Should you not have had these years ago?"

"Well, of course. But I was under age when I left Lion Court, and then I was abroad. I did not learn until I came back to London, that Montagu had seen fit to hold them for safekeeping and would refuse to give them up."

Captain Morris turned the diamond necklace over in his hands, blue fire sparking in each facet. "What will you do with them now?"

"It's a problem, isn't it? Slightly odd possessions for a man who is otherwise without a penny to his name! Until I can find a woman who deserves to wear my mother's jewelry, I rather hoped you would keep them for me in your safe?"

"Of course."

Dagonet wrapped the pearls and gave them to David Morris. The captain stood and laid them carefully away before returning to his chair. "So your cousin just handed you your property without a squeak? I don't believe it. Surely he had hidden such valuables?"

"He squealed like a stuck pig, but he could not deny that he had my mother's things, because they were happily on public display. My aunt and Cousin Charlotte were wearing them. And Sir George himself had graced his burgeoning chest with my father's French watch and diamond pin."

"Good God! I'm surprised you didn't knock him down!"

"If Catherine Hunter had not been there, I might have done. Yes, your fiancée's sister! She appears to have taken a post as companion to Lady Montagu. Why did you not tell me, I wonder?"

"Well," said Captain Morris ruefully, "it's rather damnable, isn't it? But she wasn't involved in all this, was she?"

Devil Dagonet laughed out loud. "She rather involved herself, I'm afraid. I had to kiss her."

Morris leapt to his feet. "You did not! I ought to call you out!"

Charles de Dagonet turned the considerable power of his attention on his friend. "Why? You know you would die, if you did; unless I was foxed enough to merely lie down before your chivalrous onslaught and let you slay me. Besides, I rather believe Miss Hunter can take care of herself. A remarkable young lady! She very nearly called for the butler and ruined everything; I had to stop her. Anyway, I am hardly in her good graces. I almost ran her down with my horse on the moor on my way here, and she had not forgiven me." He stood up in one fluid movement and took up a violin that had been lying on the table. "Not having seen Lion Court in seven years, I'm afraid I was victim to several rather maudlin sentiments, and I was unforgivably rude. Now I have compounded it! Nevertheless, I do promise you, David," he said with a bow, "that I shall not involve you in my sordid affairs any more than I can help it, and I certainly shall not compromise either Miss Amelia Hunter or her sister."

Then, with casual skill, he began to play.

* * *

There was to be no more music at Lion Court that
evening. Lady Montagu, proclaiming herself prostrate
with shock and distress, and dispensing with the services
of her companion, retired for the night. Her son George
disappeared into the study, where Catherine had no
doubt that he would keep company with his bottles of
port. Charlotte, after pronouncing several unflattering
comparisons between the hapless way that her brother
had handled their unwelcome visitor and the aplomb
which the late Mr. Clay would surely have displayed, also
made moves to retire. "I'm sorry that you should have
had to witness such a thing, Miss Hunter, and that you
should have invited such an insult from my cousin. I trust
it goes without saying that no word of tonight's unfortunate occurrence should be breathed outside this house? I
hope we may rely on your sensibility, if not your discretion?"

"You may trust my discretion, of course, Mrs. Clay."
How dare the woman suggest that she had invited Dagonet's kiss!

"Then that's settled. I felt I should mention it, not
knowing if our standards of behavior were what you were
used to. Mr. Clay always felt one should make sure of
these little matters. Your difference in station was obviously quite clear to my cousin. May I bid you good
night?"

Catherine, quite speechless, watched the door close
behind her. She had no desire to dwell on what had
happened. Devil Dagonet was insufferable, and his family deserved him! She was about to go to the piano and
put away the music that she had earlier selected, when
she noticed the bell rope lying where it had dropped

beside the fireplace. There was no sense at all, she supposed, in leaving it for the housemaids to discover and gossip over. Without hesitation, she pulled over a chair, and climbing from it to the side table, was able to reach the little knife that still pierced the cornice. It had been thrown, as she had been kissed, with an unsettling degree of competence. She shrugged and put it on the mantel. The end of the silk cord was still attached to an iron loop, from which ran the wire to the butler's pantry. It would not take very long, she decided, to remove the frayed stub and weave the end of the length of rope into the metal ring, thus producing a bell cord only slightly shorter than before. She was intent upon this task, which was an uncomfortable reach above her head, when the door opened and one of the housemaids came in with the coal scuttle. The bucket hit the floor with a crash.

"Oh, ma'am! You gave me such a turn! Excuse me, I thought the family had all retired. I'll come back and do the fire later."

"No, it's all right, Mary, go ahead." Catherine felt perfectly ridiculous. She had finished with the bell cord, but was still standing on the side table. Mary ignored her awkward situation and matter-of-factly retrieved the coals and set them down by the grate.

"Can I help you down, ma'am?"

Catherine nodded and put out her hand, while she tried to think of some rational explanation for why she should be climbing on the furniture, when the maid's next utterance put it quite out of her head. "It was Devil Dagonet come back, wasn't it, ma'am?" Her sharp eyes moved from the frayed butt of the rope, where Catherine had discarded it, to the knife on the mantel. "He got in after all?"

"How on earth did you know?"

"Because Potter and some of the lads was set to watch for him days ago."

"You mean he was expected?"

"Must have been, ma'am; else Sir George wouldn't have set up a guard, nor told me to keep to my room. Then Potter was found with the three lads all trussed up with rope to the trees in the drive, and Potter's been given a shiner. Dagonet was always handy with his fives, ma'am, even as a lad."

"Good heavens! He was alone against four men! But why should you keep to your room?"

"Sir George fears that his cousin wants words with me." The housemaid looked away, her hands, white-knuckled, clenched in her apron. "I'm married and taken a different name now, of course; but you see, Milly Trumble, as was drowned, she was my sister. Well, I mustn't stand here talking, I've my duties to attend."

The maidservant turned and left. Catherine stood by the fire for a moment. So Dagonet had come back for more than to steal the jewelry. He wanted to find out something from Mary. Was the girl in danger? She had a sudden dreadful misgiving that she hadn't seen the last of Devil Dagonet.

The fierce strains died away, as Dagonet laid down his violin.

"Who the deuce wrote that?" asked Captain Morris. "I don't believe I ever heard it before?"

"You wouldn't have. It's a new piece by Beethoven. Enough of music! If 'music be the food of love,' it is fit for your ears, but not my hands. I am not feeling very loving."

"I should think you feel like committing murder!"

laughed Morris, then he blushed scarlet. "Good God, Charles, I forgot. Forgive my blundering tongue."

"Fear not, dear Captain, my skin is not so tender."

"Here," replied the captain, still red. "Do me a favor and take it out on my shrinking hide. You have yet to teach me that thrust that you used at Burgos to trick Boney's men. I promise I'll do my damnedest to kill you for the sake of Catherine Hunter." He peeled off his coat, and took two slender rapiers out of a case. "Come on, humiliate me, but pray don't pink me, for I'm promised to take out Amelia tomorrow."

Dagonet smiled, totally without his usual sarcasm, and tossed off his jacket. His face was suddenly quite transformed as the muscles around his mouth truly relaxed for the first time. "Very well, but fight your best, Captain, or I shall not answer for the consequences!"

A few moments later the two men faced each other in the dining room, with the table pushed aside and the carpets rolled back. David Morris was an accomplished swordsman, but his best efforts were no match for the lightning blade of his opponent. They fought in silence, punctuated only by their grunts and disturbed breathing, the clash of the blades, and an occasional burst of laughter.

"No, no! Like this! Here and here . . . You see!" There was a clatter of steel on wood. "You are dead, sir! Kate Hunter goes unavenged!"

And Captain Morris, who had been very neatly disarmed, sat suddenly down on the floor and went off into peals of breathless laughter. Dagonet, panting slightly, reached for the lost weapon and set both blades aside.

"God's teeth, but you're a demon with a sword, Dagonet! Now, when I get my breath, for fortune's sake, show me how you did that."

"After a glass of wine?" replied Charles, crossing to the decanter. "Isn't that how it was at Burgos?"

"Oh God, don't!" cried his opponent, and grasping at his sides he rolled on the floor in helpless hysterics, while Dagonet sat calmly on the edge of the table, a wineglass in each hand. Eventually he slipped from his perch and quite deliberately poured one glass over Morris's brown hair. "I shall never make a swordsman out of you, if every time I try, you throw my past misadventures in my face and make yourself silly with laughter."

"Oh, Jupiter!" cried Morris, struggling to his feet, and mopping quite unconcerned at the wine that was now trickling down his face. "I'm sorry, but you were the one involved with those French soldiers, risking as usual your worthless life, while I watched and saw their faces. God knows how you got away with your skin!"

"Because I speak gutter French like a native, of course. My father taught me."

"It was worth the entire campaign just for that moment! Come, let's go back to the study, you'll never teach me anything now."

The fire had died away, and the talk had ranged over nearly every subject with which any educated young man might be conversant, and a few less familiar, when Dagonet stood and made for the door. "I'm to bed, David. If you're to take out the charming Miss Amelia in the morning, you had better wash your hair." His long fingers were on the doorknob, when suddenly he turned to his friend. "Listen. If it should prove uncomfortable for you, even for a moment, to have me here, you have only to say."

"What? When I owe you my life, more than once, and what's left of my sanity? Never! You may have the run of the place for as long as you wish!"

"Then I thank you."

"But I do wish you would tell me, Charles. What was the truth about Millicent Trumble?"

The softness and relaxation were swept instantly from Dagonet's features. He replied deliberately in the language of his father. *"Il vaut mieux tâcher d'oublier ses malheurs, que d'en parler."*

But David Morris had drunk just a little too much, and was just a little too tired and comfortable to take the hint. "You may not want to talk of your misfortunes, but don't tell me that you're here because you want to forget them. You're trying to find out something at Lion Court that will clear your name, aren't you? I think I have the right to ask."

"You have the right to ask, of course." The cultured voice was perfectly courteous. "But that does not mean that I have the obligation to answer. *Rien n'est beau que le vrai*—there is nothing more beautiful than the truth, and the truth is that Millicent was a very silly girl."

David's jaw had dropped open. He closed it with a snap. "I shouldn't have asked. I'm sorry. Whatever happened, it changes nothing now, of course."

"Ah, but it has changed, and will always have changed, everything. The sad, little serving wench! I should not have been so foolish as to leave myself lying around for anyone to discover. I don't know whether I killed her, if that's what you want to know. I am sure I was, however, as responsible as anyone for her death. Good night."

Captain Morris stared silently at the fire for a moment. Of course, he could trust his friend when it came to Catherine Hunter. If only Charles de Dagonet could feel that he could return that trust. He was a natural leader of men, and had been a fearless soldier, but no one—not even his closest companion, Capt. David Morris—had ever been able to get truly close to him. He didn't seem to care what others thought of him, and shrugged off his reputation as a rake and a libertine. Morris shook his head, then he leapt to his feet, and without a backward glance walked through the house to the kitchens.

"Hello, Cook. Do you have any warm water left?" And he plunged his head up to the ears in the bucket she indulgently provided.

4

Catherine enjoyed a day off once each week, and was thus to be found walking arm in arm with the Reverend Hunter through the sleepy streets of Fernbridge just a few days later. She had said nothing, of course, of what had happened the night that Dagonet had stolen the jewelry, but she was fooling herself, if she had thought she could put it from her mind. His face was constantly in her thoughts; she blushed to remember her feelings when he kissed her. How dared he? If Sir George, for the sake of his mother, was going to ignore the incident, and take no action with the authorities against his renegade cousin, it was hardly her place to question it. Devil Dagonet, she fervently hoped, was now far distant, enjoying his ill-gotten gains. She was deep in conversation with her father about something quite different, when they were hailed in a shrill voice.

"Oh, Reverend Hunter!" It was Charlotte, at the reins of a little pony cart. She whipped up the pony, drew level beside them, and pulled clumsily to a stop. "How delightful to run into you, Vicar. I hope you will not take it amiss that I should condescend to speak to you on the public thoroughfare. My dear departed husband, Mr. Clay, always had the greatest respect for the cloth, and would have wished me to acknowledge you."

The vicar murmured something polite, while Catherine tried to keep a straight face. Charlotte turned next to her. "How do you do, Miss Hunter? I suppose you have been telling your father of the horrid unpleasantness we have had at Lion Court?"

"No, indeed not, Mrs. Clay!"

Charlotte ignored her. "The most distressing thing imaginable, sir! My cousin Dagonet broke into the house after assaulting the servants, and insulted us all. He removed the jewelry that we were wearing at the point of a gun! And we women without Mr. Clay any longer here to support us! My mother has been bearing up very bravely these last few days, but you can imagine our feelings. I declare my brother is quite overset! He is too loyal, of course, to family feeling to make trouble over it. Sir George has the greatest sensibility. I intend to write to Lord Blythe with the whole. My grandfather must be told; it will be news to cause him the greatest distress, but I see it my duty. Mr. Clay was always mindful of his duty. Well, I must be off. Good day. We shall send for you and your charming wife, perhaps, some evening for cards?" And with that she whipped up the pony and rattled away.

"Well," said the Reverend Hunter, with a decided twinkle in his eye. "How honored we are to be, in truth!"

"Papa, pray do not comment, or I shall be quite undone," replied Catherine, bursting into peals of laughter. "Sir George Montagu a man of sensibility! I believe he has the hide of an ox!"

"So, what then is the tale? I am to take it that Charles de Dagonet has paid a visit to his family with disastrous consequences?"

"Papa! Mrs. Clay had made the most particular point that I should tell no one."

"Yes, but now the cat is out of its proverbial bag, you may as well tell me the whole."

She took his arm again, and they walked companionably on down the cobbled street. "It was rather dreadful. Mr. de Dagonet was apparently turned away from the front door, and no wonder! He boxed Sir Montagu's manservant, Potter, and blacked his eye, then tied him and three stable boys to the trees in the drive. He then came in at the window and robbed Lady Montagu and her family of their valuables! I thought to ring for help, but he threw a knife and cut down the bell cord. He claimed with pride the titles of scoundrel and blackguard. Papa, your old pupil is the most out-and-out rogue, I'm afraid."

"Is that everything that happened?" Her father's glance was very keen. She realized that she had never withheld anything from him before. Her face flamed. She would never mention that ruthless kiss!

"Isn't that enough? I think him a man quite without scruple!"

"We cannot always know what's in the hearts of others, my dear, nor all the circumstances of their lives. Do not judge too harshly."

"But his behavior was unforgivable. How could he show his face here again?"

Her father sighed deeply. "Millicent Trumble was a pretty, empty-headed little thing; she hardly seemed the type to attract Dagonet. I have never believed that he killed her. Only the family really know the details, but I think there must have been some kind of accident. Yet the fact remains that he was found that day passed out from drink by the path to the lake. He took a blow to the head in his fall, and was ill for some days afterwards."

Catherine looked away in revulsion. "Drink! It was the coward's way out."

"I'll never understand it. The lad was anything but a coward. Afterwards, he stood up to the wrath of his uncle and the towering rage of his grandfather with the greatest courage. He denied nothing and said nothing, except that he was sorry that Milly was drowned. Lord Blythe cut him off without a penny, and he was turned out of Lion Court with curses. He had to give up Oxford, of course. He lost every hope that he might have had for the future. A lesser man would have broken under it. Instead, he left right away for the war."

"Lord Blythe bought him a commission?"

"No, indeed not. Dagonet went to join up as a common soldier. He had nothing, my dear, and he was under age. Thank God that the recruiting officer had the good sense to recognize what he had when he saw him. Dagonet was, after all, a gentleman, and he spoke fluent French. He was attached without official rank to a secret reconnaissance and intelligence unit of Wellington's. I'm surprised he survived the campaign."

"However do you know all this, Papa?"

"Because I made it my business to find out. I was fond of him, you see, and forgiveness is part of my profession. Now, enough; here comes Amelia."

In a very fetching straw bonnet and sprigged muslin gown, Amelia Hunter sat beside Captain Morris in his smart little curricle. As the horses drew to a halt, Amelia leapt down. "Papa! The most extraordinary thing! We have just met Mrs. Clay. Devil Dagonet has been in Fernbridge! Captain Morris claims no interest in the matter, but I'll swear he guesses something about it. Do you think we're all in danger?"

Captain Morris also jumped from the carriage, handed the reins to his tiger, and the party fell into step together.

"Good heavens, Amy!" exclaimed Catherine, trying to put more conviction in her voice than she felt. Since the arrival of Dagonet, she seemed to be becoming embroiled in several small deceptions. "He must be a hundred miles away by now! I'm sure that none of us are in any danger at all."

None of them noticed that Captain Morris seemed most unaccountably relieved to change the subject.

The next morning found Catherine playing softly at the piano, while Charlotte and her mother busied themselves with some mediocre embroidery.

"I met the Reverend Hunter in Fernbridge yesterday, Mama," Mrs. Clay began, as if Catherine were not in the room. "I declare he has aged! One would not think the duties of a country parish so heavy."

Catherine tried very hard not to crash out the chords of the piece she was playing.

"Hello, Mama." Sir George came idly into the room, running a finger around his tight cravat. "Dashed uncomfortable day. Charlotte complaining again, or filling your ears with the virtues of the dear departed?"

"There is no need to be arch, George. I only commented to Mama that I had run into the Reverend Hunter. It put me in mind that we should entertain, while we are here. Mr. Clay would have seen it our duty."

"What! and sit at table with a bunch of damned stuffy neighbors and talk about the corn prices and the wool crop. No thanks!"

"Well, perhaps we could have a little evening dance, George," ventured Lady Montagu. "Just a handful of couples to stand up in the blue salon. Since your father died, I have done very little entertaining, and I rather owe it to the community."

George flung himself into a chair. "And as the lord of the manor, I must oblige? Any pretty girls to invite?"

"I think we might invite the Cartwright sisters, and Major Cartwright has friends at the Hall."

"Have that chap Morris from Stagshead!" said George, sitting up. "He's got the most bang-up team of cattle I ever saw."

"And Miss Amelia Hunter is his betrothed," announced Charlotte. "So we may invite the Reverend and Mrs. Hunter and Amelia, and thus do our duty by the parish. Oh, Miss Hunter! I quite forgot you were here!"

"I have taken no offense, Mrs. Clay," said Catherine. "I am sure my family would be honored to attend." She finished the piece with a flourish and snapped down the lid of the piano.

"Come, my dear," said Lady Montagu. "You shall make all the arrangements. I declare I feel quite the thing! A splendid idea, Charlotte. Let us set a date."

Catherine's duties, once so light, were becoming increasingly difficult. Lady Montagu had been fretful and querulous since the encounter with Dagonet, and now the plans for the dance kept her in a state of constant nervous agitation. It was obvious that the family was afraid that their black sheep might visit them again. Sir George Montagu had directed several of the men servants to keep up a constant vigil. Lady Montagu had trouble sleeping, had to be coaxed to eat, and spent several afternoons in a darkened room with the headache. That evening Catherine was called upon to read aloud in her chamber long after the rest of the household had gone to bed.

"I declare I shall never sleep! I wish you would read some of that new poetry we had earlier in the garden. Do you think you might find it?"

"The new Walter Scott? The book is downstairs, my lady. It will only be a moment to go and fetch it."

She tucked the blankets around her mistress and rearranged the pillows for her comfort, relieved to see as she quietly left the room that Lady Montagu's eyelids were already closing. Nevertheless, she went down through the quiet hallways to the parlor, where the slim volume had been left on a side table. She was surprised to find that a branch of candles was lit. Softly she closed the door behind her, and crossed to the table where she had left the book. It was not there. She had just bent to see if it had fallen, when a soft voice began to read:

"Ask me not what the maiden feels, / Left in that dreadful hour alone: / Perchance her reason stoops or reels; / Perchance a courage not her own, / Braces her mind to desperate tone."

Catherine spun around. Charles de Dagonet sat at ease where he had been hidden by the wings of an armchair, the Walter Scott in his hands. He raised an eyebrow. "You do not faint or scream, Miss Hunter? Your reason neither stoops nor fails? Obviously you are made of sounder stuff than the heroine of a romance."

She would reply calmly! She took a deep breath. "I should hope so, Mr. de Dagonet. May I ask what you are doing here?"

He laid down the book and stood, crossing to the fireplace where, gracefully leaning one arm along the mantel, he turned to face her. "Please, don't back away, my dear Kate. However seriously I am tempted, I will try not to kiss you again, or at least," his smile seemed to mock her, "not unless you attempt to rouse the household. I had rather hoped to speak to Mary when she came in to see to the fire, but I suppose it is too late?"

"This is unpardonable, sir! The servants have gone to bed; you must by now have realized it. Why do you wait here? Do you plan to steal the plate or rob the strongbox in the study?"

"Perhaps I was hoping to steal your honor? It's hard to say, isn't it, when dealing with such a dangerous renegade? But I have come only to steal what is mine." The little knife that she had left on the mantel was suddenly in his hand. He tossed it and deftly caught it again by the handle. "And Mary's confidences, of course."

"As you stole her sister's virtue?"

"Did I? How very disgraceful of me." The knife disappeared, and taking the book he read aloud: "Forgot his vows, his faith forswore, / And Constance was beloved no more. / 'Tis an old tale, and often told."

Catherine quoted from memory: " 'In vain for Constance is your zeal; / She—died at Holy Isle.' The difference seems to be that Marmion did repent in the end."

"And I do not? Are you so sure? Perhaps because her name was Milly and not Constance. So much less romantic! I have had little enough of poetry these last years, Miss Hunter; you must forgive me if I seem lacking in the nobler emotions."

Catherine took the proffered volume. Why would her hand not stay steady? "Don't you think you should leave, Mr. de Dagonet?"

"Without what I came for? I should hate to think that I have so upset the family for nothing. They are upset, I take it?"

"Your aunt, Lady Montagu, is in a constant nervous agitation, sir. Is that your wish?"

"I am sorry to discompose her. Lady Montagu is not my object, in spite of the pearls. I would far rather it was George who suffered. Even though he cares nothing for it, he enjoys being lord and master of Lion Court a little too much, don't you think? There is a certain humility lacking in his manner."

"No more than is lacking in yours, sir! How dare you come here like this?"

He laughed, but the sarcasm disappeared from his voice. "I would dare a great deal for Lion Court: every stone, every pane of glass, and every ivy leaf. The house looks too sad, and the tenants work too hard."

Catherine sat down. He had only stated what she herself had noticed. "What is it that you want?"

"A few honest words with Millicent Trumble's sister. Mary is keeping to the house; there is no way I can approach her. I don't want to frighten or coerce her, but I would like her to meet me. Would you give her a message?"

"No, I will not. How can I lend myself to your schemes?"

"Then there is no more to be said. There is no reason, of course, why you should." He stepped over to her, and executing a perfect bow, suddenly took her hand. His lips barely brushed it, and it was released. In a moment he had stepped to the window, and given her a charming smile. "George really ought to lock the windows at night," he commented lightly. "There is no telling who might get in."

He was gone. Catherine sat for a few moments staring blindly at the book in her hands, waiting for her heart to stop thudding so uncomfortably in her breast. She could quite easily see why he had gained his nickname! There was something about him that invited her trust. She realized that she had almost given in and offered to help him. Well, thank goodness she had not. There was no reason at all for her to get involved. Her resolution made, she stood and quietly left the room. The dogs had not barked at the intruder, he obviously could come and go as he pleased, in spite of Sir George's efforts; but then this had once been his home and his inheritance. When she arrived upstairs, Lady Montagu was asleep.

Amelia Hunter walked through Fernbridge the next morning without stopping at any of her favorite shops. She carried a little basket in which to collect wild berries. This strategy would take her inevitably past the gates of Stagshead, where it would be only natural for her to stop in for a few moments. She was very competently chaperoned by Annabella, who held her by the hand, except when something caught her attention and she skipped off for a moment or two before remembering that, at twelve, she was very nearly a young lady.

There was, however, no reply to Amelia's tentative knock at the brass doorknob, shaped appropriately enough like a stag, and the girls heard instead faint strains of harpsichord music from the back of the house. Even though David Morris did not play, there was a music room there, with the instruments and music stands and French windows giving onto the garden. Amelia's pretty mouth was set rather oddly as she grasped her sister by the hand, and, before she should lose her nerve, swept around the house to the gardens. Did Captain Morris have a musical visitor, and was she young and pretty? She meant to take just a peek, for the player's back would of necessity be to her, she knew, and her little boots were silent on the soft grass, but as she and Annie came up to the window, the music stopped, and the player swung around on his stool to face them.

"Miss Amelia Hunter, I presume? An unexpected pleasure! And who is this charming young lady?"

"My name is Annabella Hunter, sir. Who are you?"

"A visitor. Won't you come in for some refreshment? Captain Morris will return very shortly."

Amelia blushed under the bland emerald gaze and the charm with which he indicated the waiting chairs, but she stepped into the room.

"You ought to tell us your name," persisted Annie, also a little red-faced. "It's not polite otherwise."

"Very well," said the handsome gentleman, sweeping them both a bow. "I am neatly trapped. Charles de Dagonet, at your service."

Amelia went white, and Annie's eyes became instantly as round as carriage wheels. "Devil Dagonet!"

The door to the room had opened. "Mr. de Dagonet is my guest, Miss Annabella," said Captain Morris, smiling. "That's not a very courteous way to address him, is it?"

"I have been discovered, as you see, Morris, like Moses in the bulrushes. Now you don't need to keep my scandalous presence hidden from Miss Amelia any longer. David has been very uncomfortable about not telling you, ma'am; but the blame is entirely mine. I would have run him through with my sword, had he breathed a word."

"You're joking, aren't you?" said Annie. "Did you really jump your horse through the lych-gate?"

Dagonet laughed. "Come into the garden, Miss Annabella, and I will tell you. Captain Morris wants to speak to your sister in private."

Annie went willingly enough and sat down on a garden bench opposite the object of her curiosity, who relaxed against the convenient trunk of a tree. She could see from where she was sitting that Amy and the captain were deep in conversation. "Well?" she said, arranging her short skirts. "I don't believe you could have done it. I have looked every time that we went through it to church, and the roof is too low. You could jump a horse over the little gate and the bench where they set down the coffins, between the pillar things, but the rider would bang his head on the beams under the thatch and come off."

"That's what my cousin thought when he wagered me that it couldn't be done."

"Then how did you win?"

It was a pity that no one but Annabella could see his face just then. The expression was entirely without sarcasm, relaxed and open with a warmth of humor in the green eyes. "I hung from the side of my horse's saddle like a savage. He cleared the gate with an inch to spare, and his ears brushed the fringe of the straw. It took a very exact approach, but then he was a very good horse. My grandfather had given him to me. It was a stupid thing to do, and I was lucky not to get killed."

Annie's face was lit like the sun. "I wish I could have seen it! What did you win from the wager?"

"A promise from George; he's Sir George now, of course, so I can't tell you what it was."

"Why not?"

"A matter of honor between gentlemen."

"I bet he didn't even keep the promise!"

Dagonet laughed. "You are as sharp as you are pretty, Miss Annie."

"I'm not pretty."

"Yes, you are. You will grow up to be as lovely as your sister Amelia."

"Cathy's just as pretty as Amelia. It's cruel that nobody says so. I think brown hair is just as good as gold."

"And so do I. I am a great admirer of brown hair, but you will keep that a secret from your sister Kate, won't you?"

Annie nodded very earnestly. Her own hair was the exact color of a brown mouse, and she had always been in despair over it. "I'm very good at keeping secrets."

"Good, because I shall ask you to keep another one, and not tell anyone that I am here. Will you do that?"

"Cross my heart and hope to die." Within moments Dagonet had her in merry laughter over another story entirely.

Amelia looked around at the sound. "He has charmed Annie anyway. If you wish me to accept him as a friend, of course I will, for your sake."

David Morris smiled warmly. "I should have told you before, but he wants nobody to know that he stays with me. I wouldn't be here if it wasn't for him, you know. I owe him my life more than once. We were together more than four years in the Peninsula, Amy. Dagonet is the truest, bravest fellow I have ever known. What happened at Lion Court all those years ago, I don't know, he won't talk about it, but I will never believe that Charles de Dagonet has ever done anything deliberately cruel or dishonorable in his life."

And since that gentleman and Annabella were at that moment distracted over a joke, David stole a quick kiss from his beloved.

*   *   *

"I apologize freely, Captain, if my presence embarrassed you with your betrothed," said Dagonet, after the young ladies had gone. "It comes from being such a desperado. They will tell no one, of course. The Hunters seem to be an extraordinary family!"

"You are up to something, aren't you? You look like a pig in clover!"

Dagonet gave his friend a grin. "Who me? It is not my fault that Catherine Hunter is living at Lion Court."

"You promised me you would not involve her!"

"Kate Hunter has already entangled me, my friend. I am a helpless victim; ensnared by the Lorelei!"

"I wish I could tell when you're being serious, sir."

"I am always serious, my dear Captain, especially about the fair sex." His green eyes were bright with laughter. "Cousin George does not deserve to live under the same roof. However, if I am to win that roof back for myself, the presence of Miss Catherine Hunter cannot be allowed to stop me."

5

They were enjoying a spell of extremely hot, dry weather;
perfect for the late harvest. Two days after Catherine's
sisters had discovered a stranger playing David Morris's
harpsichord, Lady Montagu had decided to take the air
and visit her neighbor, Major Cartwright, and had taken
Charlotte and George with her in the landau. Since, in
Mrs. Clay's opinion, Catherine was not a necessary accompaniment on such a social visit, she was able to spend
the glorious day mostly as she pleased. Taking care in
record time of the minor chores that Lady Montagu had
left her, she had already walked around much of the Lion
Court estate, and stood for a while watching the tenants
take in the corn. The men formed a long line down the
field, each one bending and lifting in rhythm as he
worked to the end of his natch, the short badging hooks
flashing in the bright sun. The standing wheat fell before
them in fifteen neat patches, and in the place of the
waving golden carpet lay a scattering of half sheaves.
Each man then worked back up the other side of his
natch, until he had another half sheaf, which he bound
to the first in a single movement. The women, coming
behind their menfolk, stacked the finished sheaves to-

gether into shooks to cure, until the field became covered in neat rows of the tiny stacks. Even the children toiled long hot hours in the baking sun. Devil Dagonet was right; the tenants were worked too hard. Why were extra hands no longer hired to help?

Clouds of dust rose from the field as the grain was cut, and the lanes were powdered with fine dirt. In spite of her parasol and bonnet, Catherine was beginning to feel as if she were slowly being roasted, but she couldn't bear to go back into the house. Instead she walked up past the lake and followed Rye Water into the deep cool shade of the woods. Soon she arrived at the little grotto presided over by its stone nymph. The ornamental pool at the goddess's feet shimmered invitingly in the dappled light. Throwing off her bonnet, Catherine dabbled her fingers in the water. It felt delicious. The temptation was overwhelming. She knew the routine schedule of every member of the household; Lady Montagu and her offspring would be gone all day. There was absolutely no one who would come here. She hesitated only another moment, before beginning to strip off her half boots, and peel back her stockings. Why not?

Dagonet heard her before he saw her. Someone was in the grotto, singing in a clear pure soprano the words of an old folk ballad. The splash of water made a musical accompaniment to her song.

"We lingered where the water flows, sweet promises her eyes did make;

I gave her but a single rose, but she my heart and soul did take."

Curious, he stepped out of the trees onto the rocks above the grotto. Below him Rye Water cascaded over a little waterfall into a clear pool. Some of the water had been diverted, so that it ran over the blunted curves of an ancient stone nymph and flowed unendingly from her upturned Grecian urn. A wild briar rose had managed to take root in the face of the rock, and still held the last few flowers of the summer. Between the base of the dwarf cliff and the edge of the pool was a patch of short turf, where the well-shaded grasses were liberally intermingled with green moss. Catherine had flung aside bonnet, shawl, and parasol, and left her boots and stockings on the bank. Her dress fell straight from the high waistline just below her breasts, and the little puff sleeves bared her slender arms. She had the fine, green-striped muslin skirts gathered up in one hand and was paddling thigh-deep in the pool, while she splashed water over her neck and shoulders with the other. Under the clear surface of the pond, her naked legs gleamed enticingly in the broken sunbeams. Her back was to him; she was totally oblivious to his presence. She looked almost ethereal in the water-dappled light.

Entranced, he slipped silently down the cliff face, and stepping onto the short turf, leaned back against the cool rock. He had his jacket flung over one shoulder. The broken sunlight mottled his white shirt and tan riding breeches, and struck dull lights in his dusty boots. He could not resist it. He took up the tune and joined in.

"I am a knight without a grail, I am a tower without a dove,

I am a ship without a sail, And lost am I without my love."

Catherine spun about and saw him. The color rushed to her cheeks. He looked perfectly relaxed, as if he came across young women losing all sense of propriety every day. A wicked smile lurked at the corners of his lips, as he returned her gaze.

"What?" asked Catherine, as her breathing returned

to normal. "Only an old folk song? No pertinent quote from the poets, sir?"

"I am struck dumb, Miss Hunter. Pray do not let me disturb you. You present a charming picture. I shall be desolate, if you don't go on singing."

"Then be desolate! How dare you stand there and watch me? Any gentleman would have quietly left without making his presence known, before so embarrassing a lady."

"As I had thought you were already aware, dear Kate: I am not reckoned to be a gentleman. Don't you believe me a thief and a rogue? Besides, what well-brought-up young lady would splash around barefoot in a woodland pool with such recklessness?"

Her color deepened. "If you would be kind enough to leave, sir, so that I could recover my shoes without further impropriety, I would rectify my foolish behavior this instant."

"An impetuous action, once taken, cannot be rectified though, can it? Even if I were to leave this instant, you would still know that I had found you out. It is my humble opinion, however, Miss Hunter, that you have nothing to be ashamed of." His glance swept over her.

She decided deliberately to misunderstand. "I am all wet, sir! And I am standing over my knees in water. If that falls within the bounds of what is considered acceptable in polite society, then you have been moving in very different circles than I!"

"In Paris," continued Dagonet, blandly, as if she had not spoken, "the ladies of the court are dampening their muslins deliberately, the better to display their charms. The custom has not yet, regrettably, taken hold in England. Perhaps you can start the new fashion?"

"I am not interested in the fashions in Paris! Are you

going to just stand there making small talk, and leave me trapped in this pool?"

Dagonet dropped his jacket on the rocks and stepped forward to the edge of the water. "Of course not, I thought I might join you for a moment. It does look deliciously cool and inviting!"

"You would not dare, sir!"

"I would dare a great deal, Kate. But if you would never forgive me, the pleasure would hardly be worth it, would it?"

"My opinion of you cannot matter a whit!" Catherine had backed away a little, when he came closer. Surely he would not really step into the pool with her? Why must she do such crazy things? It had been a stupid risk to take; such behavior could only invite the wrong interpretation. And to be discovered by Devil Dagonet! He was said to be a complete libertine; hadn't he already kissed her without regard to her feelings? She took one more step back, and in that instant lost her footing. With a resounding splash, she fell back into the water. She came up gasping, and realized as she did so, that before she had moved, Dagonet was actually just about to leave. He had turned away and taken up his coat. The splash arrested him, and, without hesitating, as she fell back, he flung away the jacket and leaped into the water. He caught her by the hands and pulled her to her feet.

"Miss Hunter! You are too precipitate! This pool is not deep enough for swimming!" Before she could reply, he had swung her into his arms and carried her to the bank. He set her on the grass and handed her the shawl that she had left earlier beside her parasol. His eyes were alight with laughter. "I wish you had waited until I also could have removed my boots. It's hardly comfortable to ride with one's feet swimming inside them in pond water."

"If you had not interfered, sir, neither of us need have got this soaking!"

Water ran down off her muslin skirts and pooled about her bare feet. She was wet to the skin and was grateful for the cover that the shawl provided. Where he had held her, his shirt was also stuck to his chest, outlining the firm muscles of his torso.

"Too true! I am amply rewarded for my disgraceful lack of sensibility." He looked down ruefully at himself; his breeches and fine leather boots were saturated. "You have only to go back to the house, and the sun is so bright that you will be dry before you get there, but I must ride away in the shade of the trees with my clothes stuck to the saddle. I have done it often enough before, but it's not the most pleasant way to ride."

"What?" she said without thinking. "Do you make a habit of rescuing women from pools?"

"I was referring, dear Kate, only to the times that I have ridden soaked to the skin by the rain. A soldier cannot choose the weather in which he takes out his horse." His voice changed only imperceptibly as he went on, "The only other time that I had a woman to rescue from a pool, I apparently botched it."

The color flamed to her face. If she could have taken back her question, she would have done so a hundred times over. Poor Millicent Trumble had drowned not half a mile downstream from this very grotto! However guilty Dagonet might be, she had not meant to deliberately refer to the old tragedy.

Dagonet swept her a formal bow. "I can no more change the past than you, Miss Hunter! But my sins are of a different order entirely, aren't they? I would escort you to the house, if I were able, but it would only compound the problem for both of us. May I bid you good day?"

He leapt lightly up onto the rocks that shaded the grotto. Just before he disappeared into the woods, he stopped suddenly and broke off a briar rose. Turning it in his fingers, he said lightly, "The single rose, dear Kate. Would you take it, I wonder, were I to give it to you?" He began once again to sing the words of the old song.

"You are impossible, sir!" she stormed; but he had left, the rose in his hand.

Catherine was able to return to Lion Court wrapped in her light shawl, without meeting a soul. Dagonet obviously meant to haunt the house until he could speak with Mary about her sister's death. What was it he wanted to know? He was generally seen to be responsible, and he seemed to accept the blame without question. What could he hope to find out that could make any difference? Well, it was none of her business, and she would put him out of her mind. She bathed and changed her dress, and went downstairs to await the return of the household for dinner. She was not to be allowed, however, to forget about Devil Dagonet for very long.

"Major Cartwright just had the damned impertinence to ask me about Dagonet, Mama!" George's face was suffused with indignation. "The story is all over the village, and it makes me look a dashed fool! Why the deuce can't you learn to keep your mouth shut, Charlotte?"

"Well, I think the neighbors have the right to be warned that Devil Dagonet is in the country, George. Mr. Clay believed in speaking plain, and I follow his example. I gave only the broadest outlines of what happened. If our cousin acts the common highwayman, he must expect his name to be dragged through the mud."

"Oh, not a highwayman, surely?" said Lady Montagu

tentatively. She lay on the couch, while Catherine softly massaged her temples. "We were in the drawing room. I don't think we should indulge in calumny."

"Calumny! He has been a damned thief since he was a boy, Mama! Good lord, don't you recall how he tore out my trap lines and released all the rabbits out of the nooses? Father had him tied to the post in the barn and beat him with the horsewhip, but he wouldn't stop it!"

"Your trap lines were disgusting, George," said Charlotte. "A low poacher's trick. Why Papa should indulge you in something so unsporting, I cannot conceive. Mr. Clay would not have approved, I'm sure."

"I didn't set them where you or Mama could have found them. Anyway, it was just a boy's game; he had no right to interfere."

Catherine had gone quite white. George had set cruel wire traps for rabbits, yet Dagonet had risked a beating to destroy them! As Papa had said, Dagonet hadn't lacked courage. A boy who, whatever his athletic prowess, also wrote music and read the great poets. He must have hated to see suffering in a poor, dumb animal to have risked intervention. And Sir Henry Montagu had thrashed him for his mercy like a common criminal. A terrible and bitter humiliation, surely, for the young pride that must have lain like an ocean behind those eyes. How else had he suffered with his violent uncle? She had never forgotten her own fear of Sir Henry, when she and Amelia had encountered him at the grotto as children.

"Father beat him with a horsewhip, George?"

Sir George laughed. "More than once! Mama would have stopped it, if she could, wouldn't you, Mama?"

Lady Montagu sat up. Miss Hunter's hands had anyway unaccountably stopped their soothing rhythm. "It only made him the more determined. Which your late father couldn't understand. Dagonet had an implacable will. It was cruel treatment, yet the boy laughed at it and invited more. My poor sister's only child!"

"If you ask me," said Charlotte coldly. "Devil Dagonet deserved more than a horsewhipping. After that servant girl was drowned, he should have been hanged! A man who would take advantage of a poor maidservant in his own house is no better than a dog."

"Miss Hunter!" interrupted Sir George Montagu. Catherine looked up, her eyes blank. "Have you sent out the invitations to Mama's dance yet? There's some dashed boring names that I want to strike off the list."

6

Catherine determined, on her next free day, to tell Amelia what she had learned about the destruction of George's rabbit traps. She prided herself on being scrupulously fair, and would set at least this part of the record straight. That Dagonet had destroyed the traps in the face of his uncle's wrath was an act of considerable bravery. It did not alter or excuse what he had done since, but it did cast a more favorable light on his character. She blushed as she remembered his smile when he had found her in the grotto; the water had felt delicious, she would not regret her impetuousness. But had she not fallen, she knew that he had been about to leave her there, undisturbed. Nevertheless, he had watched her with an unforgivable insolence first. He may be kind to animals, but he had not shown her much mercy!

She and Amelia had taken advantage of the return of glorious sunshine to walk up onto the moor, fragrant with wild herbs and flowers. Both ladies wore sensible walking boots and plain muslin country dresses, for though the sun now shone like a benediction overhead, the path was muddy under their feet from the torrential rains they had suffered all week. The harvest had been safely gathered, then the first storms of autumn had come racing in from the Bristol Channel. They had been miserably trapped indoors by the downpour. The sudden bright day, in contrast, made their spirits soar. Amelia heard her sister out with a mixture of relief and embarrassment. She must believe what David had told her, and any further proof that her fiancé was not mistaken in his opinion of his friend was welcome to her ears. Perhaps Dagonet wasn't so dark after all. She was committed, however, to keep silent about that friendship and what Captain Morris had told her.

"Perhaps we have judged too harshly all along, Cathy," she said earnestly. "It is easy to blacken someone's name."

"Yes, but Millicent Trumble died because of him, Amy. He doesn't himself dispute it. And I myself witnessed him stealing the jewels from his own family!"

"We can know nothing of what truly happened, though, can we? I cannot believe him such a blackguard."

"Why ever should you defend him, Amy? It can mean nothing to you!"

Amelia blushed and looked away. Her meeting with Dagonet had impressed her more than she could say. If he was David's friend, that was good enough for her. Besides, he really was so much more handsome even than David; it was no wonder that women lost their hearts over him. Indeed, she was glad she herself was already so much in love. The two girls strolled along in silence, each lost in her own thoughts, when two horsemen cantered unseen up onto the ridge behind them.

"Pull up, Morris! 'She walks in beauty, like the night / Of cloudless climes and starry skies; / And all that's best of dark and bright / Meet in her aspect and her eyes.' My friend, your beloved walks below!"

Captain Morris rode up beside Dagonet, and looked down on the Hunter sisters. Amelia's ringlets shone beneath her bonnet like bright metal in the sunshine. "Don't act the fool, Dagonet!" he said good-humoredly. "If you must quote the latest poets at every turn, at least choose something more appropriate. Amelia's as blond as daylight."

"Why so she is! If Byron is not apt for her, then how about Wordsworth? 'But, O fair Creature! in the light / Of common day, so heavenly bright, / I bless Thee, Vision as thou art!' Let me silently depart, and you may ride down and greet the Vision and her sister, who—if you hadn't noticed—is dark."

Morris swung his riding crop and gave Dagonet's mount a sound *thwack* across the rump. Laughing, Dagonet easily kept his seat as the gray bucked, then touching his own crop to his hat in salute, he rode away down the hill. Captain Morris trotted in the opposite direction to join the ladies. In a few minutes, dismounted and leading his horse, he walked beside them up the moorland track. Amelia was radiant in his company, and Catherine walked a little ahead to allow them to be together. Yet a few minutes later, their pleasant intercourse was suddenly interrupted by the sight of a small figure flying towards them across the heath.

"Good heavens!" exclaimed Catherine. "It's one of Westcott's shepherd lads! Something must be wrong." She started towards the boy at a run.

"Please, ma'am, there's been a cave-in up at the Warrens, and master's best flock is all swallowed up!" The lad was breathless, and his voice came in gasps.

"The Warrens?" asked Captain Morris, coming up behind her, with Amelia on his arm.

"The old mine workings, sir. All this rain has collapsed the pit! It's the prize ram and ewes, drowned!"

"This is a disaster of the first magnitude! Captain Morris, you must take your horse and do what you can. Amy and I will follow as quickly as possible!"

Instantly, Morris was mounted and had taken the hysterical boy up behind him. The ladies, running as best they might in their long skirts across the rough grass and heather, reached the ridge above the Warrens several moments later. Amelia clutched at her sister's arm.

"Oh, Cathy, I can't run another step. I've the most dreadful stitch. You go on! Oh, what a horrid scene!"

Below them a gaping hole had appeared in the green surface of the moor. Behind it stood the abandoned ruins of old stone buildings, where the original opening of the mine known as the Warrens had been roughly boarded over, and near which the sheep often took shelter. The moor was riddled with ancient mine workings—a dangerous maze of underground tunnels and chambers. The recent heavy rains had weakened the roof of one of these, cut too close to the surface, and it had collapsed. The fall of the chamber ceiling must then have temporarily blocked with mud and stone the outlet in its floor into the deep mine shafts below. A swollen rivulet of water, which had once run across the surface, was now diverted into the resulting pit. Thus Catherine was looking into an open crater, the sides gashes of slick, raw earth and cracked rock, which had filled with water to make a deep, muddy pool. Where air leaked up from the deep shafts beneath, bubbles occasionally broke on the water's surface, betraying the unstable nature of the plug. And among the clumps of grass and bog plants floating in the morass of sticky, black mud and swirling water, there struggled, bleating piteously, the heavy bodies of Farmer Westcott's best flock.

As Catherine watched, a large chunk of earth and stones at the side of the pool gave way, and slumped into the mass of drowning sheep. At any moment, she supposed, the blockage below might fail beneath this new pressure, and sheep, water, mud, and stones would all be sucked down into the shafts and disappear. Beside the mine head stood the bent body of Farmer Westcott in his homespun smock, his white hair shining in the sun; and behind him was the shepherd boy just sliding from Morris's horse. A second horse, a gray thoroughbred, stood idly cropping grass a hundred feet away, and a gentleman, stripped to his shirtsleeves, was busy with a length of cable, which he had slung around a massive timber lying in the ruins. He called instructions to the other men, and the farmer and Morris ran to obey him. As he came back out into the sunshine and stood poised for a moment on the lip of the crater, Catherine had no difficulty in recognizing the arrogant turn of the head, or the waves of dark hair. It was Devil Dagonet. She slithered on down the hill, leaving Amelia clutching her ribs on the ridge top, just as Morris caught Dagonet by the arm.

"For God's sake, sir! The whole thing could cave in at any moment! You risk your life for a bunch of dumb sheep!"

Dagonet laughed and stripped off his boots. "Not simply sheep, Captain. What you see there is all of a man's livelihood and his accumulated wealth. Westcott took the blue ribbon in Minehead with that noble ram you see mired in the slough. Anyway, he was good to me as a boy."

Morris hung on to his arm. "Then let me go in with you. Two men can halve the time and the danger!"

"Your life is too valuable to someone else to risk, my friend," replied Dagonet, with a tilt of his head to where Amelia was now struggling down the hill towards them. "It is no longer yours to gamble with. Mine has no such value, alas; least of all to me! Besides, think how happy it would make George, if I should lose it!"

And with that, in one neat movement he had shaken off the restraining hand and dropped over the edge into the pool. The rope which he had discovered in the ruins was caught fast in one hand, the other end belayed around the timber and made fast to a solid block of masonry. As soon as he hit the swirling mess of muddy water, he made a dive for the closest animal. The sheep, their heavy fleeces sodden with water, lashed out with panicked hooves and dangerous, curled spikes. Undeterred, Dagonet made a loop in his rope and cast it about the horns of the nearest ewe.

"Haul!" he cried. The old man and the frightened boy were already at the rope, and Morris caught it behind them. With a resounding plop, the first creature was pulled free, and steadily hauled up over the rim. Once secure at the top, Morris released it and threw the loop back down to Dagonet, swimming below. Confused, the ewe ran helplessly about before obeying the call of her fellows, bellowing beneath her. She tottered for an instant on the brink, then attempted to plunge into the pit to rejoin the flock. Flinging herself full-length on the turf, Catherine caught her by the hind leg. Westcott was forced to abandon the rope and help her, and between the two of them the animal was herded into the ruins of the buildings, where Catherine and Amelia helped to create a makeshift gate with some loose boards, and keep the ewe confined. Catherine then ran back to the crater. Dagonet was barely recognizable for the mud streaks that covered him as he swam, but sheep after sheep was lassoed and rescued. Between animals, he was laughing.

"I can't bear it!" cried Amelia. "The pit may collapse at any minute! Mr. de Dagonet is a gentleman, not a farmer; how can he risk himself like this?"

Her only reply was a sonorous quotation. *"O fortunatos nimium sua si bona norint agricolas!"* he intoned as two or three fighting sheep struck at him with their horns, and attempted to drown their rescuer in their desperation. Amelia's Latin was not quite up to that, and she turned to her sister.

"Oh, most happy husbandmen," translated Catherine feverishly, as she herself fought with another unruly ewe, "if only they knew their own blessings." Then she laughed. "How can he think of such ridiculous things!"

"That's the lad!" shouted Farmer Westcott. "It's a good life, right enough!"

Their mood changed, the danger was forgotten, and they all worked away with renewed vigor. From grappling with the recalcitrant animals, Catherine was liberally splattered with slime. Only now that the group of saved sheep was large enough to form a flock, were their charges remaining meekly in the makeshift pen and not attempting to return to their deaths. Amelia, on guard at the gate, had dirtied her hands, but little else. Catherine, who was hauling the sheep into the pen by their horns, felt desperately breathless and bedraggled. The entire front of her muslin was wet with mud. Dagonet, however, seemed to have an inexhaustible supply of both breath and apt quotations, which Morris and Catherine occasionally returned. Farmer Westcott, not understanding a word of the gentlefolk's Latin and even less of their

French, worked happily on, and the boy, who had been helplessly shaking, had instead begun to laugh aloud as he worked, just from the merriment of their tone. Most of the ewes had been rescued, and Dagonet was grappling with the prize ram when disaster struck. A huge chunk of turf, carrying soil and rock, broke loose from the edge. As it hit the water, there was a great roar like the crash of a wave on a headland. The soup of mud and plants and water—carrying the remaining sheep, the prize ram, and Charles de Dagonet—disappeared as the shaft beneath the pool broke open and began to swallow the slough. The merry mood evaporated instantly.

"Good God! Dagonet!" cried Morris. He made as if to leap after the other man, but Amelia clung tenaciously to his arm.

"The rope, Captain!" shouted Catherine. "Haul up the rope!"

The end of the cable had disappeared beneath the boiling surface of the sinking slime, but as they all pulled together, the ram's head—eyes sealed over, but the mouth like a red gash as it bellowed—rose into view.

"Dang me, if he hasn't got my ram saved!" exclaimed the farmer. "But twenty prize rams won't make up for the loss of a lad like him."

With another haul, the ram's body reached halfway up the slope, and then it could be seen that clinging to its belly was the lithe body of a man.

"Hang on, sir, for God's sake!" cried Morris; and as Amelia and Catherine also leant their weight to the rope, both ram and rescuer were delivered over the rim onto the wet turf. At that instant the sheep kicked out viciously with its hind feet, and caught Dagonet a solid blow on the temple. He sank instantly insensible, the carved features obliterated by mud.

"Oh, please!" said Amelia, quite white. "Is he dead? I don't think he's breathing!"

There was a dreadful silence for a moment, then the carved lips smiled in their mask of grime. *"Vivre ce n'est pas respirer,* my dear Miss Amelia, *c'est agir."*

"What, sir?" said Farmer Westcott. "Can't ye speak English like a proper gentleman?"

Dagonet opened leaf-green eyes, filled with merriment. "Farmer Westcott, how very rude of me. My deepest apologies! Let me translate: life is not breathing, my dear sir, but doing."

"If you continue to act the idiot, I shall knock you out!" threatened Morris with a huge grin.

Dagonet sat up. Catherine had already moistened her pocket handkerchief in a small, clear puddle. She proffered it. "Thank you, Miss Hunter, lady of infinite courage and good sense. I'm glad that someone keeps some proportion about this absurd little scene." He wiped both face and hands clean of mud, then stood and looked over the edge of the pit. The bog and the few remaining ewes had entirely disappeared, leaving a gaping hole where the old mine shaft had opened up, like a single, malevolent eye.

"Like Odysseus, I am rescued from Cyclops on the belly of a ram," he commented dryly and pulled on his boots. "Yet I am doomed once again to ride with wet feet! At least this time, before I plunged in, I first removed my footwear." Only Catherine understood the reference, but she refused to meet his eye. The muddy square of linen was thrust into his pocket. He turned to her. "You are too generous, Miss Hunter, for I have ruined your pocket handkerchief." Then he suddenly reached out a hand and pushed her tumbled hair off her face. "You could have used it first yourself, you know. Must we always meet when our clothes are so bedraggled?"

Catherine became instantly aware of how she must look. Her thin muslin was ruined, wet with mud, and clung most immodestly to her legs and breasts. Her hair had partly come down, and though she had not realized it, in pushing it back she had left a streak of dirt across her face. It suddenly seemed infuriating that he should always see her at such a disadvantage. Dagonet gently rubbed the mud from her cheek with his finger. "You can't imagine how tempting you look," he said in a low tone. "Could we not retreat together into the old mill, for I would very much like to kiss you again."

"How dare you!" She felt suddenly as if she might weep at any minute. "Can't you be sensible even for a moment? You were almost killed!"

"So I was. That must account for my sudden amorous intent. I wish I could think that you would be sorry for my demise. Perhaps if I kiss you again very thoroughly, you might be?"

"I shouldn't be sorry, if you were to drop dead this instant!"

"That would certainly save the virtue and reputation of innumerable young ladies, wouldn't it?"

For an agonizing moment, she thought he was going to kiss her anyway. Instead, he stepped back and swept her a perfect, courtly bow before moving off to catch his horse. He swung himself easily into the saddle. "I shall alert your estimable wife, Westcott, and she can send some of the men with the dogs, and a cart for Miss Hunter and Miss Amelia. Then Captain Morris may escort the ladies safely home, and you can run the whole flock through a stream, before the mud dries and ruins your wool crop after all." The horse pranced under his practiced hand, as he laughed again. "You had better avoid the village, Captain. Miss Hunter's dress will cause a scandal! Not all members of her father's congregation will appreciate it as much as I." And with a salute from his crop, Devil Dagonet galloped away.

"Well," said Catherine, furiously. "I suppose we must all be suitably impressed, but is he always so insufferable, I wonder?"

7

That afternoon, bathed and in fresh dresses, the sisters sat together in the small vicarage garden.

"So, Cathy, you cannot now, surely, feel the same way about Dagonet? I never in my life saw anything so brave."

"Nor so foolhardy! I'll concede the bravery of what he did for poor Farmer Westcott, as I conceded his courage facing down Sir Henry over George's rabbit traps, but it alters nothing in my view of the man. I think him an arrogant rogue! I almost feel that he rescued the sheep as much for his own perverted amusement and vanity as anything else."

"Oh, however can you say so! That is too ungenerous!" Catherine's reply was a sneeze. "Now do not say you are going to catch cold before the Montagus' dance. You were all over wet and mud."

Catherine's laugh was a little bitter. "Yes, and my hair all to pieces and dirt on my cheek! I was certainly a figure of fun!"

Amelia looked at her sharply, but Catherine smiled and made an entirely different remark. She had seen herself in the hall mirror with dismay, when she had come in. It was so grossly unfair. Even when coated in mud, Devil Dagonet had been anything but ridiculous. Every sinew of his body was like steel, and he had subdued and captured the sheep with an enviable economy of motion controlled by an implacable will; all the while keeping up a stream of inane wit to prevent the rest of them panicking. She, on the other hand, had felt very much like a drowned rat, and she blushed to think how much of her slim figure had been revealed yet again by the wet muslin of her dress. She would, just once, like him to see her in silk and diamonds!

"It can't matter how we looked, Cathy," said Amelia gently. "We shall make up for it with a dazzling display at the Lion Court ball."

"You may, Amy, but not I!"

"Why ever not?"

Catherine was instantly restored to all her good humor. "It's too absurd, but Mrs. Clay does not find it suitable that I attend, and has overridden Lady Montagu on the issue. I am, after all, the paid companion. It would offend the shade of the late Mr. Clay! I may watch from the minstrel's gallery, as if I still wore my hair down, but I do not take part in the revelry."

"But that's so unfair! You love to dance, and, who knows, you might meet some eligible gentleman there."

At which, Catherine finally gave way to peals of heartfelt laughter. "Dear sister, I have compiled the guest list and sent out the invitations myself! There is to be no one there in whom I could have the slightest interest; only all our old neighbors, including the dreadful Mr. Crucible. No, in truth, it's a relief to me not to have to attend. And with so many people in the house, we shall surely be safe from the unwelcome visits of Charles de Dagonet. No mysterious, handsome stranger will turn up and ask me to dance! I intend to have a perfectly peaceful evening."

Catherine did for a while watch the arriving guests from the minstrel's gallery at Lion Court. Without question, Amelia was the loveliest young lady at the dance. She was dressed simply, in white and amber, but her perfect features were lit with excitement, and her burnished hair shone like a lamp. Captain Morris, resplendent in his regimentals, was instantly at her side. After watching them go in together, Catherine moved away to return to her own room. What she had told Amy concerning the guest list was true—she had found herself pulling back behind the cover of a pillar as Mr. Crucible minced into the hall—but she did love to dance and had no wish to subject herself to watching all the other young people of the neighborhood disporting themselves, when she could not join in.

The gallery backed onto the library, where the little balcony led to Charles de Dagonet's old room. It suddenly occurred to her that she could watch the carriages arrive from the curved windows, and admire the horses instead of the occupants. Her feet ran lightly up the stairs, and she quietly turned the handle and went in. Instantly, strong hands seized her from behind and spun her around to face her attacker. Her heart leapt to her throat.

"Miss Hunter?" said Dagonet. "Is it your fate, do you suppose, to always discover me when I skulk like a thief in the night at my old home, or is it my fate that it should be you rather than George that does the discovering?" Catherine stood helpless in his grip. The soft evening light shone across his dark hair and struck fire in the depths of sea-green eyes. Simple, buckskin breeches stretched across his lean thighs; his coat was carelessly unbuttoned, and his shirt lay open at the neck. Drums began to pound in her breast, as the strangest sensations spread warmth throughout her body. His gaze swept over her. "How fortunate that it's you, Kate," he continued gently, "or I shouldn't be able to do this." And drawing her into his arms, he began to kiss her.

His lips moved firmly over hers, and unwittingly she began to respond, opening her mouth to his questing tongue. He had meant only to charm her, disarm her a little, perhaps. It wouldn't hurt a bit to have an ally in the household, and he certainly didn't want her raising the alarm; but suddenly, as he felt her lips move beneath his, he forgot all caution. As her fresh scent filled his nostrils, he had a sudden vision of her as she had looked in the grotto and on the moor; her face, framed by a cloud of tumbled dark hair, flushed with color; her wet muslin dress clinging to the curves of her breasts and thighs. In an instant, his mouth became demanding, insisting on her response. His hands drew her closer, pulling her shapely form against his. Catherine caught fire in his embrace. Sweet sensations coursed through her body, fluttering in the pit of her stomach and filling her with desire. Her tongue caressed his, she wanted to know every corner of his mouth. As his beautiful fingers moved over her neck and back, she longed for them to explore every part of her. Tentatively she ran her hands under his coat against his soft shirt. The muscles of his torso were firm and hard. Then, discovering where the shirt lay open at the neck, she felt the smooth bare skin of his chest, downed with hair. With a gasp he broke away.

"Good God, sweet Kate!" He dropped onto the window seat, breathing hard, then threw back his head, and laughed a little unsteadily. "I deserve any punishment you can suggest! I never meant . . . no, I meant every bit of it, but I had no right . . . Oh, damn it all to hell!"

Catherine steadied herself against the wall. It took all her willpower to reply calmly. "Your cousin intends to drive you from here with horsewhips, sir, should you be discovered. Will that do?"

Dagonet laughed. "He has already tried that with sad results. No, I think he might indulge a stronger dissuasion the next time."

"If you will insist on breaking into the house and stealing the jewelry, you can't expect a civil welcome!"

"And if I kiss his mother's companion?" He caught her hand and pulled her down beside him.

"You only confirm your reputation, sir." She was fighting to steady her breathing. "How did you get in? The house is full of guests for the ball."

"Why, someone had thoughtfully left open a casement. I came across the roof as I did many times as a boy, when locked in here by my uncle, the estimable Sir Henry. I used to escape his kind ministrations and take refuge with old Westcott. His wife would shower pity upon the poor orphan waif, and feed me homemade scones and honey. I was never found out, you know. The practice in stealth and deception has stood me in good stead in my disreputable career."

"A career in thievery? Sir George Montagu could have called in the magistrates and watched you hang in Minehead."

"But he did not. How curious!"

"He saves his mother further distress, sir: it's quite simple."

Dagonet turned suddenly to her, the emerald gaze faintly mocking. *"Mea culpa!* I had not actually intended to involve the ladies in that unpleasant little scene, Kate, and certainly not you. Your father was once a great friend to me. I can only ask you to accept my apologies, if you were made uncomfortable."

"Made uncomfortable! You kissed me in front of them all! You took advantage of Sir George's family pride to steal his valuables without repercussion. What did you do with the jewelry? Did you sell it?"

"Alas, my careless tongue! I rather lost my temper, I'm afraid." He reached into his coat. "Here is the watch that I took from cousin George. Perhaps you would like to look at it?"

Catherine took the heavy gold watch with its single diamond, and turned it over in her hands. "I can see," she said, "that it's very valuable, and you have not yet sold it. Does that excuse you?"

"Open it, sweet Kate, I pray."

With a quick look at him, she did as she was bid. On the inside of the lid, opposite the watch face was some flowing script. What it said was quite clear: *Pierre, Comte de Dagonet, Paris–1775.*

"My father," said Dagonet dryly. "The rest—the diamonds and the pearls—had been my mother's. Now am I forgiven? You had no way of knowing, of course."

Catherine, blushing scarlet, gave back the watch. "I see that I am to made to look the complete fool. Does Sir George hold more of your parents' effects?"

"Unfortunately not. You see the extent of my wealth."

"Then what do you do here tonight?"

"You do not think, Miss Hunter, that you find me wallowing in sentiment, come simply to visit my childhood cell where I spent so many happy hours? 'Nuns fret not at their convent's narrow room . . .'"

"'. . . And hermits are contented with their cells.' No, I do not."

"You are a harsh judge, Miss Hunter. 'In truth the prison, unto which we doom / Ourselves, no prison is . . .' "

"It was no prison at all! You may have learned Wordsworth, sir, and set sonnets to music, but you still had no problem at all in scandalizing the neighborhood and seducing the maidservants, did you?" She felt filled with confusion and anger. She had almost entirely surrendered to his wiles!

"Ah, so I am yet again to be reminded of my misspent youth? I suppose it matters not. I have become the complete libertine, of course, Miss Hunter: a rake, with no regrets and not a single selfless act to my name."

"Must you always mock? I did not ask for either this meeting or this accounting! No one's character is entirely black. I have learned from Sir George that you used to destroy his cruel rabbit traps. That surely was an act of mercy?"

If he noticed that she was being a little inconsistent, he gave no sign. Instead, his face was unreadable, though the sea-green gaze never left hers.

"Rabbits? Oh, yes! My cousin's traps. Perhaps you think in your romantic view of my youth, that I gave a thought to the poor suffering conies? Maybe I just wanted to annoy George?"

"And be thrashed for it?"

"Oh, it was worth anything to annoy George."

"And is that why you're here tonight, to annoy Sir George?"

"Of course! I intend to speak to Mary. That will annoy him very much."

"And Farmer Westcott's sheep? How was Sir George discommoded by that?"

"He was not. But don't think for a moment that you

can find an example of my behaving selflessly. Isn't it possible that I just like to amuse myself?" Which since it was so close to what Catherine had herself said to Amelia, reduced her to silence. "Now, if we have discussed the undoubtedly enthralling subject of my character for long enough, perhaps you will excuse me? Mary should be through with her duties for the night, and under the confusion of Lady Montagu's little entertainment, I can have her at my untender mercy. If I stay here a moment longer, I may be tempted to remember myself and kiss you again. It is unaccountable that I did not do so in the grotto, isn't it? I have had plenty of time to think about it, and I am mystified. You were certainly tempting enough!"

Catherine wished she had something to throw at him, but instead she was left standing helplessly in the little room. Her heart was beating uncomfortably. She knew perfectly well that he could only have destroyed George's rabbit traps, at the risk of such vicious punishment, because he had hated their cruelty. And the drowning sheep! He had very nearly died, and that was not only for Farmer Westcott and his wife's scones. No, the truth was that, in spite of his reputation, Devil Dagonet simply would not stand by and watch any creature suffer, if he could save it. She could not help but admire that. Then how had Millicent Trumble drowned? She would very much like to know the answer. She knew perfectly well that his kisses meant nothing to him, but they had stirred feelings in her she didn't know she possessed. In spite of herself she had become involved. She had never been kissed like that before, it would take more than a moment to regain her composure. There was no way she could quietly go back to her room and go to sleep now. Instead she went down through the house to the parlor and paced restlessly about. Faint strains of music echoed from the ballroom. She was lost in her tumbling thoughts, when the door opened silently behind her.

"We are both destined to be frustrated tonight, Kate. All my efforts to uncover the past are in vain; and you must hear the music without treading a measure. Mary will not speak to me; you are excluded from the ballroom." Catherine whirled around. Emerald eyes surveyed her under slightly lifted brows. "I have something for you. I almost forgot."

He walked up to her and formally presented her with her handkerchief, which she had last seen covered in mud up on the moor. Some unknown hand, perhaps Mrs. Westcott's, had laundered and starched it. How could she have so casually dismissed that bravery? And the jewelry had been his mother's: it was George who had no right to it. She had judged harshly, indeed. She blushed. 'Thank you, sir," she said stiffly. "I have been unjust, haven't I? I have no right at all to question your behavior."

"On the contrary, Miss Hunter, you alone have every right. If nothing else, I owe you something for your brave warning on Eagle Beacon, when we first met. It was my behavior which stands very little scrutiny on that occasion. And in the grotto, I caused you an unwarranted ducking! I can hardly apologize for kissing you, because I cannot find it in my black heart to regret it; but I have abused your trust, and put you in an untenable situation with your employer. Though you have twice caught me in the house, you have not betrayed me. Surely you can agree that it is I who am in your debt." He was moving aside some of the small pieces of furniture which cluttered the room, until there was a clear space of polished boards beside the piano. The distant band had struck up the strains of a waltz. Dagonet came back to her, and with a disarming smile, swept her an elegant bow. "And now," he said with a flourish, "may I have the honor of this dance?"

"How can you be so absurd, sir?"

"You don't like dancing?"

"That's not the point!"

"Then it is my dissolute self? Can you not forgive me? Miss Hunter, you break my heart! Now I do regret everything. You are afraid of me?"

She was laughing. "Of course not!"

"Good, for though I may be practiced in the art of seduction and abandonment, you are quite safe. I have the greatest respect for your father, and even I am unfortunately too much the gentleman to kiss you again in the drawing room. So you have no excuse. We may be outcasts from the revelries, but there is no reason why we shouldn't enjoy the music."

He took her hand and swept her into his embrace; instantly they whirled into the steps of the waltz. As she might have expected, he was a perfect partner. His hold at her waist was no more than courteous, her hand lay lightly in his. Catherine relaxed and allowed herself to follow his lead, her plain skirts eddying behind her. She had never felt so graceful or light-headed before. Around and around they spun together, in a delicious partnership of joy. She was floating on the wind. The waltz had never felt like this with any of the bumbling young men of her father's parish. At last the music died away, and Dagonet released her and bowed. The spell was broken. The next measure was a lively country dance.

"Alas," he cried. "We need at least four others to make up the figure." Within moments, he had placed the piano stool, the fire screen, an occasional table, and a large vase in the appropriate spots to represent the missing dancers. He swept her another gallant bow, and Catherine, thoroughly caught up in his mood, collapsed into helpless giggles.

"Do not give way, dear Kate, to unseemly emotion! The country dance is that most sensitive of occasions, where the parties step past each other in stately dignity, yet may exchange the speaking look, the longing glance. Hearts have been won and lost in the country dance: many a young lady's future happiness destroyed because the measure did not bring her a chance to throw an arch look at the gentleman of her fancy!"

"The men, of course," laughed Catherine, "have planned their siege of the most eligible heiress like a military campaign. They jostle for the honor of some notice from her limpid eyes, or a soft wave of her fan. The winner has his name on her card for the dance: he gets the curtsey at the beginning of the measure, yet then must see her handed down through the ranks of the losers! All his effort doesn't win him much."

"But if she will but look at him under her eyelashes, all is forgiven and forgotten!"

He began to weave between the side tables and the fire screen in a perfect satire of the most pompous members of the parish. The dreadful Mr. Crucible came instantly to mind. Helpless with laughter, Catherine joined in. Their dance became a pantomime, yet it was one performed with grace and wit, and to her immense surprise, the most innocent joy. She followed his movements, playing her part in the charade as if they were old childhood friends. Their hands touched and separated as required by the dance, and at the end he swept her a gallant bow and she sank into her most graceful curtsey. His face was alight with laughter.

"And the waltz, of course," he continued, as the music changed and he again swept her into his arms, "scandalously allows the gentleman to hold the lady of his choice in his gloved embrace. She, secure in the view of the whole world, may enjoy the chaste encounter without threat to her virtue, while driving him to distraction with her grace and charm."

"Unless, as has often been my unfortunate lot, Mr. de Dagonet, she has no particular liking for the gentleman, in which case his proximity is uncomfortable. Or she may think she likes him, but he treads on her toes, and she limps for a week."

"Then she should have refused him to start with, instead of thoughtlessly placing herself in such a man's power." The waltz ended, but he did not release her. "I trust I did not step on your toes, Kate?" She looked up at his face. She had never before seen him so relaxed, the sea-green eyes suffused with wit. He reached up a hand and gently stroked away a wisp of hair from the side of her neck. His smile invited all her trust and confidence. Wildly, she hoped he would kiss her again. But as she gazed up at him, the clear eyes darkened, and the long muscles beside his mouth stiffened as if in pain. He ran his finger gently over her lip, as he felt his heart contract with tenderness and desire. "Oh, dear!" he said, with a wry smile. "I hope we have not just made a dreadful mistake."

The door crashed open behind them.

"Good God, sir! What the deuce is the meaning of this?"

It was George. Dagonet leapt away from Catherine, thrusting her towards the couch, and himself backed towards the piano. Sir George, his face swollen with rage above his intricate cravat, advanced upon him. He wore his best embroidered satin waistcoat and fashionable black and white striped coat and breeches. His stout legs, encased for the evening in pink stockings, were embellished at the knee with ribbon rosettes. He was perfectly correctly dressed for a ball, except that in his right hand he carried a naked blade. Devil Dagonet was quite unarmed.

"You were ever proud to beat me at fencing when we were boys, sir, were you not?" hissed George.

"Yes, but then, cousin dear, I also had a weapon. Will you kill me outright, or only maim me a little?"

"Damn you, Dagonet! I would not do you the favor to relieve you of the burden of your worthless life!"

Dagonet vaulted over the piano. "Too bad. Bonaparte wouldn't do it either, though I tried to give his men every opportunity for seven long years. You were always too conservative with your occasional generous impulses."

The sword slashed, and Dagonet ducked gracefully around the wing chair, where he had once sat and read Walter Scott to Catherine. A deep gash appeared in the upholstery, and stuffing flew into the room. Catherine gasped and ran to the piano. She picked up a book, which she intended to throw at George, if the opportunity once presented itself.

"I only intend, sir," growled George, clumsily stumbling over the vase, which had so recently represented Mr. Crucible at the country dance, "to insult that insufferable vanity." The sword passed within inches of Dagonet's cheek.

"Well done, George! Your care of me is touching. Even my barber is not so solicitous of my looks; why, he nicked me on the chin just last week."

"I'll do more than a nick, sir! I'll give you a scar that will make women faint!"

"They already do, cousin, and willingly: into my arms!" laughed Dagonet. "You'll have to do better than that."

And as the blade whistled harmlessly over his head, he bent to take up the coal tongs, stepped past the fire screen, and cleanly disarmed his assailant. The weapon clattered to the floor, and, in an instant, the sword was his. Dagonet looked at the weapon in mock surprise. "How generous you are, cousin, to provide me with a weapon, after all. Now, how should I use it, I wonder? If anyone else in the room also had a rapier, we might fence like gentlemen, but our quarrel is still unevenly matched."

George, panting heavily, his color draining from his face, backed away.

"You will not strike at an unarmed man, sir!" he sputtered.

"Why not?" asked Dagonet seriously, testing the blade. "You just did. However, the neighborhood would only hear your version of events, were I to take revenge. *'Les absents ont toujours tort.'* So you may escape once more with your miserable hide intact." He strode to the window, carrying the sword, and lifted the sash, while Sir Montagu stood, his jowls dark with sweat, by the Sheraton sideboard. "Good night, George! Take care of Miss Hunter, I came across her all unwitting and could not resist taking advantage of her helplessness. The most shocking experience for a young lady!" And with Catherine thus neatly absolved of any responsibility, he was gone.

George collapsed onto the sofa. He had lost several buttons from his waistcoat, and one rosette was twisted around to dangle ridiculously from his kneecap.

"Allow me to fetch you a brandy, Sir George," said

Catherine, setting down the book. "I assure you I am quite unharmed, but I fear you may have overexerted yourself."

Sir George ignored her, and, getting his breath, ran instead to the window. He stuck out his head and a moment later pulled himself in, grasping his sword by the hilt. The bottom six inches were stained with the dirt from the flower bed. He turned, blade in hand, but Catherine, deciding that discretion might well be the better part of valor after all, had already left the room. She had more things to think about than George's discomfiture. She was very much afraid that she was falling prey to the practiced charms of a rake. "The absent are always in the wrong," indeed. Somehow, she must find out the truth about Devil Dagonet.

She was not able to find Mary alone and draw her aside for several days.

"Yes, ma'am?" asked Millicent Trumble's sister. "Did you want something?"

"Mary, I want you to tell me: what did Charles de Dagonet want from you the night of the ball, and why did you refuse him?"

Mary looked uncomfortably at her hands. "I can't rightly say, ma'am."

"Was it about your poor sister?"

"Yes, ma'am."

"Was she is love with him?"

Mary looked straight at Catherine and dimpled. "Oh, yes, Miss Hunter, we all was. He's still a dreadful handsome gentleman!"

Catherine smiled. "Mary! And you a married woman!"

Mary grinned and shook her head. "He wanted me to tell him what I knew of what happened, ma'am, when Milly was drowned. And if I still had any of her things."

"And do you?" Mary nodded. "Then why wouldn't you speak to Mr. de Dagonet and explain that to him?"

"Because all I have is a letter he wrote to her. I keep it hid. No one but me's ever seen it. Sir George asked me once if I knew anything about Milly's death that I hadn't told, but I kept mum. He forbid me to speak to Mr. de Dagonet anyway, on pain of dismissal."

"But if you had a letter, wasn't it your duty to show it to Sir Henry Montagu at the time?"

"I couldn't do that, ma'am, for it would have hanged Master Charles then and there."

"How could you protect him, Mary, after what happened to your sister?"

Mary's round face looked as stubborn as a child's. "Milly wasn't any better than she should have been, ma'am. It wouldn't have served no purpose to make things worse for Master Dagonet."

"Tell me the whole, Milly. I would like to help Mr. de Dagonet, too."

"I wasn't really in Milly's confidences, ma'am. She was a right pretty little thing, but she was younger than me and kept herself apart from the rest of us. Peter Higgins was real sweet on her; he followed her like a puppy wherever she went, but she wouldn't have no truck with him. She said she was destined for better things than to marry the gardener's lad. I can see her now toss her head in the kitchen, and say she had a gentleman who was going to take care of her. I didn't think she would have drowned herself, not our Milly."

"How was she found?"

"John Catchpole, ma'am, the stable man, found her

floating in the lake. He found Devil Dagonet, too, passed out cold from drink in the woods by the path, the bottle still in his hand. I remember the day they were both carried up to the house. John Catchpole was paid off afterward and went away. Sir Henry wouldn't keep him on. Poor Peter Higgins ran off, too. He was just a lad really; I dare say it broke his heart. Anyway, they were both gone from Lion Court before Master Dagonet was out of bed. He was sick as a dog for a few days, and still white as a sheet when he had to face Lord Blythe. They threw him out of the house, but none of it would bring our poor Milly back."

So two innocent servants had lost their positions, too, because of Charles de Dagonet! John Catchpole and Peter Higgins: Catherine wondered what on earth had become of them. It took another several minutes before she could persuade Mary to bring her the note. The evidence was damning indeed. *Dear Milly*, it read. *If you are in so much trouble, meet me tonight by the Rye Water Lake, and I'll see what I can do about it. You're too pretty a miss to be crying your eyes out in the stables.*—Dagonet. The handwriting flowed strong and confident across the paper. It was identical to that she had seen in his room, creating music for sonnets by Shakespeare.

"So he had arranged to meet her that night! Oh, Mary, she was your sister. Didn't you want revenge?"

"Revenge, ma'am? It was as much Milly's fault as his, I dare say. I wouldn't have wanted to be the one to send Master Charles to the gallows. He was too fine of a lad for that."

"Then why on earth did you keep the note?"

"Because he wrote it! There, I've said too much already. I never should have kept it." And with a sudden gesture, the housemaid threw the letter onto the fire.

Catherine wanted to weep. She had hoped so much to find that Mary had something that proved Devil Dagonet innocent of Millicent Trumble's death. He, instead, had known that she had something incriminating, and had been determined to wrest it from her. There had been no need for his concern; Mary was still so besotted with a girlish infatuation for him, she had suppressed evidence of his guilt, and now destroyed it. Dagonet was an out-and-out rogue: he would use anyone for his nefarious purposes, and never look back. Is that why he had been so charming with her? Why he had kissed her? So that she would also shield and protect him, while he rifled the house and made Mary give up the letter? Women were only too easy a prey for a rake like him. She blushed as she recalled the strange, wonderful sensations she had felt. What if he had kissed her again? She, too, sensible Catherine Hunter, had very nearly come under the spell.

8

Capt. David Morris had returned from the ball and walked whistling into his study at Stagshead. He was faintly inebriated, just a little tired, and very happy. For him and Amelia, the bumbling neighbors with their country manners, the unsubtle flatteries of Sir George, and the odd remarks of his sister Charlotte, had never existed. They had danced oblivious to their surroundings. That they had spent the evening entirely together was quite unexceptionable. They were to marry in just under a week. Morris stopped, however, quite suddenly, when he saw his friend awaiting him in front of the fireplace, dressed carelessly in buckskin breeches and dusty boots.

"What, Charles? Have you been out?"

Dagonet gazed at him for a moment, and smiled. "Congratulations on your happiness, my friend. You have spent the evening in the arms of your beloved, inviting nothing but the fond and sentimental best wishes of the parish. You have my felicitations."

Morris colored just a little. "Of course, I spent the evening with her. If you knew what it was to be in love with a fine young lady like Amelia Hunter, you wouldn't be so damned impertinent."

"Ah, my dear Captain! That is a state that is never to be my lot, is it? It's the great advantage of being a notorious rake, you know. One's grosser emotions will never be mistaken for anything so fine or delicate as love. The lightskirts will flock to your side, and you never have to endure the innocent embraces of the virginal daughters of good family. Marriage is out of the question, and you'd be a scoundrel to engage the affections of a decent woman, let alone return them. It's the most enviable position!"

Morris threw himself into a chair and released the knots in his cravat. Dagonet should not destroy his mood, damn him. "Pour yourself a drink, for God's sake, Dagonet," he said. "You're too dashed odd for words. What has happened, anyway?"

"Everything has happened, my dear Captain. And nothing that brandy will heal." His tone was still light and bantering, but Morris realized that he was controlling himself with a certain amount of effort. Dagonet began to stride back and forth before the fire.

"You went to Lion Court, didn't you? What the devil do you expect to find there, old fellow? Can't the past lie forgotten?"

Dagonet whirled to his friend. His green eyes blazed like fire. "I carry the past like the Old Man of the Sea. It awakes me at night like a succubus! Those last days at Lion Court haunt me day and night, and not because I can't forget, but because I can't remember! All I know is that a silly girl was drowned in the lake, and I was found stinking drunk in the woods! But I don't even know who discovered me, and I don't know why I was there in the first place. Millicent Trumble was nothing to me. It is a void as great as the mouth of hell. Did I kill her? There is no reason why I should have; but try living with that question, my friend. My uncle and grandfather obviously believed that I did; but no one would tell me their reasons. Who has the answers? No one outside of Lion Court, and few inside it! My uncle is dead. George, then? If he knew, I am the last person he would tell. Most of the servants knew nothing of it at the time. Only Mary, the girl's sister, is left! She might know something, and she won't talk to me!"

"So you saw her at last? How did you get in? The place was crawling with servants for the ball."

"I crept in over the roof, my friend, like the renegade that I am. It was no trouble to corner Mary in the hall behind the pantry, but my famous charm was useless. If she could have helped me, I believe she would; but she only blushed and mumbled. My pursuit of her confidences has thus been in vain. Maybe she has nothing to tell? Then I am condemned to never learn the truth!"

"You could have made her talk, Dagonet. You know it."

"Yet I would not." He relaxed suddenly and smiled, yet the green eyes were empty of mirth. "Miss Hunter will talk to her for me, I fear."

"You're a damned rogue, sir!"

"More than you know, Captain, but I am the victim of my latest trap!" Dagonet threw back his dark head and laughed. "No more of my maudlin troubles! Let me get that damned brandy."

Each morning that week found Amelia once again at Stagshead. She and David sat together on the small couch in the music room, talking over every dance, every moment that they had shared at Lion Court. She felt transported with bliss. Today, Captain Morris had her hand in his and was gently playing with her fingers as they conversed. At the harpsichord sat her usual chaperone, little Annabella. Amelia was far too correct to sit alone with David, even if they were almost man and wife. Annie, however, made no objection at all to these frequent visits. She was engaged this time in playing hilarious duets with the object of her latest infatuation, Devil Dagonet. It had not been difficult to keep her word, and not tell even Mama that the famous prodigal was staying with Captain Morris, since it was so much fun to be with him, and if Mama found out, she might put a stop to it.

"No, no!" squealed Annabella. "It doesn't go like that! It goes like this!" Her short fingers plopped out the tune.

"Does it?" said Dagonet, as seriously as if he were addressing a duchess. "How odd. I thought my part went like this." And he played the first few lines of an old song that sent Annie into peals of laughter.

They were all thus entirely engrossed, when Catherine arrived at the French window. She had walked all the way down from Lion Court in a stiff breeze, so that her face was flushed with color and tendrils of dark hair blew annoyingly around her face. She had gone over and over in her mind everything she knew about Charles de Dagonet. It wasn't too hard to guess where he might be staying. Who else had also spent years in the Peninsular Campaign—with whom else had he been on such easy terms as he rescued Farmer Westcott's prize flock—but Capt. David Morris? An instant before she appeared, Dagonet heard her boots on the gravel walk. He stopped playing with a light word to Annie, and went to face her. His features remained a perfect mask, but Annabella leapt gaily from the stool and ran to her favorite sister.

"Cathy! It was to be a secret, even from you; but now

you've found out! This is Devil Dagonet, and he's my very best friend in the world!"

Amelia had shown the grace to blush scarlet, though there was no real reason why she should, and David, with only a trace of awkwardness, began to ask Catherine to come in. They were interrupted by Dagonet. His tones were perfectly modulated, with just the merest hint of amusement. "Alas, discovered again! Miss Hunter has come to see me, my friend. Let me take her for a turn in the garden."

Before any of them could object, he had seized Catherine by the arm, thrust her onto the terrace, and closed the door behind them. "The shrubbery is splendid this time of year, ma'am. May I show you the finest of Captain Morris's rhododendrons?"

"Let go of me! How can you! The flowers have been over for months!"

Undeterred, he propelled her away from the house. When they reached the thickest part of the plantation, he spun her to face him.

"Now, Kate dear, tell me why you hate me so much."

"How can you ask? Destruction runs before you like a pack of hounds, doesn't it, sir? You will use and toss away anyone in your path, if it suits your own purposes. It must have seemed a fine joke to enlist me for your cause. And how can you involve Annie and Amelia in your deceptions? I do despise you, Mr. de Dagonet, but I would not give you the honor of such a strong emotion as hate."

Dagonet released her, and she began to pace up and down the little gravel path. Quietly watching her, he leant casually against the trunk of a great beech tree. He had himself under an iron control. "Mary has told all; and I am condemned?" His expression was totally unreadable, but his tone was light. "Your face is an open book, Kate. Deception is impossible for you, isn't it?"

"As it is natural for you? What do even your kisses mean? A fleeting amusement for a Casanova—to practice your seductions on the daughter of a country vicar? You began with a fifteen-year-old maid in your own home. How many women have you left with broken hearts over the intervening years?"

"I have been completely ruthless, of course." The sun danced in his dark hair as the wind tossed it over his forehead, but the green eyes were dark with shadows.

"Ruthless enough to have me do your work for you with Mary? Why didn't you bully or beguile her yourself? She would still have protected you forever. She did show me the note, but don't worry about it anymore, sir. She has destroyed it."

"What note? I am in the dark, sweet Kate."

"The one you wrote Millicent Trumble the day she was drowned. The note inviting her to meet you beside Lion Court Lake."

And at last Catherine had the satisfaction of seeing him turn stark white beneath his tan. It was a moment before he spoke again, but his voice betrayed nothing but an idle curiosity. "What other charming revelations did she make to you?"

"Nothing that you cannot know yourself, Mr. de Dagonet. The bottle was still in your hand, I understand, when John Catchpole found you in the woods. It must have been a dreadful day for him. Your uncle paid him off the same week, and an innocent servant had to make a new way in the world."

The color was still drained from his face, but he replied quite calmly. "Then I am found out at last in my true colors, Miss Hunter. But I have succeeded, haven't I, in my schemes, for you have told me what I wanted to know; and how could your opinion of me possibly matter?"

"It matters not a whit, sir, since I do not imagine that we shall meet again."

There was silence for a moment, before he replied. "Then this is goodbye, Kate. I shall leave Fernbridge tomorrow. Have no concern for your sisters. Amelia has eyes for no one but Captain Morris, she has hardly been aware of me; and as for Annie, I have been a childish adventure that she will forget with the next storm. I amused her, but I have done her no harm."

With a formal bow, he was gone. She watched him stride off up the gravel walk, before she turned away and left the garden. She could not face her sisters; Dagonet would have to make her excuses for her.

The excuses were made with a remarkable grace, and Amy and Amelia left together without the slightest idea that anything very terrible had gone wrong. Captain Morris, however, was not to be so easily put off.

"Did Miss Hunter discover what you wanted, Charles? Did Mary hold the clue to your reinstatement in society?"

Dagonet dropped into a chair. His face was set like stone. "I am doubly damned, my friend. She succeeded only too well! It would appear that I arranged to meet Milly Trumble that day, though why I should have done so, I have no idea. I wrote a note, in fact, which Mary had kept. I have thus not been proved innocent, but undoubtedly guilty; and so my nefarious schemes have backfired in my face. I have, however, learned something else that was unknown to me."

"Which is?"

Dagonet laughed bitterly, and leaping to his feet, began to collect up his few belongings that lay scattered about the room. "The name of the man who found us that day: a certain John Catchpole! My uncle's favorite henchman, and a man remarkably good with horses! I am off to Newmarket, Captain. The races start next week, and it's about time that I mend my sorry finances in the betting tents."

Morris stood up and took him by the hand. "I'm devilish sorry to see you go, sir!"

"Never fear, David. Like a bad penny, I'll turn up when you least want me; but credit me with at least enough sense to make myself scarce before your wedding. You're marrying into a very fine family, you know."

The men shook hands and Dagonet made for the door. At the threshold he stopped and turned back for a moment. "You may set your mind at ease, Captain, about Catherine Hunter: the brave and beautiful sister of your beloved. Her heart and virtue are quite safe. I have made sure, you see, in my competent way, that she despises me."

Amelia was a radiant bride, and the weather and the arrangements conspired to give her a perfect day. She received the well-wishes of the entire parish, and then she and Captain Morris left Stagshead for the Lake District for their honeymoon. Mrs. Clay and Sir George Montagu had ridden away from Lion Court in the large carriage shortly before the wedding. George declared himself unutterably bored with Exmoor and announced he was off to Scotland for some shooting. Charlotte had received an invitation to visit from a bosom acquaintance, with whom she would be able to indulge in many happy hours of shredding the reputations of others. Life at Lion Court settled back into its humdrum existence. Lady Montagu spent a week or two bemoaning the departure of her children, then quietly slipped into her old routine. The name of Devil Dagonet was never mentioned, but Catherine saw his face everywhere in the house. She could not rid her mind of him. How could she have been so foolish, as to almost lose her heart to such an out-and-out rogue? If she thought, however, that she could be free of any mention of him for very long, she was mistaken. She entered the parlor one morning to find Lady Montagu in a state of considerable agitation.

"Oh, Miss Hunter! The most unexpected thing! I am quite overset, my dear. Lord Blythe wishes me to go to Bath this instant!"

"I trust your father still enjoys his good health, my lady?"

"Oh, yes indeed. His health is still quite sound; remarkably so for a man of his age. No, he received a letter from Charlotte, oh, weeks ago!" She glanced down at the sheet in her hand and read: "Your daughter, ma'am, has had the effrontery to send me the most impertinent piece of gossip." She looked up at Catherine, her brow wrinkled with distress. "He has been fretting over it for all this time, and now demands that I go and give him an account of the whole. How Mrs. Clay could have been so careless as to so upset her grandfather, I don't know, but she wrote and told him of our terrible visit from Charles de Dagonet. I must go! You will accompany me, won't you, Miss Hunter? We must leave at the earliest convenience. Bath! It means so much packing and trouble that

we might as well go right on to London, for I am promised to visit Charlotte in November."

Thus, two mornings later, Catherine left Exmoor for
the first time. Comfortably seated beside Lady Montagu
in her cumbersome coach and firmly setting aside all
thoughts of the dangerous Mr. de Dagonet, she set off for
Bath. With the further promise of London, she was in the
highest spirits, and she could not deny, even to herself,
the greatest curiosity to meet the notorious old Lord
Blythe, Marquis of Somerdale, grandfather to both
Dagonet and Sir George Montagu, his stout cousin.

9

The town of Newmarket, not far from Cambridge, was the heart of the horse racing world, and a Mecca for all those young men of fashion who had nothing better to do with their time and their money than lay wagers at the October meetings. The course was a constant pandemonium of noise and color; fashionable sporting gentlemen rubbed shoulders with the professionals of the turf and the serving classes, all mad with the frenzy of outguessing the odds. The air reverberated with the excited cries of men and horses. Charles de Dagonet stood a little apart from the milling crowds, his broad, elegant shoulders propped against a railing, and quietly surveyed the scene. He had no intention of placing bets on the horses. The pay he had received in the Peninsular Campaign had been modest enough, and now he had no income at all. With his slender resources, he could only mend his fortunes in a situation where skill played a greater role than chance, and that was at the gaming tables, not at the track. It was not long before the event for which he had so patiently been waiting occurred.

"Good God! Dagonet! When the deuce did you return

from France, sir? The last I saw, you were at Wellington's coat tails in Paris. That was in June!"

Dagonet swept a graceful bow which instantly inspired a surge of envy in the young man facing him. "Good day, Wrackby. I am returned to England, as you see, and have spent the intervening time making housemaids mumble and stealing jewels. I trust I find you in good health?"

The young Viscount Wrackby made as if to clap Dagonet on the shoulder. Then he recalled that Devil Dagonet wasn't the kind of chap with whom you got too familiar, so he wrung his hand instead, memorizing the reply he had just heard, to share later with his cronies.

"Oh, never better! You're the very fellow anyone could the most want to see. Kendal and Frost are here. You remember them from Paris? Come, after this match, we'll give you a game of dice! There's a tent set up over yonder. You know that Crockford's opened a hazard saloon in Newmarket town? It promises to outshine his own Hell in St. James's Street!"

A few moments later, Dagonet was walking with a group of the most fashionable dandies, any one of whom would have given half his fortune if he could only affect quite that air of casual menace, to the spot where they could best see the start of the next race: a match between a colt and a filly.

"You'll lay a pony on Mr. Lane's bay colt out of Scalper, Dagonet?" Wrackby lowered his voice to a whisper. "A cert, sir! The filly has been made safe! The ring men shout themselves hoarse over a fixed thing."

"I'd not back him," said Dagonet, with a smile. "My humble guess is that the filly will win."

Lord Kendal instantly followed his lead, and stared at Wrackby for a moment through his quizzing glass. "Indeed, she will, sir! The colt has no wind; without wind he has no air; and with no air, sir, he's no Dandy and no gentleman, but a scurvy rogue. We'll have none of him! I'm for the mare." He took out his book, where all his bets were recorded.

"But Golden Rule has took poison! I had it from one of the touts. The bay colt has more wind than the filly, sir! I'll lay you a hundred on him!"

"And the blacklegs are in on the game, Wrackby," said Dagonet. "Save your guineas, and I'll take them off you at hazard."

Wrackby hesitated; Dagonet had the infuriating habit of almost always being right, and now Kendal would benefit, but it was too late. There was a roar as the two horses came under starter's orders. The bay colt was fretting and dancing under his jockey. He was a sleek, nervous horse, and the filly who was supposed to be poisoned certainly looked sleepy in comparison.

"Such a steed was Cyllarus, tamed to the rein of Amyclean Pollux," drawled Kendal. He did not seem in the least concerned that the filly was so quiet.

"Hardly Amyclean Pollux, my dear chap," said Dagonet smoothly. "The jockey's an English John Bull. The colt is mishandled, wouldn't you say?"

"Never say so, sir!" interrupted Wrackby. "Mr. Lane has the best lads in England."

"Not unless he has the hire of one John Catchpole. I never saw a better man with a horse."

"Catchpole?" said Frost. "I've heard of him, I believe. Used to run Lord Bentwhistle's stables in Hertfordshire. An Exmoor chap, wasn't he?"

Dagonet smiled. "The very man. And is he still there?"

"Devil take me, if I know, sir!"

"I care nothing for your Exmoor men, Frost," interrupted Wrackby. "I still say it's the nag, not the filly, wins the money. I'll stake you all a dinner he'll win by two lengths."

Lord Kendal turned and quizzed the viscount until he blushed. "What, sir? He's not worth a doxy's promise!"

The horses were off. Within a hundred feet, the bay colt had stumbled and checked, and Golden Rule, who was supposed so reliably to lose, won by several lengths.

"Now, I'm ruined! I had a hundred guineas against her!"

"And a dinner, sir!"

Some time later, bemoaning their losses with a curious lack of conviction, the dandies retired to the gaming tent, and ordered the most expensive wine they could find. Led by Dagonet, the conversation soon became a debate over the virtues of the various training methods espoused by different horsemen, but nothing more was to be learned about John Catchpole. Still later that night, after a comfortable meal consisting of soup, sauces of lobster and oysters, various dressings, sausages and roast beef, followed by jellies, tarts, nuts, cheese, and fruit, all liberally washed down with claret and port, the gentlemen found themselves around the gaming tables at Crockford's, wagering deep against the rolls of the dice. At four in the morning, mysteriously still almost sober, though admired as the wit of the evening by his fellows, Charles de Dagonet walked thoughtfully back to his lodgings the richer by four hundred guineas, and a vital piece of information about a certain Exmoor man. The next morning early, he set out for the famous Hertfordshire training stables of one Lord Bentwhistle.

"And what the devil do you have against my grandson, miss?" snapped Lord Blythe.

Catherine looked steadily at the old man facing her across the neat parlor in his rented rooms in Bath. He was nothing like she had expected. Devil Dagonet's irascible grandfather was as round as a plum, and about the same color. The florid cheeks were haloed by a shock of snow-white hair and whiskers. His left leg, in a soft woolen stocking to relieve the pain of his gout, was propped up on a needlepoint stool. At every other sentence he pounded the floor beside his chair with a silver-topped cane, and the brass buttons on his chest leapt with the effort.

He glared at her. "Well? I can tell you don't care for him. He's a damned rascal, and what's worse, he broke his word to me; but the jewelry was his, and there's no female on this earth can resist him."

"Then I hope I am the exception, my lord," said Catherine.

"Do you, by God?"

At which point, Lady Montagu tried to intervene. "Father, you cannot imagine how dreadful it was! Dagonet threatened me with a pistol! In my own house!"

"*My* house, madam."

"Yes, well. Miss Hunter cannot do other than despise him. He had the temerity to insult her in front of us all."

The old gentleman glared at Catherine once again. "So he kissed you! If I were sixty years younger, I'd do the same myself."

"I see where Dagonet gets his arrogance, my lord! Had you done so, I should have reserved just the same distaste for you."

"You're a damned impertinent baggage, young lady!"

Catherine's blood was up. "And you, my lord, are a despotic old man."

Lady Montagu's mouth had dropped open, but to her

immense surprise, before her father could reply, her companion suddenly began to laugh. "This is too absurd, my lord!" choked Catherine. "You must forgive me!" Then suddenly the Marquis was laughing too, in a great shout of good humor, leaving Lady Montagu to wonder how on earth the unprepossessing Miss Hunter had managed to win over her father with less effort and more completely than she or her own children had ever done.

Later that day, Catherine sat alone at the harpsichord. Softly she sang the tender words to the old song:

"We lingered where the water flows; sweet promises
   her eyes did make.
I gave her but a single rose, but she my heart and
   soul did take.
I am a knight without a grail; I am a tower without
   a dove;
I am a ship without a sail; and lost am I without my
   love."

It was the song she had been singing when Dagonet found her in the grotto. She shook her head, furious that the words should bring her a memory of his sea-green gaze. It was no use. However carelessly he had used her, she must know more about the mystery of Devil Dagonet. What she had learned from Mary clarified nothing, really. From what Lord Blythe had said earlier, there had been some matter of honor, of a promise made between gentlemen. That had certainly been part of the reason for Lord Blythe's rage, and for Dagonet's banishment. The old Marquis was of exactly the type and the generation to forgive or even admire an entanglement with a woman. What had he said to Lady Montagu? "I never gave a damn about the girl, ma'am. And I don't give a damn about young Charles showing up at Lion Court. Do that pompous son and insufferable daughter of yours good to get a shaking up. I'm damned if I wouldn't have liked to see their faces! But Dagonet broke his word to me, and he can go to the devil where he belongs, as far as I'm concerned. I just don't want any more impertinent letters on the subject from your daughter, ma'am!" Then, seeing Catherine's expression, he had turned to her. "And what the devil do you have against my grandson, miss?" At which point, Catherine realized quite how much the old man had been hurt by the discovery of his grandson's betrayal, and quite how much there was that she could not fathom about Devil Dagonet. How could he be both musician and swordsman, soldier and horseman, risk his life for the sake of helpless creatures; yet carelessly destroy the hearts of women? What had really happened by Lion Court Lake; why had he arranged to meet Millicent Trumble? He might be a ruthless rake, but to her chagrin, she was forced to admit she could not stay indifferent; somehow she must discover the truth.

During the rest of her stay in Bath, however, her resolution was not to be tested. Lord Blythe did not again refer to Dagonet or to the reason for his disgrace. Instead Catherine played chess or cards with the old man; entertained him at the harpsichord; and argued the issues of the day. The brown trees and leaf-strewn pavements of October gave way to November's damp streets and bare branches. They had been in Bath almost a month, when at last she and Lady Montagu packed up to go on to London. Lord Blythe hobbled out with his cane to see them off.

"Good-bye, Papa," said Lady Montagu, fussing with her gloves. "Shall we see you in London this winter?"

"Bah! I'm damned if I'd make the journey for the sake of your whey-faced offspring! Now, if Miss Hunter would promise me a game of chess, I'd come for the sake of one more checkmate."

"You'll not get it, my lord!" replied Catherine with a laugh. "I'm determined not to be beaten again."

The old man's face was suddenly wistful. "We're a good match, young lady. It was Dagonet who could never be bested. I'd like to see you in a match with him! But then, you don't care for him, do you?"

"I think my feelings match yours, Lord Blythe. He can go to the devil, as far as I'm concerned."

He gave her an extremely shrewd glance. "Yes, I was afraid your feelings might match mine, my dear. He's a damnable fellow! But if he should ever cause any hurt to you, he'll answer to me for it!"

Catherine was furious to find that her voice was a little unsteady. "How could he possibly injure me, my lord?" she lied. "I am immune to Devil Dagonet."

10

It was still early in October when Charles de Dagonet rode casually into Bentwhistle Park. All the way from Newmarket, he had not allowed himself to think once about Catherine Hunter. Whatever tender feelings she might have unexpectedly aroused, he could never allow her to be part of his life. As long as the mystery about his past conduct remained, there was nothing he could in honor offer her. He was an outcast and made his living at hazard. She was the respectable daughter of an old benefactor, and the sister of his best friend's wife. It was to be sincerely hoped that she was so disgusted by him that she had forgotten all about him. He entered the stable yard and was accosted at once by a groom, who doffed his cap respectfully at the sight of the powerful-looking gentleman mounted on a silver-gray thorough-bred.

"May I be of any help, sir?"

"You might provide a trough for the gray, young fellow, and walk him out a little. Here's a guinea for your trouble. Then I should like a word with your head stable man. I'm in the mind to purchase a new mount."

"Why, thank you, sir! Much obliged. That'd be Mr. Grimes, sir."

"Mr. Grimes, is it? I don't recall the name, but then, I've been away in the Peninsula. Has he been here long?"

"These five years, sir. Since I first started as a lad."

"He must be a good man, then, for I just saw a couple of Lord Bentwhistle's nags win up at Newmarket. Seems I remember some of the horses from the old days, too. Who was the trainer then?"

"A Mr. Catchpole, sir. But he's gone now from Hertfordshire. There was some kind of trouble about him; had something on his mind, most like, and he took to drink. The master turned him off without a reference."

"Did he though? Whatever became of the chap?"

"Went to London, as I heard tell, sir. Came to a sticky end, I wouldn't be surprised. He was a rough customer after a bout with the bottle. Though good enough with the horses, he took to beating up us lads. I had a hard knock or two from him myself. Well, the master wouldn't stand for it, and Catchpole was turned off. None of us was sorry to see him go, and that's a fact. Never heard of him since, and good riddance." The groom spat into the cobbles. "Why, here's Mr. Grimes now, sir. Good day to you."

As the groom led the gray away to water, Dagonet turned to the newcomer and engaged him in a knowledgeable conversation about thoroughbreds. They were occupied for over an hour, but as it turned out, there was nothing in Lord Bentwhistle's stables that interested him after all, and much to the regret of Mr. Grimes, Devil Dagonet rode away without making a purchase. He had what he had come for, however, and the silver thoroughbred was turned at a spanking trot for that great city where anyone with something on his mind could disappear for five years or longer: London.

Catherine and Lady Montagu arrived at Mrs. Clay's Leicester Square residence quite exhausted. The journey to London from Bath had taken two long days, and the weather had been terrible, so that the turnpike was mired in mud. All her life, Catherine had longed to see the capital city, but as they drove in, there was a solid downpour of rain, and Lady Montagu insisted on having the windows drawn tight and curtained. Thus she saw nothing of all that glory, splendor, and bustle that she had dreamed of admiring. She caught the briefest glimpse of the gracious square with its imposing modern facades as she was hurried into the house, and they were greeted by Mrs. Clay herself.

Lady Montagu was instantly whisked into the elegant parlor, which boasted a roaring fire that crackled and flamed in the most inviting way, while Catherine, in her damp coat, was directed to oversee the servant's disposal of the luggage. As the ladies left her in the hall, she could not help but overhear Charlotte comment to her mother.

"Really, Mama, why did you have to bring that impossible country companion? Dagonet saw right away what kind of woman she is. I trust you will not expect me to entertain her in my drawing room. Mr. Clay was always so particular about maintaining the highest standards of propriety amongst one's acquaintance." They entered the drawing room together. "Let me introduce Lady Pander, who has been so good as to keep me company until you arrived."

Through the open door Catherine caught a glimpse of a sharp-faced woman in dark blue silk. After the initial introductions, Lady Pander launched into a description of the society that had already arrived in London for the season. "Lady Beauville is reliably said to have been seen traveling with the Viscount Fenchurch, quite unchaperoned! I trust it can't be true, but I do have it on the best authority that Miss Hope was compromised by Lord Albers, and yet he won't marry her, they say; my dears, she is quite ruined! Of course, I shall not spread the tale, but it's on everybody's lips."

Catherine immediately surmised that this vicious gossip must be Charlotte's bosom friend, but the confidences of the ladies were immediately interrupted by the arrival of Sir George Montagu. George gave Catherine the merest nod, before the footman showed him into the drawing room. There was an instant effusion of bowing and scraping and murmured polite greetings, then Catherine heard George's voice rise to a bellow. "Yes, it is true; the talk of the whole damned town! Begging your pardon, Lady Pander. He's here in London, and lording it up with a crack high-perch phaeton and pair; been here almost six weeks! I met Lord Kendal the other day, and the fellow had the nerve to tell me that Dagonet was fast becoming the favorite in the Prince's set. He's even been elected to White's. He's gambling deeper than any of them. Yet the money's coming from horse trading! They say he's taken up with the lowest crowd in the city: horse dealers and touts and such like!"

"La!" cried Lady Pander. "How delicious! You can't mean it!"

"You understand, Lady Pander," interrupted Charlotte. "We have quite overthrown any connection. Charles de Dagonet is no longer considered to be a member of this family!"

"That's what I told Kendal, ma'am," continued

George. "I informed him that after the behavior which Dagonet had displayed at Lion Court that caused the Marquis to disinherit him, we could trust he would never be accepted again by polite society. And Kendal had the effrontery to fix me with that dammed quizzing glass of his, and insult me to my face!"

"What did he say?" asked Lady Pander.

" 'I wish I'd had the presence of mind to drown all my past mistresses, sir. I could have saved myself a great deal of trouble.' Those were his very words."

There was a shocked silence for a moment. Catherine could imagine Lady Pander's smirk, as she saved up this *on dit* to spread around town.

"Well," commented Mrs. Clay, at last. "My late husband would not have found Dagonet defensible. Mr. Clay had the highest of standards. But what can you expect from someone who is half French? Bad blood will out. That the other gentlemen tolerate him for their amusement in the gaming hells is all very well, but we can rest easy that we shall not encounter our cousin at Almack's or in any well-bred drawing room!"

Catherine would hear no more. She had disposed of Lady Montagu's overflowing baggage, and taking up her own modest valise, asked the housekeeper for directions to her room. She was not in the least surprised to find herself placed in the attics.

The next morning, she arose early and ruefully looked out of the window at the bare rooftops of other houses. The faint noise of the capital city drifted up to her: horses and carriages, the cries of street vendors, the flutter of pigeons. The servants had been long awake, of course. The housemaids started at five with the fireplaces and the rugs, before beginning on the silver and boots. It would be another hour before they began to bring hot water and chocolate to the ladies. How on earth was she supposed to fit in with this household? And how could she possibly pursue her determination to find out the truth about Devil Dagonet? Everything she knew of him was damning, except that he was kind to animals and good with children. Little Annabella had been entranced by him. Yet he was still an unmitigated rogue. Just because he had kissed her so expertly and dallied with her with such unaccustomed gallantry, she had been about to lose her heart to him. No doubt he was an accomplished seducer, a man without scruple. He had only tried to win her affection in order to use her to aid him in his scheme to influence Mary. How easy she had been for him! The thought made her wince. A green girl straight from the vicarage, she had been no match for his practiced wiles. And yet, there was something else about him: as if he himself was keeping some great secret. She remembered that cold little room over the entry at Lion Court, with its books and music; the gallant courage it must have taken to stand up to his uncle with such defiance over George's rabbit traps. How could such a boy have so easily become a rake, and now be living by his wits as a gambler? She shook her head. She must know more about this enigmatic man. What had really happened at Lion Court Lake? Why had Dagonet been found there, sodden with drink? Why had the mention of Milly's note made him blanch in Captain Morris's garden? There was only one clue, the name of the man who had discovered him at the lake: a certain John Catchpole. Her thoughts were interrupted by one of the maids.

"Miss Hunter? There's a lady to see you downstairs, ma'am, a Lady Brooke."

She knew absolutely no one of that name, and it was far too early for a polite morning visit. In amazement, Catherine followed the girl down to the drawing room. A very pretty young lady was sitting by the fire. She was dressed in extremely fashionable, ebony silk mourning, with a black hat and veil perched on her golden curls. As the door opened, she leapt from the chair with a delighted squeal, and flung herself into Catherine's arms. It was Amelia.

"Amy! What on earth? What has happened?"

"Oh, Cathy, it's so good to see you! I knew you would be up! Everything is wonderful! David couldn't come, but he sends his best." She quickly indicated her black dress. "Don't mind the mourning; it's not for anyone you know. Everyone is as well as could be."

Catherine warmly returned her sister's embrace. "Then I'm very relieved. But where is this Lady Brooke I'm supposed to meet?"

"Right here!" With a merry grin, Amelia indicated herself. "Come and sit down, and I'll tell you all about it."

The two girls sat by the fire and Amelia, her blue eyes shining, began her tale. "David has come into an inheritance. It's the most unexpected thing! His great uncle, Lord Brooke, died recently of an inflammation of the lungs, and the heir was suddenly killed within the week in a hunting accident. David hardly knew the Brookes, and, of course, I had never met them, so you can't expect me to be too sad, you know; but no one else is left of the family, and Captain David Morris is now Lord Brooke of Somerset, and your own little sister, married barely seven weeks, has become Amelia, Lady Brooke! There is a town house in Grosvenor Square, and vast estates near Taunton, and no end of complication and business. David is to be running back and forth forever, but we had to travel to London to see the old Lord Brooke's man of business, and so I am to be in our town house for the winter! We both insist that you will come and keep me company, since he is to be gone so much. Do say that you will. And you must come this instant, since David leaves again in the morning."

Catherine hesitated for only a moment. Of course, she would accept her sister's invitation. Life as companion to Lady Montagu was rapidly becoming intolerable. As she smiled and gave a little nod, Amelia leaned forward and grasped her hands. "I'm so glad, Cathy. We shan't go about much in society, because of the mourning, except among the family, but David will be much relieved to have you with me. And I thought to write Mama and have her send Annie up to London to stay for a while. She would adore the sights of the city, and I need to stay in practice entertaining children." Her face was suffused with a subtle blush, and she laughed. "You see, I know it's early to be absolutely certain, but I think—no I'm quite sure really!—I'm to have a baby in the summer!"

While Amelia waited, Catherine repacked her modest case. At breakfast, she gave her notice to Lady Montagu. That lady expressed the severest regrets that dear Miss Hunter was no longer to fetch and carry for her, but she agreed that she must indeed be with her sister during such a delicate time. Mrs. Clay was not sorry to see Catherine Hunter leave her house, but she was extremely sorry that she had ever been rude to her, now that she was Lady Brooke's relation. In a last-minute effusion of sanctimonious protestations, she tried to establish a friendship. Catherine was polite and tried to hide her secret amusement, before she and Amelia drove away together in the grand Brooke carriage, emblazoned with its ancient coat of arms. In contrast to the little attic room where she had spent the previous night, Catherine was shown into a gracious bedchamber at Brooke House, overlooking the square. The huge drawing room was dominated by a large pianoforte, which the new Lady Brooke demanded she play as often as she liked. Neither of these things quite accounted, however, for the delicious happiness that filled Catherine as Amelia showed her around. The one thing that mattered the most was her sudden, newfound freedom. As Amelia's guest, she could come and go as she pleased, and there was nothing to stop her in her quest to find out the truth about Devil Dagonet.

She was not to find the time immediately, however, for Amelia insisted on buying her a new wardrobe, and the sisters spent long hours at the most fashionable mantua-makers, where Catherine must be measured and prodded just as if, she commented in an aside that made Amy giggle, she were a horse being fitted for harness. Then she must accompany her sister on the visits that duty required they make to various relations of the old Lord Brooke. They had been subjected to several of these—where they sat in hushed drawing rooms, and made polite conversation—when Amelia received an invitation to dine with an ancient aunt of David's, one Lady Easthaven.

Catherine did not go to a great deal of trouble with her toilette, expecting another dull evening. She selected an attractive, pale gold silk dress that Amelia had given her, but she dressed her hair herself, and had no jewelry. However, she knew that she was perfectly presentable to be the guest of another aged relation. They left for Lady Easthaven's large mansion on the outskirts of the city in

good time, and were allowed into the house by a particularly erect and pompous butler. They were shown into
the drawing room, where Catherine was surprised to see
a small company already gathered. It was obviously
going to be a society evening, rather than the quiet family
meeting that she had expected. The tiniest of wrinkled
ladies, in an old-fashioned hooped dress and a great deal
of rouge, hurried over to greet them.

"My word! Delighted! Delighted! Lady Brooke, you
are most welcome to the family, my dear. And Miss
Hunter. Welcome, welcome!"

They were introduced one by one to the guests, Lady
Easthaven keeping up a steady stream of bright conversation.

"Surely we are missing two gentlemen?" whispered
Amy, when she was able to get her sister's ear. "We shall
not be able to sit down to dinner without having extra
ladies."

"Perhaps Lady Easthaven does not worry about such
niceties," replied Catherine softly. "She would seem to be
quite the eccentric."

At that very moment, the door opened again, and the
two missing gentlemen were shown into the room. The
first was obviously a very serious dandy. He stopped and
quizzed the company through a small glass, and bowed
to the ladies.

"My dear Lady Easthaven," he said lightly. "I have
worn my neckcloth in a *trône d'amour* in your honor, and
now I cannot turn my head without cutting my cheek on
the points of my collar. Nevertheless, I cannot fail to see
in my stiff scanning of the company, that you have two
young ladies here whom I have never had the pleasure to
meet. You will sit me next to whichever is unmarried, I
trust?"

He stared steadily at Catherine, but she had no eyes at all for him. She had colored deeply and was gazing at the other gentleman. Dressed simply in neat evening clothes, his sea-green eyes were laughing back at her.

"You are embarrassing Miss Catherine Hunter, Lord Kendal," said Devil Dagonet. "If you will put down that damned quizzing glass, I will introduce you."

A moment later, Dagonet was bowing deeply over her hand. "How refreshing to see you in a clean, dry dress," he said.

"If I can avoid spilling my wine down my skirts, I shall attempt to keep it that way, at least for the evening!" she shot back. "Whatever are you doing here, sir?"

"Why, I came, as I imagine you did, to eat my dinner. Not every member of the ton has the fine scruples of Mrs. Clay, but then few have had the good fortune to have enjoyed the impeccable example of her dear departed husband. Lady Easthaven is not so nice. Besides, she is an old friend of my grandfather's, and has known me since childhood. She has the bizarre idea that I am not capable of wrongdoing, and would like to marry me to an heiress."

Catherine was not able to reply, since Lord Kendal was demanding her attention, and it was that gentleman who escorted her into dinner. Dagonet was seated at the far end of the table, beyond the three-tiered mold of game mousse, and she was forced to give her attention to her immediate neighbors. She could not help but notice, however, as the elaborate formal dishes were brought and removed, that he seemed to have his companions in delighted laughter for most of the meal, particularly a pretty young lady in a sapphire necklace.

When the gentlemen joined the ladies in the drawing room after dinner, Lady Easthaven lost no time in demanding that she be provided with music, and Dagonet was called upon to play. Catherine watched him with interest as his fingers roamed over the keys for a moment. In the next instant, she was transported. Why should she be surprised that he played with such subtlety and power? There was not another sound in the room except the sweeping notes, until the company burst into applause at the end of the piece.

Dagonet spun around on the piano stool. "It is customary, Lady Easthaven, for the ladies to entrance us with their talents." The lady in the sapphires sat up a little straighter. She had informed him at dinner that she loved to both play and sing. Her brow contracted as he continued. "Miss Hunter sings, I believe?"

Catherine was trapped. She went graciously to the piano, where Dagonet was laughing up at her. Before she could express any preference, he began the opening bars to the old folk song that she had sung in the pool.

"How dare you choose this?" she hissed.

With a wicked grin, he began the words:

"We lingered where the water flows, sweet promises
　　her eyes did make;
I gave her but a single rose, but she my heart and
　　soul did take."

She was forced to join in, and supply the lady's part:

"I am a maiden lost in sadness, lost the hand
　　without the glove;
Lost my laughter, lost my gladness; lost am I
　　without my love."

As soon as they finished, under cover of the applause, she leaned over and was able to speak to him.

"Lady Easthaven is wrong, sir. You delight in wrong-doing."

His reply was casual. "Why ever should you think so, Miss Hunter?"

"Because you are determined to always discompose me. How could you force me to join you in a love song! I think that it is time I got my own back."

She sat next to him on the piano stool, and launched into a well-known ballad of betrayal. Without a moment's hesitation, Dagonet supplied the harmony.

"I pray you will not, dear Kate," he whispered under cover of the music. "My wicked habits are no concern of yours!"

Catherine turned to glance at him, and suddenly felt her heart turn over. It was simply unfair for a man to have such a profile! And they were sitting altogether too close for any kind of emotional equilibrium. "But perhaps I will make them my concern, sir," she hissed. "Such a reprobate should be brought to his accounting!"

"Are you threatening me, Kate?" His voice was perfectly level, but his expression was unreadable.

Catherine forced herself to look away, before her wayward body betrayed her. "If I were, it would only be just, don't you think?"

They were not to be able to speak privately again. The demands of the company must be met. Dagonet next played a duet with the lady in the sapphires, then another guest took a turn at the instrument. Within another couple of hours, the company broke up and Devil Dagonet returned alone to his lodgings in Jermyn Street.

What Catherine meant to do, he had no idea, but he could not let it worry him. He must devote himself to his quest. John Catchpole had disappeared very thoroughly into London's noxious underground. In subtle pursuit of his quarry, Dagonet had built the reputation of being just another young blade with a passion for horseflesh, who had no objection to rubbing shoulders with the more questionable members of the trade. He was steadily building the contacts and the trust he would need to discover where that certain Exmoor horseman had gone, and what he had been doing, after he had left Lord Bentwhistle's stables.

As George had announced to the scandalized ladies, Dagonet was gambling heavily, and was indeed firmly a member of the Prince Regent's inner circle. Beau Brummel and Lord Kendal took delight in his wit and style, and as George had discovered, couldn't care less about any unsavory past, as long as he was prepared to drink deep and wager high. Lady Easthaven was beyond reproach, and was also using her influence in society on his behalf. Contrary to his cousin's description, however, he was not financing his high-flown life style by trading horses. Rather, his skill at the gaming tables was giving him the blunt to continue to follow the faint trail left by John Catchpole. Without that gentleman's suspecting anything, Dagonet was already extremely close to his quarry.

There was only one area in which he didn't quite seem to fit his enviably expanding reputation among London's dandies, and that was that he wasn't known to be keeping a bit of fluff of his own. The ladies of the demi-monde found him infinitely charming, but none of them, to their great chagrin, had been able to fix his fancy. Nor was he showing any interest in the lovely young heiresses that Lady Easthaven was determined to put in his way. Dagonet himself was damned if he knew why. The ladies were beautiful and enticing enough. It couldn't still be any trace of his feeling for Catherine Hunter: his self control

TAKE ADVANTAGE OF THIS SPECIAL OFFER, AVAILABLE *ONLY* TO ZEBRA REGENCY ROMANCE READERS.

You are a reader who enjoys the very special kind of love story that can only be found in Zebra Regency Romances. You adore the fashionable English settings, the sparkling wit, the captivating intrigue, and the heart-stirring romance that are the hallmarks of each Zebra Regency Romance novel.

Now, you can have these delightful novels delivered right to your door each month and never have to worry about missing a new book. Zebra has made arrangements through its Home Subscription Service for you to preview the three latest Zebra Regency Romances as soon as they are published.

3 **FREE** REGENCIES TO GET STARTED!

To get your subscription started, we will send your first 3 books ABSOLUTELY FREE, as our introductory gift to you. NO OBLIGATION. We're sure that you will enjoy these books so much that you will want to read more of the very best romantic fiction published today.

SUBSCRIBERS SAVE EACH MONTH

Zebra Regency Home Subscribers will save money each month as they enjoy their latest Regencies. As a subscriber you will receive the 3 newest titles to preview FREE for ten days. Each shipment will be at least a $11.97 value (publisher's price). But home subscribers will be billed only $9.90 for all three books. You'll save over $2.00 each month. Of course, if you're not satisfied with any book, just return it for full credit.

FREE HOME DELIVERY

Zebra Home Subscribers get free home delivery. There are never any postage, shipping or handling charges. No hidden charges. What's more, there is no minimum number to buy and you can cancel your subscription at any time. No obligation and no questions asked.

TO GET YOUR 3 FREE BOOKS
FILL OUT AND MAIL THE COUPON BELOW

3 FREE BOOKS

Mail to: Zebra Regency Home Subscription Service
120 Brighton Road
P.O. Box 5214
Clifton, New Jersey 07015-5214

YES! Start my Regency Romance Home Subscription and send me my 3 FREE BOOKS as my introductory gift. Then each month, I'll receive the 3 newest Zebra Regency Romances to preview FREE for ten days. I understand that if I'm not satisfied, I may return them and owe nothing. Otherwise, I'll pay the low members' price of just $9.90 for all 3 books and save over $2.00 off the publisher's price (a $11.97 value). There are no shipping, handling or other hidden charges. I may cancel my subscription at any time and there is no minimum number to buy. In any case, the 3 FREE books are mine to keep regardless of what I decide.

NAME

ADDRESS _____ APT NO.

CITY _____ STATE _____ ZIP

(   )
TELEPHONE

SIGNATURE
(if under 18 parent or guardian must sign)

RG0894

Terms and prices subject to change. Orders subject to acceptance by Zebra Home Subscription Service, Inc.

GET
3 FREE
REGENCY
ROMANCE
NOVELS—
A $11.97
VALUE!

was too great for that. A picture of her as he had seen her in Morris's garden came unbidden to mind, the wisps of dark hair blowing about her flushed cheeks, those magnificent eyes flashing fire. He had deliberately behaved to her like a dog! No wonder she had hated him! It had been his intention that she forget all about him. To meet her at Lady Easthaven's was perhaps inevitable; but it seemed, to his relief, that she was still determined to hold him in dislike. In the future he would make sure that they did not meet, for he fully intended never to see her again. The threats she had made at Lady Easthaven's were surely empty.

It was exactly one week later that Dagonet discovered what she had done. It was still early when he returned to his lodgings and, pulling off his cravat, threw himself back in an armchair. He had already won a great deal that night, but his tongue felt rooted to the roof of his mouth with the foul taste of too much wine and spirits, too much wearying wit and meaningless laughter. Nevertheless, he would change his clothes and go out again. His manservant, before he retired for the night, would have left a fresh shirt and linen laid out in the bedchamber. Dagonet did not expect his servants to wait up for him, when he was about to spend a night on the town.

Meanwhile a jug of hot coffee sat by the fire and several days' newspapers lay piled on the table. He sipped the welcome coffee, and was idly perusing the classified personal columns, when he suddenly leapt up from the chair. Damn it! However could she have done something so foolish? Innocent, brave, impetuous Kate! Good God, didn't she realize the danger that might be involved? He scanned the advertisement's tiny print one more time:

"Wanted: information about one John Catchpole from Exmoor. Reward offered. Contact Miss Hunter at Brooke House, Grosvenor Square." The newspaper was already several days old. Rapidly throwing his coat back on, and thrusting into its pockets his small pistol, Dagonet swallowed the rest of the coffee, took up his sword cane, and ran from the house.

11

Several hours earlier that same day, Catherine headed towards the stews of Whitechapel in a hired cab. The note had come when she sat alone at the piano. Amelia was out, visiting some more distant relatives of the previous Lord Brooke; David was still down in Somerset; and little Annie was due to arrive from Exmoor any day. Perfectly content in the beautiful room, Catherine had played through most of her favorite pieces, when the footman had entered with a slightly scruffy note on a silver salver. Rapidly perusing it, she thrust it into the pile of music, then, penning a hurried note to Amy, in case she should return early from her duty visit, she scrupulously followed its directions. These involved a considerable walk from the gracious quiet square to a fountain in a public thoroughfare. There she had met a large silent man in a black coat and round hat, who had offered to escort her to where she might meet with the object of her curiosity: John Catchpole. She heard the name Lower Hobb Lane mentioned, but she was too unfamiliar with London to recognize it. They were now swaying together in the cab behind the uneven trot of a run-down horse. Without speaking a word, her companion rapped suddenly on the roof of the vehicle with a large, stout cane that he carried. The horse stopped, and taking her elbow, the man propelled her from the cab.

"We walk from here, miss. Stay close. No one'll bother you, if you're with me."

With those words, the fellow had dived into the crowd. Catherine looked about herself with horror. The streets were alive with human activity, but the conditions in which these activities were being carried out were those of the utmost squalor and misery. An open sewer ran down the middle of the narrow lane into which she followed her guide, and without concern half-naked children and dogs rooted around in the filth. Her ears were assailed with a cacophony of raucous shouts and bellows, as the inhabitants of the foul closes yelled their comments to each other. Coming from the clear sea air of Exmoor, Catherine had never seen anything so appalling. As a vicar's daughter, she had witnessed poverty up close before, but poverty tempered by the wholesome country environment and the mercy of her father's ministrations, nothing like this. Even in her simple, elegant dress and pelisse, she stood out dramatically from the crowd, most of whom were dressed either in rags or various styles of tawdry finery that proclaimed to the world their unsavory profession. What on earth had she risked by coming here with this total stranger? Bravely squaring her shoulders and ignoring the curious and hostile glances she was getting, Catherine followed the black coat and round hat into a bewildering maze of ramshackle dwellings. Finally the man disappeared into a narrow doorway, through a passage and up a flight of stairs. At the top stood an ancient wooden door that appeared to have been beaten with chains, where he gave an elaborate knock and bent to whisper in the keyhole. The door opened a crack and the man turned to go. He brushed past Catherine without a word, and disappeared into the teeming alleyway that they had just left. With her heart pounding in her breast, Catherine went on up the stairs and pushed at the door. It gave way before her, and she stepped inside.

A large woman with a vast mop of greasy hair pushed up into a gray cap was waiting, and closed the door behind her. She was clutching a copy of the newspaper where Catherine had inserted the advertisement, but since she held it upside down, it was immediately apparent that she could neither read nor write, and was thus not the author of the note. "Are you this Miss Hunter?" she inquired suspiciously. At Catherine's nod, she continued, "What is John Catchpole to you then? I don't know as he ever had any truck with fancy ladies this last five year or more. Here, that's an awful pretty little bag." With a single movement, she had seized Catherine's reticule, and emptied the contents on the dirty table. There was not much there; handkerchief, comb, a handful of coins, all of which the woman scooped into her apron pocket. "Here, follow me."

The greasy mobcap led the way up another flight of stairs that led off the room, to the very top of the house, where Catherine was directed into a tiny attic. She was immediately left there alone, and to her horror heard a key turned in the lock. None of the chairs looked particularly inviting, so she stood steadily by the window and composed herself to wait. Her heart was beating heavily, and she willed herself to stay calm. There was no reason at all why these people should harm her, she reminded herself. She had deliberately not brought much money with her, so that she could promise a reward on her safe return to Grosvenor Square. Surely the expectation of receiving a decent sum would ensure her safety? She would not be afraid! She was within minutes perhaps of achieving her goal: the truth of what had really happened at Lion Court all those years before, when Millicent Trumble had been found drowned and Dagonet disinherited. Would John Catchpole's tale clear Dagonet or condemn him? She swallowed nervously. Why should the answer matter so much?

The minutes passed, however, with no further development, and soon coalesced into hours. Using the hem of her dress, Catherine cleaned off one of the filthy chairs as best she could, and sat down. The light was beginning to fade rapidly outside the window, and since the glass was broken, it was getting extremely cold in the little room. There was no lamp or candle to be seen, and before long Catherine lost all track of time. She tried the door handle to no avail; as she had suspected, it had been securely locked. The window was stiff with rust, but she was at last able to open it. It looked out over a sheer drop of five or six stories into a black-shadowed courtyard. There was certainly no escape that way. Somehow it made her feel less of a prisoner, however, to have it open, so in spite of the cold, she left it ajar.

She had perhaps nodded off, when a sudden thudding of booted feet on the stair brought her instantly upright. There was a glow of light around the frame, then the door was thrown open, and a man's shape blocked it. The light of a candle threw his coarse features into sharp relief. Catherine leapt to her feet, and forced herself to speak calmly.

"Mr. Catchpole, I presume? I have been kept waiting here in the dark for an unconscionable length of time, sir, but I appreciate your having the goodness to see me."

"What is John Catchpole to you, miss?" The man's voice was slurred with drink and a thinly veiled menace.

"What the hell is John Catchpole to you, that you should print his name in a public newspaper for anybody's eyes to see? Perhaps you didn't think that John Catchpole might be a very private man?"

"Not so private that you didn't respond to my advertisement, sir. You were under no compunction to do so."

"Nor do I have to be here now. But any cove might have a simple curiosity about a person that would bandy his private name about in the public newspaper."

Catherine decided to take the bull by the horns. "My name is Catherine Hunter, I am sister to Lady Brooke, but I am from Fernbridge in Exmoor. My father is vicar there. I believe you once were familiar with the locale?"

"And if I was?"

"Then I think that perhaps you were unjustly dismissed from the service of Sir Henry Montagu, after the drowning of Milly Trumble. Perhaps it's not too late to set things straight, if wrong was done to you."

To her amazement he threw back his huge head and laughed aloud. "Much wrong! Much wrong!" Then he lowered at her like a wounded bull and grasped her by the wrist. "You're poking your pretty little nose in where you've got no business, ain't you? That's a good way to get it bitten right off. What do you know about the matter?"

"I know nothing, sir, but I hoped you might enlighten me. There is no reason why you should not tell me about Millicent's death, and I am not in the least cowed by your threats. The reward that I promised awaits you in Grosvenor Square, but you won't get it, unless I am returned there tonight unharmed."

"You're a cool miss, aren't you, my pretty? You know nothing, know nothing? Is that true now? Why I believe that it is!" The grip was unrelenting on her arm, she could feel her flesh beginning to bruise under his fingers. When he at last released her, she fell back against the chair where she had been sitting. "There's just one aspect that you didn't cover though, ain't there? Supposing it were a hanging matter, eh? Just suppose that. Suppose it were a matter of a certain cove swinging at the Old Bailey; that might change the way that cove thought about someone that would bandy his private name about."

Then, for the first time, Catherine was truly afraid. Fools do indeed rush in where angels fear to tread, she thought suddenly, and I have been a consummate fool. Why on earth did I think he would just tell me about it, or about anything? She had not had any way of knowing, of course, when she had placed the advertisement, that Catchpole had sunk in the world, and was now obviously engaged in criminal activity. She had naively thought that he would still be employed somewhere as a decent groom or stable man, and would freely explain to her the mysteries that remained about Devil Dagonet. Now, she realized, she was in fact in mortal danger. No one knew where she was, except the silent man who had led her here, and he must be in the employ of John Catchpole. She could expect no help there. The woman downstairs had taken all of her money, so that even if she were to escape from this dangerous house, she could not pay for a cab to take her home. Besides, between here and any respectable cab rank lay those noisome streets and their inhabitants; alone, she would never get through them alive. Her pelisse or dress would be worth a year's living to such poor wretches.

"I see no need at all to talk of hanging, Mr. Catchpole. I came for some simple information. If you won't give it, then there's no more to be said, and I would appreciate an escort home. You will be rewarded. Should I not return soon, Lord Brooke will be scouring the streets for me."

"Ah," said her captor with a wink. "But Lord Brooke ain't home, is he? And I can think of a certain lady as would give me more for you than the pin money you have set aside. You're a nice little piece, and maids are worth plenty to certain members of the gentry, who'll ask no questions either before or after. Meanwhile, since it seems you don't know nothing, John Catchpole's going to make himself scarce." With that he thrust her back into the chair, and left the room. Her only consolation was that the candle still guttered on the table, so that she was not left entirely in the dark.

Dagonet went straight to Brooke House, where he demanded from the imperious butler the honor of seeing Miss Hunter or Lady Brooke without delay.

"The ladies are not at home, sir."

"Did they go out together?"

"I'm sure I couldn't say, sir." The butler had been inherited with the house from the old Lord Brooke. It was well beneath his dignity to give information to any handsome gentleman who might happen to knock. He began to close the door, when suddenly a pistol was thrust into his starched chest and the gentleman's green eyes blazed with a dangerous fire.

"I have no time to waste on social niceties, my man. I am an old friend of Lord Brooke; Charles de Dagonet, at your service. You will tell me when and how Miss Hunter left the house."

The butler sputtered. "I will ask the footman, sir."

It was fortunate that the footman had been brought up

from Stagshead, and recognized the determined visitor immediately. "She left about three o'clock, sir. Right after I brought up the note."

Dagonet instantly pushed past the men and dashed up the stairs to the drawing room. Now where? Pray God that she hadn't taken it with her! His keen gaze swept over the room. There was a conventional note to Amy on the mantelpiece. Without compunction, Dagonet read it; Kate didn't say where she had gone, or when she would be back. Some books lay scattered beside the sofa, and an embroidery frame stood near the fire. Perhaps Kate had been reading or sewing, when the footman interrupted her? Dagonet sifted through the basket of silks, and felt beneath the cushions of the chair and then the sofa; there was nothing there. The pages of the books were thoroughly shaken. One of them, he noted grimly, was Walter Scott's long poem, *Marmion*. The tragic tale of poor Constance hid nothing. Perhaps Kate had burned the note, after all? The fire danced merrily in the grate; there was absolutely no way of knowing. Dagonet unconsciously ran his hand through his hair. Could she have simply gone out on a social call? Was all his alarm for nothing?

Then his eye lit upon the piles of music at the piano. Someone had been playing, and had left in a hurry without bothering to put the sheets away. Who else but Kate? In a stride he was at the instrument. His long fingers quickly sorted through the pages, until they came across the scruffy little note that Catherine had received that afternoon. "In regards to meeting the gentleman you advertised for," it read. "Please meet a man in a black coat and hat at the following place, who will take you to him . . ." So she had indeed gone after Catchpole, and had met someone at the cab rank. Would Kate have been taken to the spot that Dagonet, after all his long research, had discovered? It was the only lead he had. Scrawling a quick addition to the note that Catherine had left Amelia, Dagonet ran downstairs, had a quick word with the footman, and strode out past the scandalized butler. In minutes, he was at the cab rank and following, had he known it, in the very footsteps of the driver who had earlier conveyed a young woman and a man in a black coat to the outskirts of Whitechapel.

"I daren't take my rig any further, sir," the cabby said, as the horse drew up.

Dagonet leapt lightly from the cab, pressed an extremely generous sum into the driver's outstretched hand, and gave him some rapid instructions. He then disappeared into the warren of lanes and allies that earlier had swallowed up Catherine and her guide. Thank God, thought Dagonet, it's not unfamiliar ground. His weeks of tracking John Catchpole had made him familiar enough with the area; but Catherine's life might depend on whether he had discovered the right house. Many of the inhabitants of the noxious warren were now drunk on cheap gin, but if any of the footpads gave thought to interfering with the gentleman who was now striding through their midst, they soon decided to give it a miss. The cane that was carried in his left hand obviously housed a sword, and there was something about the easy athletic way he carried himself that said he probably knew very well how to use it. Several of the women, however, approached the dashing young stranger, and hung on his arm for a moment with offers and promises. He gave each one a smile and a joke that pleased and flattered, while relieving the doxy of both her grip and her hopes. They let him go on by with a sigh. Dagonet did not fool himself for a moment, however, that he would stand a chance should the mood of these denizens change. He would rather face a dozen of Boney's soldiers than a London mob out for blood.

Catherine sat silently in the attic room and contemplated her fate. It did no good now, of course, to wish she had not done something so impetuous. How could she have been so naive? It had seemed so simple an adventure, when she had placed the advertisement. She was more convinced than ever that John Catchpole had something to tell, and something to hide, but whatever chance there had been to discover it was now ruined. Meanwhile, she was well and truly trapped, and she dreaded to discover what the ruffians in this terrifying house planned to do with her. The candle had burned almost to a stub, when a slight sound at the window made her spin around. She sprung to her feet. A man sat nonchalantly on the windowsill. His clothes were mired in soot and his shirt lay open at the neck, but there was no mistaking that air of insolence with which he was contemplating her.

"As you see, ma'am, I once again must visit you by way of the roof. Forgive my appearance, I pray. I was forced to use my cravat as a rope, to allow me to drop onto the exceedingly narrow windowsill of your prison. I am, however, much indebted to you for again leaving the window open."

"Dagonet! How did you get here, sir?" Her heart had begun to pound.

He stepped into the room. "I believe I have more claim to ask that question of you. How dare you come here and place yourself in danger?"

Her chin went up. "There has been enough of deceit

and mystery, I believe. Too many people have suffered already! I came to talk with John Catchpole."

"You have absolutely no right at all," he replied coldly, "to interfere in my affairs. If I did seduce and murder a kitchen wench seven years ago, it is no earthly concern of yours. I am quite capable of investigating my own sordid history for myself."

"Without much success," flared Catherine. "I, at least, have met and talked with Mr. Catchpole, which seems to be more than you were able to achieve."

His eyes were as icy as a northern sea in winter. "And have, no doubt, caused him to bolt! What did you learn, I wonder? Anything?" Catherine was silenced. She had never seen him like this before. "Anyway, having spent the best part of the last several weeks discovering the existence of this house and carefully stalking my quarry so that he should not be alarmed, I find the trap sprung and the game gone. Even if I so wished, I don't have the luxury of pursuing him, since I have you on my hands. The house is well guarded, and though I came in from the roof, we cannot return that way. A distance I was able to drop to the windowsill is still more, I fear, than either of us can jump back up."

"You have no need to rescue me, sir. I am certain I shall shortly be returned unharmed to Brooke House." Since this was very far from what she was certain of, Catherine's voice may have lacked a certain conviction, but it did not lack for emotion. For some unaccountable reason, she was very angry. How could he be so impossible? "Mr. Catchpole assured me of it himself!"

"Did he?" Dagonet raised an eyebrow in an infuriatingly insolent manner. "I very much doubt it. Nevertheless, however much you deserve to be left to your unkind fate, I owe more to Lord Brooke than to leave his wife's sister unattended in Whitechapel. Thus, however unwelcome it may be to you, ma'am, I intend to remove you from this house. We shall have to leave through the door, since as I have explained, there is no other exit, so if you would be kind enough to rattle at the knob and call out in a distressed way, we shall endeavor to enlist your charming captors in our escape attempt."

There was no more to be said, so Catherine did as she was bid, hammering and screaming at the door. Before long, nailed boots could be heard ascending the stairs.

"What's the racket for? Shut your trap in there!"

"I shall throw myself from the window!" cried Catherine. "You cannot stop me!"

Instantly the key turned in the lock, and the door was thrust open. As a large ruffian burst into the room, Dagonet, who had placed himself behind the opening, gave the man a single blow to the back of the neck, which felled him like a tree.

"Well done, Miss Hunter. First move to us! Knight takes rook," stated Dagonet grimly, and seizing Catherine by the hand, he began to lead her down the narrow stair. Voices could be heard at the bottom of the passage. Two men clad in heavy wool coats were crouched over a card table in the room where the fat woman had stolen Catherine's money. The greasy mobcap, however, was nowhere to be seen. Dagonet paused for a moment, and thrust Catherine firmly behind him. There was another door at the far side of the room, which stood partly ajar. In absolute silence Dagonet took the pistol from his pocket. Catherine suppressed a gasp. Surely he wouldn't risk firing a gun and bringing in the entire neighborhood! As if reading her thoughts, Dagonet unloaded a bullet from the chamber, and, taking perfect aim, threw the lead pellet against the door on the other side of the room.

As it swung open from the blow, and the bullet rattled in the room behind, the men leapt up and ran over to investigate. At that moment, Dagonet, pulling Catherine by the hand, crossed the now empty room. It was the work of a moment to open the beaten front door, enter the final passage, and emerge into the night. "Second move! Knight takes two bishops."

"Countermove," said Catherine urgently. "Red queen threatens checkmate!"

Rapidly approaching them was the large form of the woman in a gray cap and dirt-stained apron. As Catherine tried to step deeper into the shadows, the woman saw her and let up a screech.

"Jenkins! Mullet! The girl's getting away!"

There was the sound of nailed boots thudding down the stairs, as Dagonet and Catherine took off running up the street, the fellows in the woolen coats in hot pursuit. In a matter of minutes, they had momentarily outrun the hounds, who were both heavier and older, but Dagonet suddenly pulled up.

"Damnation! We're into a blind alley! Checkmate in two moves."

Sure enough, the last turn they had taken had put them into a short entry passage for the doors to various questionable residences, from some of which the sound of drunken singing welled out into the night. Unlike many of the lanes through which they had come, it was well lit with smoking lanterns. A throng of merrymakers, including several inebriated gentlemen who rubbed careless shoulders with pickpockets and footpads, staggered over the cobbles. The light shone down on them all indiscriminately. If their pursuers looked down into the passage, they would certainly be discovered. At that moment, a doorway opened and a girl stepped out. Her hair was a lurid bronze above her scarlet cloak, and the eyes that raked over Catherine were blurred with drink. Dagonet caught her around the waist, and she smiled up at him. "Here, darling," said Dagonet. "The lady has taken a sudden shine to that pretty cloak of yours, but this will buy you twenty just as good." At the glint of gold, the woman stripped off her cloak willingly enough, before she reeled away into the street. In another moment, Dagonet had flung the cloak around Catherine's shoulders, and, running his hands over her hair, sent a shower of hairpins into the gutter. "White queen blocks check!" he laughed, as her hair cascaded over her shoulders, completing her disguise. "You look like a perfect hussy!" And with that he pulled her into his arms and began to kiss her ruthlessly on the lips. Her spine melted into butter. As the ruffians arrived panting in the opening to the passage, all they could see was a crowd of drunkards and a gentleman entertaining himself with a local doxy. With a curse, they turned and went thudding away up the street.

As he released her, she stumbled against him. Her eyes were blind with angry tears; not because he had kissed her, but because she couldn't keep herself from responding. How many women had fallen prey to that practiced embrace? Gentle fingers wiped the tears away from her cheek. "Forgive me, sweet Kate. A simple ruse. Even I could not fight off our pursuers, should their local friends flock to their aid."

"Then a pretense would have been sufficient, sir!" snapped Catherine.

The laughter died from his eyes. He gave her a short bow. "Of course, I offer you my most humble apologies. However, perhaps we could postpone our quarrel until a little later? We are not yet out of the woods."

Taking her again by the hand, he led her out into the maze of streets. It had begun to drizzle. They ran together through a labyrinth of stone and brick, more than once slipping up and down flights of steps that ran in and out of filthy courtyards. They had just passed through one of these, when a muffled shape stepped from the shadows and a huge, nail-studded cudgel whistled within inches of Dagonet's shoulder. He whirled Catherine up against the wall, and with a deadly whisper his sword sprung from its cane. "You'll have to aim better than that, my friend!" cried Dagonet. "Come, try again! You mean to gain my purse, perhaps, but you'll have to sweat a little for the honor. This blade is an old companion!"

Catherine flattened herself against the wall; then saw to her horror another man springing towards them. As Dagonet fought off the first attacker, the second pulled a pistol from his pocket and took aim. Without hesitation, she picked up a loose cobble from the street and flung it with all her might. As it thudded into the man's shoulder, the pistol shot flew wild. Dagonet laughed aloud. " 'Fair maid, is't thou wilt do these wondrous feats?' " he quoted lightly. There was a flash of the blade, and the first attacker's belt was severed. As his trousers collapsed around his ankles, he tripped and went sprawling on the filthy stones. A quick blow from the cane, and the man lay insensible.

Dagonet turned to face the second footpad. His breathing was barely disturbed, except by his laughter. "You don't return my quote, Kate? Doesn't Joan reply: 'My courage try by combat if thou dar'st'?"

" 'And thou shalt find that I exceed my sex,' " continued Catherine boldly. " 'Resolve on this,—thou shalt be fortunate if thou receive me for thy warlike mate.' King Henry VI, First Part? Oh God! Look out!"

The pistol had been raised again within three feet of Dagonet's chest, but it suddenly flew from the ruffian's hand and clattered to the ground. The man swore and raised his cut hand to his lip. As Dagonet presented the blade again, he spun around and took to his heels. With a grin, Dagonet turned to Catherine.

"You look like an Amazon, dear Kate. Would you be able to swing that ferocious weapon, do you think?"

Catherine looked with amazement at the cudgel in her hand. She did not even remember picking it up. Instantly she dropped it. "Saint Joan might have done! But I really don't know, sir." Her breath was coming in gasps, and she laughed. "I am not used to warfare. Don't rely on me for a 'warlike mate.'"

His tone was perfectly serious, but he raised an eyebrow, and his eyes were like deep pools. "You think I could not win such a partner?"

"You would receive nothing from Joan of Arc, sir. She goes on to say she 'will not yield to any rites of love.' Your quote may be better chosen than you know."

"Checkmate, Miss Hunter." He sheathed the sword and gave her a self-deprecating grin. "You are impervious to all my deadly charm and poetry. Now, let us get out of this stinking hell."

If only it were true! she thought ruefully, as she followed him around two more corners. There stood a horse and cab, patiently waiting by the curb. In a moment, they were trotting away, and Whitechapel was left behind.

12

They did not, however, pull up before Brooke House in Grosvenor Square. Instead Dagonet led her into an elegant unknown hallway, and up to what had to be his own rooms.

"Where are you taking me, sir?" she asked stiffly. "I would prefer to be returned to my sister."

"I think not, sweet Kate. You have not seen yourself, and Lady Brooke's butler was starchy enough when I appeared at the door in the guise of an elegant gentleman. I do not think that at present he would suffer me to escort you into the hall."

It was true. They were both mired from head to foot. The hem of Catherine's gown was torn, where she had caught it with her heel or on a nail, and it was thick with a crust of muck. Her loose damp hair curled in abandon around her face, and she had somehow cut her hand, perhaps on some projecting piece of masonry. She had not noticed it at the time. Dagonet was equally besmirched, and his cravat, of course, had been left hanging from the rotten gutter of a house in Whitechapel. For the first time, Catherine recalled that yawning chasm below the window where she had been imprisoned. She shivered. Where had he found the courage to attempt to drop from the roof onto that minute windowsill? Had he no care at all for his own life? They entered the spotless study. The coals of the fire had burned down to a faint glow. The empty coffeepot stood amongst the newspapers, where Dagonet had left it. He ignored the wet footprints they were tracking across the exquisite carpet, and set Catherine down in the armchair.

"You know this is highly improper, sir," said Catherine unsteadily. The room smelt wonderful, of leather-bound books, and lemon and beeswax furniture polish: a clean masculine smell. Her eye ran over the ranks of books, and the violin case that rested on the side table. Somehow it didn't look like the den of an accomplished rake and gambler.

"More improper than spending the evening in Whitechapel alone with a gentleman; flinging rocks, brawling like a barmaid, and racing in a distinctly unladylike way through the streets? Sit there and relax. You are quite safe, dear Kate."

He knelt and rapidly stirred up the fire, adding fuel until it was blazing merrily, then, taking the coffeepot, he left the room. Minutes later he returned with a basin of warm water and a towel, and hot coffee.

"Here, drink this, it'll do you good."

Gratefully she took the cup of steaming, fragrant liquid. He had added a generous shot of brandy, but she gulped it down. Suddenly she realized that she had eaten nothing since early afternoon. The hot coffee sent a warm glow through her limbs.

As soon as she had finished, he took her hand. "You are cut. Here, let me see that."

She was too tired to remonstrate. For no reason she could fathom, she had the strongest desire to cry, but with determination she bit back the tears. It was true: she was safe! The full enormity of their ordeal threatened to overwhelm her. She would not break down in front of him! She was rescued by the next unsuitable quote. " 'Woe to the hands that shed this costly blood!' "

"Don't be absurd, sir, it is only a scratch. I believe a piece of masonry was the offender; and it didn't have hands." What a relief that her voice was as casual as his!

"Nevertheless, it needs tending." He had obviously already washed his own hands in the kitchen, and now, kneeling before her, with deft, gentle movements, he washed hers, cleaned the cut, and bound it in a strip of white linen.

"Where on earth did you learn to be such an accomplished nurse, Mr. de Dagonet?" she asked lightly.

Immediately she wished she could take back the words, for even his self-control was not sufficient to prevent the fleeting pain that crossed his features. "On a battlefield," he said curtly. A moment later, however, he was smiling up at her before he rose lightly to his feet. "Now," he said, "there should be sufficient hot water ready to clean you up properly, and return you to your sister looking more the thing. Follow me."

She obediently went with him into the next room. With horror she discovered it to be his bedchamber. She turned on him, eyes blazing. "Sir, this is unconscionable!"

"What, that you should bathe, while I scrape some of the mud out of your hem? You know I rarely get to see you in a clean dress. Dirt seems to be your most common sartorial accessory. For a rake like me, I really should need to see you in diamonds in order to ravish you. You will find soap and towels laid out and, I admit to my sorrow, lady's hairpins and a comb on the dresser. I shall deliver the water and then not disturb you, on my honor. Make yourself as presentable as you may, while I do the same in the kitchen, and then I think we can appear without scandal at Brooke House. I left a note for your sister. She will not be in the least worried about you. Only the butler will still raise his eyebrows, that I should return you so late from the theater. I have had your evening cloak sent round here with the aid of one of Morris's clever footmen from Exmoor. It is there on the bed. No one will discover a torn spotted muslin underneath."

He grinned innocently as he left the bedchamber, and she stripped off her dress, gratefully washing her face and limbs in the hot water. She hung her dress outside the door, and good to his word, it was returned in ten minutes with the worst of the filth sponged away. As she dressed again and put up her hair, she looked around the room. It was almost austere in its elegant simplicity. Had he entertained paramours here? She felt the color rising in her cheek. It somehow didn't seem likely, the room was so plain, but then he had to have acquired the hairpins somewhere. What did she know of the ways of a man like him? He seemed to deny nothing that was said about him, however heinous; yet there was some deeper mystery about his past. Something he himself didn't know; something he also had hoped to learn from John Catchpole. Surely that must rattle that insufferable self-confidence?

Dagonet did not seem in the least rattled, however, when, an hour later, dressed in impeccable evening clothes, he delivered her to Brooke House in his phaeton. His tiger, unconscionably awoken from his bed in the stables, stood stiffly behind. She had not been able to do quite as well with her own appearance, her hairstyle lacking perhaps its usual polish, but keeping up the hood of her cloak, she knew she was passable.

Amelia had not, however, gone quietly to bed. Instead she flew down the stairs and straight into Catherine's arms.

"Cathy, the most dreadful thing! Annie is taken deadly sick, and she's all alone in an inn in Marlborough! Polly arrived these three hours since with the news. She didn't know what else to do, she said, than to come to us, but Annie has the fever, and no one is there to take care of her but the chambermaid! We must go right away!"

"Quiet yourself, Amy, I pray. Let me see Polly. Of course, I shall go to Annie, but you cannot travel so far in your condition."

"But how are you to go, Cathy? David has the chaise in Somerset, and the curricle is at the shop, having the right wheel repaired! I was run into this afternoon on my way home, and Peter Coachman says it will be days before it is safe to drive again! We have no carriage here at all!"

"Then I shall take a hack post chaise. It is not so far to go. I shall be quite all right, and Annie will no doubt be up and well again even before I arrive."

"Begging your pardon, Miss Hunter," interrupted Dagonet's calm voice. "But Marlborough is more than eighty-five miles. A hack post chaise will not be available until morning, and will take you the best part of fourteen hours. You will thus not arrive at Annabella's bedside until late tomorrow evening, at the earliest. If you would allow me the honor of escorting you, we can leave now and be there before breakfast."

Catherine immediately began to remonstrate; but after the maid Polly, who had been assigned to accompany Annie on the long journey from Exmoor, had given her story, it was obvious that there was no time to be lost. Polly was in tears through much of her tale. The people at the inn had seemed very nice, and she had left Annie with them with no compunction at the time, but then she had not had any idea that it would take her so long to reach Brooke House; the distances between England's cities meant very little to a girl who had never gone more than five miles from home before. There was no doubt, however, that Annie was very ill indeed. Polly had left her in a high fever calling deliriously for her mother and sisters, while the maidservant at the inn tried to keep the blankets on her, and withhold the water she was crying for, on the theory that it was necessary to starve the fever.

"Good God!" exclaimed Dagonet. "Damn ignorance and prejudice! They will kill her! Kate, we must go now, however repugnant it may seem to you. In the phaeton we can be there in five or six hours, if we keep our weight to a minimum. It means no tiger, no maidservant, and no luggage: an appalling breach of propriety, of course."

"What on earth can propriety matter in the circumstances!" said Catherine desperately. "How soon can we leave, sir?"

"Cathy, you cannot travel at night!" Amelia's blue eyes were awash with tears. "Think of the danger! And your reputation, should this be discovered!"

"I shall be quite safe with Mr. de Dagonet, Amy," replied Catherine. "All that matters is that I must get to Annie with maximum speed. The dark will cover us, no one need know that I have lost all sense of maidenly modesty. Come, think of poor Annie all alone in that inn."

Amelia reluctantly agreed; it did not occur to either of the ladies at that moment to question Catherine's statement that she was in no peril to travel alone through the night with a notorious rake. Instead, Catherine turned to Dagonet for an answer to her question.

"In half an hour. Lady Brooke, you will see that Miss Hunter has some hot soup, and provide her with the warmest possible clothes." He turned to Catherine. "Have your maid pack a small overnight bag, and lie down for at least a few minutes. You are going to need all your strength, I'm afraid."

A few minutes later, his tiger was hanging on to the back of a phaeton traveling far too fast for safety through the empty streets of London. Dagonet took the stairs up to his lodgings three at a time, and hammered at his manservant's bedroom door. The tiger had already received his orders and was busy saddling the gray in order to ride ahead to the posting inns and arrange for changes of horses. The manservant opened his door rubbing at his eyes, his nightcap askew on his balding head. "You called, sir?" he managed to say between yawns.

"Wake up, for God's sake," snapped his master. "I want clothes for travel, a small bag, and something to eat."

The man snapped to attention and hurried off to do his master's bidding. Mr. de Dagonet had been a most reasonable employer so far, but there was no accounting for the ways of the gentry. Where was he off to in the middle of the night? Running away from gaming debts, no doubt! Dagonet ignored the sour looks of his servant and strode into his bedchamber. As he began to strip off his evening clothes, he noticed the red cloak where Catherine had left it lying across the bed. He stopped for a moment, then carefully picked it up, and hung it on the back of the door. Brave Kate! Damn it all! She had certainly delayed his hunt for the truth about the drowning of poor Milly Trumble. It would not surprise him if

John Catchpole left the country. Either way, she had made a mockery of his vow never to see her again. Thank God she was still angry with him. How else could he stay true to his honor, and prevent himself from showing the tenderness he had felt ever since Exmoor? With a curse, he shrugged into the linen shirt and warm jacket that his manservant had laid out, and carelessly thrust his arms into an extremely fashionable, many-caped driving coat. There was no time to think about it now: though they were about to race together through the night to Marlborough, he would have enough on his hands with his mettlesome team and a vehicle that, though undoubtedly fast enough, was designed rather for parading in the city streets than going at breakneck speed down the turnpike. It would take plenty of skill just to prevent them turning over at the first bend. He had no doubt, however, about the danger to Annie should they not arrive in time. He had learned a great deal about fever amongst his wounded comrades in the Peninsula; enough to know that the ignorant ministrations of a Marlborough inn maid would be more than enough to put Annie's life at risk.

Minutes later, he took the reins of the phaeton once again, and cantered back to Brooke House. Catherine was waiting in the hall. As he had ordered, she wore her most serviceable woolen dress and a fur-lined cloak of Amelia's. At her side sat a tiny bag containing the merest necessities. Amy had given her enough money to buy anything that she might need once they arrived in Marlborough. She had even forced herself to eat soup and bread, and lie down for a few minutes. She would not think about what she was about to do: leave London alone with the notorious Devil Dagonet. All that mattered was Annie.

She was handed up into the phaeton, and Dagonet tucked a leather travel rug around her knees. There was a hot brick waiting for her feet. One of Lord Brooke's servants was holding the horses' heads, and at the gentleman's signal he sprang back. The horses plunged ahead, taking Catherine unaware, so that she rocked dangerously against Dagonet's arm.

"Pray, attempt to keep your seat, Miss Hunter," he said coldly. "I shall not need your help at the ribbons. This carriage is unstable enough without your interference."

Furious, she sat bolt upright. She realized that she was exhausted from her foolish venture into Whitechapel, but she would not give him the satisfaction of seeing a moment's weakness. She had appeared to enough disadvantage already in front of this arrogant rogue!

"Never fear, Mr. de Dagonet," she said stiffly. "I trust that I have interfered in your affairs enough. I do not, however, imagine for a moment that having offered to take me to Annie, you now intend to land us in the ditch." She must not let him discompose her! In an attempt at reconciliation, she went on, "I must hope that you can believe that I am not insensible to the debt that I owe you. My thanks are due as well."

He gave a wry smile. "I hope you do not think that I race through the night for your sake, Miss Hunter. I happen to be very fond of your sister Annie: a child of infinite good sense."

She must persist, in spite of his determination to throw obstacles in her way! "I do not refer only to that, Mr. de Dagonet. I also owe you thanks for rescuing me from Whitechapel."

He laughed. "The merest chance, my dear Kate. I came to see John Catchpole, and discovered you instead.

I should have left you there, of course, but it appealed to my sense of the ridiculous to attempt to extricate you. Besides, it gave me the opportunity to kiss you again. You looked very fetching in that courtesan's cloak."

"You are determined to mock me, sir! I insist on giving thanks where they are due. I happen to know that you inquired for me at Brooke House, before you appeared so casually on that fifth-story windowsill. Indeed, I am led to understand that you threatened the butler with a pistol."

"A regrettable habit of mine. My manners have always lacked polish."

"How can you say so? You are reliably reported to be a rival with Beau Brummel! But why did you not use that pistol against the footpads who attacked us? To use a sword against a gun was surely a crazy risk to take? I can see that my life would have no value for you, but your own must be more dear."

"On the contrary, ma'am. I value it very little. Strange as it may seem to you, however, I do have an aversion to taking the lives of others, even a couple of incompetent footpads. A pistol tends to have a very final effect. Besides, the sword is infinitely more entertaining."

"And amusement is the overriding purpose of your life?"

"Perhaps. Besides I abhor incompetence. For their bumbling, those footpads deserved humiliation a little more than death, wouldn't you say?"

"And you, of course, are always competent!"

"I have tried to be, Miss Hunter. In my experience, competence counts a great deal more than good intentions. The times when I have had the second without the first, are those that have haunted me for the rest of my life."

"Then you must allow me to be grateful that you had both tonight."

She was not to have the indulgence of a reply. He merely shrugged, and they clattered on together without exchanging another word. However she might try, he was not going to allow her to thank him for her rescue. Yet she was under no illusion about the fate that might have awaited her had he not. But perhaps it was only an amusement to him. And had his own interest in John Catchpole not been involved, would he have risked his life to save hers?

Within half an hour they had left the city behind, and were racing past sleeping villages and farmsteads. The earlier drizzle had stopped, and an almost full moon had risen to cast its pale glow over the frosty countryside. In two days it would be December. The surface of the turnpike was frozen hard, and echoed hollow beneath the horses' hooves. Dagonet kept the team at a steady canter, and they had settled into their pace. There was an eerie beauty to the scene, the dark trees standing silent sentinel beside the road, the silhouette of their empty branches stark against the night sky. Catherine glanced at Dagonet beside her. His dark hair was blown back from his forehead, and the classic profile was set like marble in the moonlight. In their soft gloves, his capable hands kept the horses well up into their bits. He was, of course, supremely competent. What must he think of her? She had behaved abominably; ruining his chances of interviewing John Catchpole himself. He was perfectly right, it had never been any business of hers. She must appear an insufferably interfering busybody. The thought caused her more pain than she wanted to admit.

When they suddenly clattered into the first posting inn, they had been traveling for almost two hours. The lights and the bustle took Catherine by surprise; the rhythmic movement of the carriage had lulled her into a state dangerously close to sleep. Dagonet directed her into the warm parlor, while he oversaw the change of horses. There was hot chocolate waiting by a roaring fire. She set aside her cloak for a minute, and allowed the flames to thaw out her frozen limbs. Whether she could manage another four hours she wasn't sure, but she certainly wasn't going to let Dagonet see that she was tired. He seemed to have inexhaustible reserves of energy. It was not five minutes before he was handing her back into the carriage, where a fresh hot brick awaited her feet.

"Are you all right?" he inquired. "We shall be another hour before we change horses again at Reading. These post horses will not be able to keep up the pace for as long as my own team."

"I am perfectly fresh, thank you," she lied, and once again they drove away in silence.

They had just passed the little village of Hare, dipping down across the Thames bridge and up the steep slope of the climb out on the other side, when Dagonet was suddenly forced to haul the horses to an abrupt halt. Due to the gradient of the hill, he had already steadied them into a slow trot, when three horsemen burst out of the black shadowed woods beside the road and galloped across their bow. The phaeton skidded sideways, as the post horses shied and jibbed. Catherine grabbed desperately at the edge of the seat to prevent herself from being thrown out. Each man wore a dark greatcoat, but that was not what made Catherine's heart thump in her chest. Their faces were covered with black cloth, so that nothing was visible of their features but the glitter of their eyes, and each man trained a pistol unerringly at the phaeton.

The moonlight danced off the barrels, well-greased, primed, and ready to fire.

"If I could trouble you for your purse, sir?" said the nearest of the highwaymen, politely bowing a little from the waist to acknowledge Catherine. "It's rather late to be out on such a cold night, wouldn't you say?"

"I might say the same about you, sir," replied Dagonet coolly. "Too cold, surely to keep a very steady aim."

"I'm reputed a crack shot, sir!" replied the highwayman instantly. "In any weather!"

"You would seem to be a sporting gentleman." Dagonet's tone was only slightly mocking. "I wager you my purse that you are not such a good shot as I."

Instantly one of the other horsemen rode over to his friend and began to remonstrate. "Come on, Joe. We can take the gentleman's purse for free. There's no need to wager over it!"

But Joe had one aim in life, even beyond that of stealing gold: to uphold the reputation of his fellow gentlemen of the road and conduct himself with the true aplomb of an aristocrat. Weren't the broadsheets full of the gallant exploits of Dick Turpin and Sixteen String Jack? They may have died at Tyburn Tree, but their names had gone down in history. He ignored his friend. "Any of us can outshoot you, sir!" he replied to Dagonet. "I'll wager your purse against the maid!"

It took Catherine a few moments to realize that he meant her. She turned with mute appeal to Dagonet, but he was not looking at her. This is what came of traveling with a gentleman unchaperoned! The highwaymen took her for a loose woman, some casual fancy piece, rather than a lady. Well, Dagonet would set them straight. She gasped when he replied in cheerful tones. "Done, sir! Two shots each at the highest leaf on that holly bush over there by the mile stone. If your shot is better than mine, the gold and the lady are both yours!"

"It's too far!" remonstrated the second highwayman. "Can't be done!"

"And he can't do it either: the prize will be ours, never fear," said the leader. "Take your shot, Jim!"

The moonlight shone brightly over the scene. The holly twig was quite clear against the sky. Caught up now in the game, the highwaymen lined themselves up so that Dagonet would have no advantage of position, and in turn took two shots each at the target. The man called Jim tried first; his shots both went well clear of the bush. The third accomplice had no better luck, in fact his second shot fell short of the tree altogether.

"You're more wind than threat, sirs," stated Dagonet as casually as if he made conversation over tea. "If you can shoot no better than this, you will have to turn into honest men."

The leader laughed aloud. "My turn now, sir. I hope you're not too fond of your little doxy, but she'll have a good life with Merry Joe!"

So saying he turned and took careful aim at the innocent bush. The first shot grazed through the top leaves, and sent a rattle of berries to the ground.

"Well done, sir," encouraged Dagonet. "But not good enough yet! I'm tired of her anyway, she has a foul temper and a more doleful tongue than Cassandra. You'll find her a sorry burden, sir!"

"But a welcome armful, no doubt, on a cold night!" returned Joe as he took aim again. Catherine watched with her heart in her mouth. If this shot was successful, would Dagonet actually give her up to these men? She would rather die! It seemed that minutes went by as the highwayman sighted along the barrel of his pistol. There was a flash and a roar, and more leaves spun up into the night sky. It was, however, no better than the first attempt, and with a curse the highwayman spat into the road.

"I'm damned if it can be done, sir. Do better than that, or the purse and the lady are mine."

"You're an admirable shot, my friend," laughed Dagonet. "Perhaps I should concede defeat?" Catherine sat beside him in an absolute fury. How dare Dagonet so casually wager her honor with these ruffians! What did their purses matter? She sat in a rigid silence, as Dagonet slipped out his pistol and took aim. The shot exploded past her ear, and the very top leaf snapped off the holly bush and spun into the air.

Before the highwaymen could register that they had lost the wager, Dagonet had pulled out another pistol and trained its barrel on the three horsemen, conveniently grouped together. "My win, sirs," he said, entirely without emotion. "And now, since you have so very kindly emptied your pistols of both bullets, and since I have another in this chamber and two more in its companion, which makes one dose of lead for each of you, you will dismount without any suspicious moves and take the bridles off your horses."

Dumbfounded, the ruffians could only do as he directed. Moments later, their bridle-less mounts went galloping away. Dagonet then required Merry Joe and his companions to remove their boots, which he collected and deposited in the phaeton.

"Now, good evening to you, gentlemen!" The highwaymen were each given a stylish bow, before Dagonet whipped up the team and they cantered off. The men were left cursing and shaking their fists in the frosty air, while their boots were tossed from the carriage along the roadside, where it would take the ruffians several hours to find them.

As soon as they were well away, Catherine turned to Dagonet. "How dared you, sir! What would you have done had that Merry Joe turned out to be a better shot! How could you offer to leave me with them!"

"He did not turn out to be a better shot, dear Kate. Your question is entirely hypothetical."

"This is insufferable, sir! You could not have known that. What would you have done—handed me over to them in an attempt to save your precious purse?"

"You seem to forget, madam, that you were entered into the wager at the highwayman's suggestion, not mine. But you did not need to be alarmed, you were never in any danger."

"Your arrogance passes belief! Had you lost, you would have been honor-bound to leave me with them! It was an unconscionable risk, but then perhaps your sense of honor is not so fine tuned, and you would have gone back on your word without a thought. Either way, the situation was untenable!"

"My word is, you must believe of course, always open to negotiation. Only a gentleman considers his word inviolable." The reply was flung at her like a knife. "You forget, Miss Hunter, that I am not a gentleman, but a rake. My reputation precedes me wherever I go. I am surprised you are not cognizant of it. In any event, I was lucky in my shot, so whether I would have preferred to leave you to Merry Joe, or break my questionable word as a gentleman, we shall never know."

"Any normal sane person would have thrown over their purse, rather than risk a bullet!" Catherine insisted.

"Undoubtedly. But then any normal sane person has

credit. I have none. If we are to complete this journey, my gold had better stay in my own possession."

With that she was silenced once again. She would never understand him.

13

By the time they made the last change of horses at Newbury, Catherine was almost sleepwalking. There was no way she could rest in the open carriage; no cushioned headrest that would allow her to relax for a moment. Hour after hour, they had galloped on through the dark. Only the thought of little Annie lying helpless in the Rose and Crown at Marlborough, gave her the determination to climb back into the phaeton one last time. Dagonet had done everything possible to see to her comfort. Every posting inn had been ready with a hot drink and a fire, each time a new brick was placed in the carriage, but nowhere had they stopped for more than a few moments. The little tiger on the gray thoroughbred had prepared the way for them with expertise, and there had been no delay in getting fresh horses. It reminded her of a military campaign, but then, of course, Dagonet had been a soldier. Had there really been any danger that he couldn't shoot the leaf from a holly bush, when he himself had picked the target? How many numbing hours of practice had it taken to be so sure of his aim? In any event, the ruse of the wager had effectively disarmed three men, and left him with three bullets. If his word meant nothing to him, he could have escaped with his purse, whether he had won the wager or not. Still, she shivered as she remembered the glint in Merry Joe's eye. As she tried to step up into the phaeton, she stumbled from pure weariness. Dagonet caught her arm.

"An hour and a half, Miss Hunter. Can you do it?"

She nodded and, throwing up her chin, climbed aboard without assistance. She had no idea, when she awoke an hour later, how she had come to be asleep at all, let alone with her head on her companion's lap. He had one arm around her, steadying her shoulders, and a fold of the fur cloak was cushioned under her hair against his thigh. The whip was set into its holder, and he drove on with the reins in one hand. The other hand rested gently against her back. I must sit up! she told herself firmly. This is outside the bounds of anything that is suitable! Yet it felt so secure and safe to be cradled against that strong body. She was so warm under the leather wrap that had been arranged so that the wind should not disturb her. Without moving she watched the countryside pass by. Why did it all look so different? Suddenly she realized that it was snowing.

"When did the snow start?" she asked sleepily.

"Just past Hungerford."

At the sound of his voice, she realized quite how compromising her position must appear to him, and she sat up. He did not, however, remove his arm from her shoulders. They were passing though the bleak, open hills of the Marlborough downs. The valley of the River Kennet that the road had followed for most of the journey had dropped away to their right. Flurries of snow stung her face as she looked about. Steadily the landscape was disappearing under a white blanket.

"Go back to sleep, Kate," said Dagonet. There was

something in his voice that was indefinable. "I'll wake you in time, before we enter the coach yard!"

"I cannot think it quite the thing that I should be supported by your arm, sir."

"Why? Is it uncomfortable?"

"No, but . . ."

"Then I should think you have no grounds for objection. Without your presence to keep me awake, perhaps I should also tumble into sleep—even fall from the carriage—leaving the horses to run on unguided through the snow."

"I think you jest, sir."

"But you cannot be sure, can you?" His fingers had unconsciously begun to stroke the back of her neck. "Come, you will be no use to Annie, if you cannot hold yourself upright when we arrive."

With that, she gave in and put her head back on his thigh. She fell asleep once more to the delicious feeling of his long fingers gently brushing through her hair.

The Rose and Crown commanded the premiere position in the main square in Marlborough. When the phaeton pulled up in its large courtyard, the inn was already bustling with the activities of the new day, although the light of dawn was several hours away. Instead, there was a blaze of light from lanterns slung all around the stone walls. The ostlers ran back and forth in a soup of slush from the still falling snow. Horses nickered in anticipation, as their grooms forked hay down into their stalls. No carriages were being prepared for departure. If this weather kept up, they were going to have a multitude of travelers staying on at the inn until it improved. Several of the stable lads looked up in astonishment as an extremely fashionable high-perch phaeton drawn by post horses entered through the narrow archway. A gentleman in a many-caped greatcoat instantly threw the reins to the nearest boy, and handed down a lady completely muffled in an expensive fur-lined cloak. Without a word, he ushered her inside and confronted the innkeeper, who hurried up to them.

"Good morning, sir," said Dagonet. "You will show us immediately to the room of Miss Annabella Hunter. This is her sister." The hood of the lady's cloak fell back to reveal a pale face framed by dark hair. Black circles shadowed clear hazel eyes. "I shall also require a private parlor, and an extra bedchamber."

"Well, I'm glad you're here, ma'am, and that's a fact. The chambermaid has sat with the little girl all night, but she's right poorly. You look fair knackered out yourself!"

"We have come from London," said Catherine. "Please show us to her right away."

The innkeeper began to usher them up the stairs. "I don't know as I can accommodate you as to the extra rooms, sir. We're full up already, and what with the storm, I figure as how many of the guests will be staying on an extra night or two. Truly, there's not a room to be had in the house."

"Then you will require some of those guests to move." Dagonet slipped a sum of gold into the man's hand. "I cannot believe that you cannot find at least one spare bedchamber."

"Why, thank you, sir. I'll see what I can do." With that he indicated a door at the end of the corridor.

Catherine hurried in. Annie lay tossing and turning in a disordered bed at the side of the room. The only other furniture was a small couch, some stools, and a table with a pitcher and washbasin. Obviously the funds that her father had been able to provide for the journey had not stretched to the better rooms in the inn. A chambermaid rose at their entrance. "Oh, she's right poorly, ma'am. I wouldn't be surprised if she was to slip away at any minute."

It was apparent that the child was past recognizing them. Her breath was coming in thin, disordered gasps. The little room was insufferably hot, and Annie's forehead blazed like a brazier to Catherine's touch. Dagonet was stripping off his coat and gloves. "You will bring me some clean snow in a bucket," he snapped to the chambermaid. "And a pitcher of fresh drinking water from the well, but first I want it boiled for ten minutes. Also have sent up a small amount of fine sugar and some salt."

"Boiled water, sir?"

"You heard me. Do it now."

As the chambermaid scurried to obey the imperious gentleman, he stepped to the window and threw wide the casement. Fresh snow-laden air flurried into the room for a moment, then he closed it again, leaving the merest crack to let in some outside air. The curtains at the bed protected Annie from any direct draught, and the room began instantly to become more comfortable.

He joined Catherine at the bedside, and felt Annie's forehead and pulse. "The fever will burn out the disease, but it's far too fierce. She will be consumed, unless we can get her temperature down. She also needs liquids, her lips are parched!"

There was a rap at the door and the chambermaid entered with a jug of water and a bucket of snow. "I've kept her well wrapped up, sir, and starved her as best I might, though she cried pitifully for water."

Catherine thought that Dagonet would greet this sally with curses. But instead he said gently, "I'm sure you're a good girl and did your best. Now bring us plenty of nice clean cloths, and some coffee and breakfast for the lady." The chambermaid hurried willingly away. Taking the boiled water, Dagonet mixed into it a small amount of sugar and salt and began to carefully tip a few drops between Annie's lips. She gulped reflexively and he gave her some more.

Catherine's stamina had finally given way. Tears were coursing unnoticed down her cheeks, as she held her little sister by the hand and tried to talk to her. "What can I do?" she asked Dagonet.

"Just what you are doing," he replied quietly. "Don't think that she cannot hear you speak to her."

"Why boil the water?" asked Catherine.

"I have no idea. It seems to help. Perhaps the boiling purifies it, like the fever purifies the blood."

When Annie could drink no more, Dagonet dipped the cloths that the maid had brought into the now melted snow and began to sponge the child's limbs. She whimpered, and Catherine stroked the damp hair back from the hot forehead. They were interrupted by the chambermaid one more time, when she brought in a tray laden with hot fresh rolls, buttered eggs, and steaming jugs of chocolate and coffee.

"I can't eat!" protested Catherine.

"Nevertheless, you will," stated Dagonet. "You will take off your coat, wash your face and hands, and eat your breakfast. We must both keep our strength, and there is nothing more you can do right now for Annie."

She hesitated only a moment. Of course, he was right. Once she had eaten, indeed, she felt much better. Taking Dagonet's place at the bedside, she insisted that he breakfast in turn. To her amazement, he first stripped to his shirt and plunged his head and hands into the cold water

in the bucket. He stood up and went to the washstand for
a towel. The water ran down over his fine linen shirt,
making it stick to his muscled torso. Catherine looked
away. Preoccupied with Annie, not once had she given
any thought to him. He seemed invulnerable, but he had
after all just driven through the night with no sleep at all,
as the snow coated his head and gloves. Prior to that,
because of her impetuousness, he had been forced to
crawl over the roofs of Whitechapel and fight off footpads. Meanwhile, she had done nothing but sit beside
him in the carriage, her hands warmly wrapped in the
robe, and then fall asleep on his lap. Nevertheless, when
the innkeeper arrived to inform them that he had indeed
discovered a vacant bedchamber, it was Catherine who
found herself being put to bed there by the chambermaid, while Dagonet kept vigil beside Annie.

She awoke in a daze. A bleak light streamed in at the
window. Snow still fell steadily into the streets. It must be
mid-morning or later! Hurriedly she climbed out of bed
and dressed. Her room was only a few doors down the
corridor from Annie's, and she quietly opened the door
and went in. Dagonet sat where she had left him. Annie's
little hand was firmly grasped in his long fingers. There
didn't seem to be much change. The child's breathing
still came in shallow gasps, her face was flushed and
beaded with sweat.

"Is there any improvement?" asked Catherine quietly.

Dagonet looked up at her. His face was shadowed with
dark memories. "No, not much. But no change for the
worse. I think the crisis will be tonight. Are you rested?"

"Yes, thank you." Their conversation was as stiff and
awkward as if they were total strangers. He had told her

that he had learned to be a nurse on the battlefield. What terrible scenes had he witnessed there? She realized that all she had ever seen of war in the newspapers were dashing tales of victory and glory. No doubt there was great courage and bravery, but at what price in suffering? She sat at the bedside. "Will you go and rest now?"

He stood up and grinned at her. "Unfortunately, there is not another chamber for hire for any amount of gold. I can hardly use your room, Kate dear. That would offend the delicate sensibilities of our kind innkeeper, and set tongues to wagging as surely as if you were there to share the bed with me."

She would not let him discompose her! "There is the couch, Mr. de Dagonet." She indicated the small sofa that sat near the fire. "I shall take no offense, sir. You might be in need of your faculties later. Even you cannot go without sleep forever."

Without a word, he took a blanket from the dresser and lay back on the couch. In an instant, he was asleep. The dull light softened the chiseled features, and wiped away the tension around the fine lips. Catherine watched his steady breathing. Countless women must have done so, she thought with a blush, in happier circumstances. One of his hands lay relaxed on the blanket. He has the most beautiful fingers, fine and strong: equally at home with a sword or a violin, on the reins of a horse or the body of a woman? Her color deepened at the thought, and she forced herself to look away. So he had enjoyed the favors of many lovers. Can I blame them? It's no use at all, is it, Catherine Hunter? Whatever he has done and whoever he really is, I'm very much afraid that you're in love, like some silly moonstruck milkmaid! Nothing would cause him more amusement. Even the vicar's daughter is a conquest! He might even condescend to be kind, and I certainly couldn't bear that. No, whatever else might happen between them, she would salvage her pride. He must never discover that a strange new emotion was tearing at her heart. As soon as Annie was out of danger, she would do her best to make sure that the fascinating Charles de Dagonet disappeared entirely from her life.

14

Sir George Montagu was feeling particularly pleased with himself. Dashed if it wasn't tough on a fellow to have his female relatives about! Now at last he had London to himself. Sister Charlotte had decided to travel down to Bath again with her bosom bow, Lady Pander. Why a respectable widow should want to gallivant around the country in the middle of winter, he had no idea. She was probably planning to curry up to old Lord Blythe again. Well, good luck to her. Grandfather couldn't stand her, and never would. It also relieved George's ears of any more tales about the late Mr. Clay, whose mediocre qualities had been so unexpectedly improved by his death. And poor old Mama, Lady Montagu, would not stay on in London when she heard that Charlotte was planning to leave; nor would she go home to Exmoor without Miss Hunter. She declared that she would never live in Lion Court again, if she had to be alone there, and had gone to visit another old friend on the outskirts of the city. Thus he no longer had to make his daily duty visits to her, and listen to her bemoaning the loss of her tiresome companion. He had always had the feeling that Miss Hunter had no respect for him, none at all, and that could be laid fair and square at the feet of cousin Dagonet. Damn the fellow! It was bad enough that Dagonet should laugh at him to his face, but to know that the vicar's mousy daughter had witnessed his humiliation was beyond anything. It had even appeared that Dagonet was courting her! They had been dancing together, that night at Lion Court; George was convinced of it. George couldn't imagine why, she was certainly not pretty! George preferred his women with a little more meat, and not half so clever.

There was one place, though, that he had one over on his infamous cousin. George's reputation for respectability was impeccable, and thus he had entrée to all the most exclusive rings of the marriage mart, including Almack's: that ultimate arbiter of acceptability. And just last week he had met Miss Ponsonby by the lemonade table; slightly plump and very blond, adorably simpleminded, and the possessor of a fortune worth ten thousand a year. He believed the impressionable Miss Ponsonby had smiled rather kindly upon him, and her mama obviously felt him to be a most eligible suitor. A respectable match like that would be a triumph over Dagonet! Miss Ponsonby would make a very good mistress for Lion Court. Not that George really cared that much about the place: ramshackle old building like that, needed knocking down and replacing with a nice modern structure. Nevertheless, the income from the estates was more than welcome, and it was very satisfying to know that it was going to be his and not Dagonet's. Besides, there was a seat in Parliament that would fall to the owner of Lion Court soon enough, once old Cartwright were out of the way. And that would be a feather in his cap! Now, however, he had heard from a reliable source that Devil Dagonet had fled London to escape gaming debts, and that was the final cause of George's smug expression. For as long as his dashing cousin remained in the city, there was no telling when or how he might suddenly choose to torment or humiliate him. It was a relief to have him gone. George thus felt perfectly safe as he returned from St. James's Street. He was so amazed, that he almost stumbled when he was accosted from the depths of a shadowed doorway.

"Remember me, guv?"

George peered at the fellow for a moment. An unpleasantly large and overbearing person with heavy features, certainly not a gentleman and a little the worse for drink, stood threateningly in the shadows. "I don't believe I ever saw you in my life, my man! Now you will kindly allow me to pass."

The man stepped further into the light. "George Montagu, ain't it? Sir George now, I should say!" He leered into George's face, which had turned a violent shade of red.

"By God! John Catchpole! Dash me if I could recognize you for a moment there. It's been—what?—seven years or more. Down on your luck, are you? Well, you'll get no help from me."

"No help, eh? After what I done for you back then? No help?"

"I don't know what are you talking about, my man!"

"I'm talking about Milly Trumble, that's what I'm talking about! Pretty handy for you, poor Milly going down in the lake like that, wasn't it?"

George's color was fluctuating from red to white. "You are rambling, sir. I know nothing of the matter. I wasn't even at the lake. I know absolutely nothing!"

"Know nothing, know nothing! That's what she said!"

"She? Whatever do you mean?"

"Why little Miss Hunter, that's who I mean. And was

it you who sent her?" The look that crossed George's features gave John Catchpole an instant answer. The man laughed aloud and doffed his cap, before saying over his shoulder, as he went striding off up the street, "Look to your back, Sir George! Better look to your back! You might be hearing again from a certain John Catchpole."

And the proud suitor of Miss Ponsonby was left standing, mouth agape, on the pavement. He was thunderstruck. Miss Hunter! What on earth had she got to do with the drowning of Millicent Trumble, with Dagonet, or with the stable man dismissed so long ago by his father? And more to the point: how much did Mr. Catchpole know?

George might have been equally amazed had he known how his name was to be shouted at the Rose and Crown at Marlborough. After a day with very little change, when Dagonet and Catherine had steadily nursed her through the fluctuating fever, Annie had woken enough to recognize them. Her eyes blazed like diamonds in her round, flushed face, and she sat up in bed and struggled against Catherine's restraining hand. She was on the edge of delirium, and she demanded that only Dagonet should nurse her, she wanted Dagonet to give her a drink. When Catherine stepped back, however, with a silent appeal to that gentleman, Annie instantly demanded that Catherine mustn't leave her, and she clung pitifully to her sister's hand.

"It's all right, Annie," said Dagonet. "We're both here. Now drink this, then lie back down like a good girl."

Annie had dropped back into a restless sleep, but as the night wore on, the fever mounted, and she sat up in the disordered bed with a start and shouted, "It was George, wasn't it? Sir George Montagu! I've thought and thought, and I know it wasn't you, it was George. George! George!"

"Hush, Annie, we're here, Catherine and Mr. de Dagonet. Sir George Montagu is in London." Catherine tried to bathe the burning forehead, while Dagonet took Annie by the hand.

Annie's little fingers hung onto Dagonet's like claws. "I know you didn't do it!" she cried. "I know it! I know it! You must tell me. I've thought and thought and thought, and it's the wager, isn't it? You must tell me about the wager!"

"Hush, Annie," began Catherine, but the little girl began to thrash in the bed. "Annie, you must lie still!"

"I won't lie still! I won't! Devil Dagonet didn't do it!"

"Didn't do what, Annie?" asked Dagonet quietly.

"You didn't drown that Milly girl. I won't believe it. You must tell me the truth! It was to be George's baby, wasn't it? And that's what the wager was all about, when you jumped through the lych-gate! It was George! You must tell me. You must tell me."

"If I do, will you be quiet and lie down and go to sleep?"

Annie clung to him; she was rapidly becoming hysterical. "Why did you jump through the lych-gate? You must tell me about the wager! I don't care about all that gentleman stuff! It was George's fault! Milly was in love with George!"

And quietly, his face set in a mask, Dagonet replied, "Yes, she was."

Catherine would have left immediately, but Annie clasped at her dress and wouldn't let her go. "You can't leave! All that gentleman stuff about honor and all that is silly! I want to know about the wager! Dagonet must tell me! He must!"

"Annie, if there is some matter of honor between gentlemen, of course Mr. de Dagonet can't tell you about it; you know that." But Annie would not lie down. The fever raged behind her glassy eyes, and her dry skin was stretched tight over her little skull.

"Nonsense," said Dagonet firmly. "Annie's right, it's very silly. And Miss Annabella won't tell a soul, so it doesn't matter."

Immediately Annie became quiet. She clung to Dagonet as if she were drowning, and only he could rescue her. Dagonet's voice was entirely without emotion as he began, and Catherine, to her immense discomfort, knew that she was going to hear the truth about something that, however much she had wanted to know, she had no business hearing.

"Milly was a silly girl, Annie. She thought that George loved her and would take care of her. So you were right about that part. But it wasn't very suitable, was it? And I knew that our grandfather wouldn't like it very much. I was a very arrogant and conceited young man, you know, and I thought I could make George leave her alone. He said he would not unless I could jump my horse through the lych-gate. If I won the wager, I must tell no one about him and Milly, but he would give Milly up, so that she could fall back out of love, before any harm was done. If I lost, he would keep Milly, and I would not interfere, and I would give him my best horse, too."

"But you won!" said Annie. "And you kept your word, but he broke his! Because you didn't tell anybody, and he kept being Milly's lover, so that she was going to have a baby! And even when everybody thought it was you, you didn't tell, because you had given George your word!"

"That was very silly, wasn't it?"

"I knew it! I knew it! I thought and thought, you see! You took the blame for George, but I knew you couldn't have done it! You had too much honor and George had none. I knew it was the wager!" And with that she broke into a sudden, drenching sweat. In silence, Catherine bathed and dried the skinny limbs, as Dagonet stripped off the bed and laid clean sheets. A few moments later, Annie dropped into a sound sleep, her breathing deep and even. The fever was broken.

Catherine sat back on her stool. Her face was white.

"So you have been in the habit of wagering over women's virtue for a long time! A poor serving girl for a horse!" Instantly she wished the words unspoken. How could she be so unfair! Annie owed her life to Charles de Dagonet, and she could be no more generous than that? He could not have prevented George from seducing Millicent Trumble; all he had tried to do was to put a stop to it. Had George possessed any honor, the wager would have succeeded! How else was he to try and influence his cousin's behavior? Yet somehow she could not help herself.

He stood and went to the window. His voice was perfectly smooth and cultured. "I do not excuse it."

"And your precious word of honor? Your word to George is broken now!"

"It doesn't matter, does it? You will tell no one what you have learned, and neither will Annie. I believe I already told you that, not being a gentleman, my word is negotiable."

Yet, of course, it had not been negotiated to save his own reputation or against his grandfather's wrath. Only to save a little girl from her delirium. Had he told what he knew about George and Millicent Trumble at the time, he might now have been the possessor of Lion Court. But he had given his word to his cousin, and though George had broken faith, he had not, even though he would pay a terrible price for it. Yet still, there was that inexcusable arrogance! To wager that he could jump his horse through an impossible obstacle! Did the fact that he had succeeded change that?

"And the drowning? Was George responsible for that, too?"

"He was not there." Dagonet's voice was almost casual, but he kept his back to her. "He had spent the day in Fernbridge with Lady Montagu and friends. His alibi cannot be questioned. No, the drowning may still be laid at my door, though I never did enjoy the humble charms of the fair Milly." He turned and faced her, the controlled voice unchanged. "I don't know what happened. You found out yourself that I wrote Millicent a note inviting her to meet me there. I don't know why. I remember nothing of it. I was apparently so stinking drunk at the time, that I have blacked out the entire day. Clumsy of me, wasn't it?"

Catherine's thoughts made a confused whirl in her head. If he had not been involved with Milly, why meet her? Had she asked him for help, when she found out that she was with child? Did she believe Dagonet could intercede for her with George? Nothing else made sense. Catherine tried to remember the exact wording of the note that Millicent Trumble's sister, Mary, had shown her at Lion Court. Most of the words came back. She realized now that there was nothing in it that implied that Milly had ever been Dagonet's mistress. That construction of events had somehow been superimposed afterwards, and because of his word of honor to George, Dagonet had allowed it to pass unquestioned. She remembered her father's description of the scene at Lion Court, when Lord Blythe had come down. It had taken an extraordinary courage and determination for Dagonet to withstand all that wrath, when he had not in fact been Milly's lover. Which meant that even if George had been entirely unconnected with the drowning, it had still been incredible that he had allowed his cousin to take all the blame for what had happened. That he had stood by while Dagonet was thrown from the house, and then benefited by becoming their grandfather's heir, made his behavior all the more vile. No wonder that there was bad blood between the cousins! And in spite of all that had now been revealed, they were no closer to knowing the truth about Milly's death, or what had made Dagonet apparently drink himself into a stupor. Which meant that whatever it was that John Catchpole was hiding, was all the more critical.

"Perhaps when you sent the note, you meant well by it," she ventured.

"Yet Milly died. Rather spoils an attempted reconstruction of my role as that of rescuer of the fair maiden, doesn't it? I should have saved my horse the trouble at the lych-gate. It was unconscionable to put such a fine animal at risk. Now, if you'll excuse me, Miss Hunter, I am going out. Annie will sleep peacefully now. The danger is over."

With that he threw on his greatcoat and walked quietly from the room, and Catherine was left to her thoughts.

15

Dagonet walked the silent streets of Marlborough totally unaware of the snow that was coating his hat and shoulders. He was well aware of the cruel irony with which fate was determined to couple his actions. He had sworn to himself not to get involved again with Catherine Hunter, and here they were trapped together by circumstance at an inn. He must remove her from his life! The fact that she now knew the truth about who Millicent Trumble's lover had actually been, changed nothing. Her honor was sufficient that she would let the knowledge go no further. Annie, if she remembered at all when she awoke in the morning, was also to be trusted. His oath to George still held. The world would still believe the worst of him. If he only knew himself how poor, foolish Milly had drowned! As he had told Catherine, he had always prided himself on his competence. Yet the girl had died! For seven years the image had haunted him. Poor Milly, frantically pacing beside the water, and then perhaps casting herself in when no help arrived. When he had discovered from Catherine about the note, it had been a terrible blow. If he had arranged to meet Milly when she was so desperate, and had then carelessly let her wait in vain by the lake, it was the unforgivable action of a blackguard. His sense of honor informed him that he was as responsible for her death as if he had pushed her.

George must have spurned her without a backward thought, when he knew she was pregnant. Dagonet had been furious when he had discovered that George had seduced her. She was only fifteen, for God's sake! He himself had enjoyed some amorous adventures, of course, but only with women who knew exactly what they were doing, not with a helpless maidservant, five years younger. He could still recall the day he had faced George down over it. His cousin had begun by denying everything, and then had become defensive.

"You're the one with the reputation for being a rake, not me! You have a mistress in Oxford, don't you? I told grandfather you did!"

"Lord Blythe doesn't give a damn about my mistress, George! But he would give a great many damns, if he thought that either of us had so lost all sense of honor as to take advantage of a maidservant in his house. Thanks to your tale-telling, I have already had to face him over my so-called libertine behavior, and it wasn't pleasant. He doesn't care if we are involved with women, but he cares a great deal whether we conduct ourselves with any sense of decency. I gave him my word of honor that no innocent maid would suffer over my actions, but I won't answer for yours! You must give the girl up right away."

"I'm damned if I will! It's no business of yours! You can't make me do it!"

"I'll do anything you say, if it will save her."

"Then I'll make you a wager! Take that precious stallion of yours and jump him through the lych-gate at the Fernbridge church, and I'll never touch her again. I'll give her up, and you'll give me your word that, whatever happens, you won't tell a soul. Fail, and the horse is mine."

"You are a bloody bastard, aren't you, George? You have always envied me the horse, but your attempt to win him might cripple him instead. The jump can't possibly be done."

"Well, that's my offer. Take it or leave it!"

And, of course, he had done it, and George had his promise. He had not realized until he had stood facing the wrath of his uncle and grandfather, that George had not kept his side of the bargain and not given up poor Milly after all. And thanks to Catherine's talk with the girl's sister, he now knew that he had arranged to meet her when she had no one else to turn to, and he had failed her, too. Poor little wench! He could never forgive himself. He had known at the time how he had been found, and that he must somehow be involved and had foundered. Milly Trumble had died all alone at the lake, while he lay in the woods with a bottle. That his grandfather and uncle had thought that he was also her lover hadn't mattered at all, compared to the enormity of that. Why? Why had he failed her? He must find out! John Catchpole was his only hope. In the meantime, there was Kate Hunter. He had never met anyone like her, but unless he could first clear his name, he must give her up!

When he returned to the Rose and Crown, he went straight to Annie's room. Catherine still sat where he had left her. As he entered, she leapt up.

"I have behaved abominably, sir!" she began.

"Have you? I'm not sure how you can think so. Does Annie still sleep?" He went to the bed and checked the little girl's pulse and forehead. He smiled at Catherine.

"She will rest now until morning. I have asked the chambermaid to sit with her, and engaged a private parlor for us. We have not had a proper meal since we arrived. You look like a positive ragamuffin, as usual; so go and change your dress, and we shall celebrate Annie's recovery in style."

Catherine looked down at her crumpled frock and gave him a rueful grin. It was the same dress she had traveled in. "I don't have a change with me."

He tossed her a package. "Here you are. I hope it fits. I'll be ready in fifteen minutes."

It was closer to twenty minutes, before Catherine was prepared. The pale amber silk fit her perfectly. Wherever in Marlborough had he found such a garment at such short notice? She brushed out her hair, coiled it at the nape of her neck, and wove a white ribbon into it. No doubt some poor shopkeeper had fallen victim to that iron determination, and been forced to open his store. Without question, he had also been the object of enough charm to make him feel privileged to have done so! She had no jewelry with her, but she knew she looked well. In spite of her exhaustion, Annie's recovery had done wonders for her spirits, and her color was high. Why not have dinner together? She owed him her little sister's life, and had given him nothing but harsh words in exchange. Surely she could guard her heart, yet still be civil?

They went down the narrow stair, and the innkeeper showed them to a private dining room. As he opened the door and Dagonet ushered Catherine inside, she was horrified to find that two ladies already sat at the table.

"What is the meaning of this? We asked for a private parlor!" began the first, raising heavily plucked brows. "We were just shown in here by the maid. Innkeeper! There must be some mistake!"

The innkeeper began to mumble and bow, but Catherine was not in the least concerned with his embarrassment. In order to quench her own, she was trying to back out of the room. It was too late. The other lady had turned her head and was looking at them, mouth agape.

"Miss Hunter! And Charles de Dagonet! I declare I shall faint!" It was Charlotte Clay.

"Oh, how completely perfect!" The speaker, Charlotte's companion, rose to greet them. Her sharp features were alight with mischief. "Here alone together? And so late at night? Were you not Lady Montagu's companion, Miss Hunter? I have never had the pleasure of meeting the gentleman you are accompanying, but I am, of course, aware of him by reputation. I happened to see your name in the register, sir. I didn't see yours, Miss Hunter? But, Charles de Dagonet: not an easy name to overlook. You had booked only the one room, sir, had you not? I am so pleased to make your acquaintance at last, after hearing so much about you! I am Lady Pander."

Dagonet bowed over the hand she proffered. "My pleasure, my lady. Your reputation is also well established, of course."

Charlotte Clay ignored these barbed pleasantries. "Whatever do you do here, sir? Oh, how dreadful! With Miss Hunter! And sharing a room! Have you lost all sense of the proprieties?"

"I might ask the same, Mrs. Clay. Your inquiry is indelicate, don't you think? You are also delayed by the storm, I take it."

"We are on our way to Bath, Mr. de Dagonet. And are quite trapped here, or I should leave this instant. You shall not turn aside my comments. I believe in plain speaking! You and Miss Hunter here together! What else is one to think? Everyone has been caught by this snow for days! Oh! If Mr. Clay should have lived to see the day when I should sleep under the same roof with such blatant indecency! My salts, Lady Pander! I am quite overcome!"

Catherine wished the floor would open and swallow her; amber silk, white ribbon, and all. This was a disaster. Her reputation would never survive Charlotte's account of this meeting at the Rose and Crown. Lady Pander would make sure it became the *on dit* of the day! If it had been anyone else but Devil Dagonet, perhaps she could explain it away, but to be caught staying at an inn with a notorious rake, with no other chaperone than her little sister, was unpardonable. It would be humiliating for Amelia, too, who must now cope with these vicious gossips in high society. She could never live it down!

"Your concerns are all due to a misplaced sensibility, Charlotte. How could you think so ill of Lady Montagu's friend?" It was Dagonet. His voice was bland with unconcern, but surely this time even he could not rescue her? Lady Pander and her friends would tear her reputation to shreds, like a mouse in the claws of an eagle. How could he seem so relaxed? His expression was so open, she was totally unprepared for his next statement. "I have neglected to inform you of the happy event, dear cousin," Dagonet went on in dulcet tones. "But Miss Hunter and I are married."

Catherine turned to him, eyes blazing. Oh, this was even worse! "Whatever are you saying? We are not—"

He cut her off with a warning squeeze to the arm. "We are not telling anyone yet, is what my wife wishes to say. A quiet country wedding was better suited to our tastes. Until the event is formally announced, we know we can rely on your discretion, Charlotte, and Lady Pander's is, of course, well known."

Without letting go of her arm, he made polite good-byes and whisked her out of the room. In the next instant he turned on the innkeeper, who had stood mouth agape throughout this exchange. "Now, sir. If you would kindly show us to a parlor that is not already occupied, perhaps we can eat our dinner."

At the whiplash in Dagonet's tone, the innkeeper leapt to obey, cowering and mumbling apologies. A few minutes later, they were shown into an empty chamber and the door closed behind them. Dagonet leaned back against the polished wood and began to laugh. Furious, Catherine whirled on her companion.

"How dare you! How could you tell them we were married?" She stalked up and down the dining room. "It's too absurd! The word will be all over Bath by the end of the week, and all over London in two! Whatever possessed you?" She turned and marched up to him. He stopped laughing and bowed, but his eyes were alight with a keen sense of the ridiculous.

"What word would you prefer passed from mouth to mouth by those busy ladies, Kate dear? That you are my wife or my mistress? There is no other choice, I'm afraid, thanks to some bungling inn maid."

It was true, of course. No other interpretation could be put upon their presence here. Dagonet grinned at her. He appeared to keep his voice level with no effort at all. "If you prefer to be known as my mistress, you can deny our marriage, and it will make no difference. Just a little extra garnish to the story. Otherwise, we can be married without delay, and there will be no scandal."

"How can you stand there so calmly and smile about it? This is beyond anything! I don't want to marry you!"

"I'm sorry you find the idea so repulsive. It was, I admit, the opposite of my intention when we began this evening together. Nevertheless, I offer you my hand and heart, sweet Kate, and my disreputable name, for what it's worth."

It was the most painful moment of her life. She could see that they were both trapped. It must be the last thing that he wanted, to be saddled with an impetuous girl that had already interfered too much in his life. Under any other circumstances, his proposal would have been the fulfillment of her heart's desire. She was no longer under any illusion about her feelings for him, but she would not burden him with them, when they were not returned. Now he was being gallant, but he could not mean it.

As if he read her thoughts, he continued, "I do mean it. You can have no idea what you and your family will face, if you are thought to be my mistress. It will not be possible to deny it and be believed. You will lose all respect and decent treatment. The world is full of vultures, Kate. Marry me, and they will think you misguided, but not wicked. I give you my word, it will be a marriage in name only. After a decent interval, it can be annulled."

How could she admit that if his motivation was any other than to save her reputation, she would not want a marriage in name only? She no longer believed him guilty of any wrongdoing in the death of Millicent Trumble. Some other explanation was bound to be discovered, if they could only get John Catchpole to tell his story. Dagonet was the finest man she was ever likely to meet; could she now throw this generous gesture back in his face?

"I do appreciate your motives, sir. But surely there is some other way out?"

"There is none. If you are thought to have been my mistress, but return to London alone, I shall then be accused of abandoning you. That is, of course, no more than much of the ton would expect of me, thanks to my talkative cousins, but it will put David Morris in a dreadful spot. As your sister's husband, he will probably feel obliged to call me out. He's a very good friend, I would rather not face him on the dueling field." She hesitated, and he went on very gently: "There is also your father to consider. I think I owe him more than to ruin his eldest daughter."

She smiled at him a little ruefully. "We're both trapped, aren't we, sir? I know you don't really want to marry me, but I think I must accept your proposal."

"Good, then that's taken care of, and we can have our dinner at last." He bowed over her hand and kissed her fingers, then rang the bell for the waiter.

Catherine could never fathom afterwards, how she could then have sat across the table from him and enjoyed such a merry meal. Perhaps it was because of Annie. The full import of the danger to her sister and the final relief from it, bubbled up in her like champagne. Perhaps it was because Dagonet was simply the best dinner companion anyone could wish for; his wit had, after all, entertained the Prince Regent and Beau Brummel. She gave back as good as she got, however, and when at last he escorted her to her room, and left to relieve the inn maid from her watch over Annie, she felt quite reconciled to being Mrs. de Dagonet, even if in name only.

The next morning, the snow began to melt, and travelers began to leave the Rose and Crown in droves. Lady Pander and Mrs. Clay presumably continued their journey to Bath, where the news of Catherine's marriage could be expected to spread with great rapidity. Catherine gave them no more thought. Annie was much recovered, but still weak, and would come back to London with them. She had forgotten nothing that Dagonet had told her. She insisted that George must also have drowned Millicent Trumble, and all that Dagonet could tell her of George being reliably known to have been elsewhere, could not convince her otherwise.

Catherine meanwhile had to give thought to facing her father. A message had been sent to Exmoor, and in a few days, the Reverend Hunter duly arrived. She need not have been so concerned. After spending an hour closeted with Dagonet in a private parlor, the vicar announced himself content with the decision.

"It is not how I imagined marrying my eldest daughter, my dear, but you are in safe hands with Charles."

"Then you think he is innocent?"

"I have always believed him innocent. I knew him as a boy, remember? But until it's all cleared up, the suspicion is like a poison spring at the center of his being, and he is being destroyed by it. You can't allow it to happen, Catherine. Exmoor and Lion Court need him. He can't be allowed to go to waste."

"He's indifferent to me, Papa, but I'll do what I can." She put her arms around her father and hugged him. The next day he married them himself.

16

Dagonet had hired a comfortable four-horse chaise to take them back to the city, while his tiger slowly brought the phaeton up behind. Annie slept much of the way, her head pillowed on Catherine's lap.

"Well, sir," Catherine commented lightly to Dagonet as they pulled away from Marlborough. "What now?"

"You will return to Brooke House, dear Kate, with Annie. I have John Catchpole to hunt down. I do not imagine that he is still to be found in Lower Hobb Lane in Whitechapel, but he has probably not gone too far. This time, however, I would prefer not to have your assistance."

"Now that we are man and wife, sir; do you not think I have an interest in proving your innocence?"

"If that is what is to be proved!" he said with a wry smile. "You have just sworn to honor and obey, Madame de Dagonet. My first orders are that you do not interfere again with our unpleasant Mr. Catchpole."

"But you do not expect me to keep the promises made under duress, sir. I do not take orders from you! I also swore to love. You do not mention that."

"Because love cannot be ordered, ma'am," he said coldly. "Whereas obedience can."

Annie listened to this exchange with interest. She had woken up several minutes before. There was no polite way she could let her sister and her hero know that she had eavesdropped, so she stayed on the rocking coach seat, with her head in Catherine's lap, without moving. Cathy may be forbidden to interfere, she thought as she allowed herself to drift back to sleep, but I'm not, and I'm going to show that Sir George Montagu is the villain.

Capt. David Morris, now Lord Brooke, returned to the city to find that his friend was indeed married to Amelia's sister, but that nothing else seemed to have changed. Dagonet still kept his bachelor apartment, and Catherine was still a guest at Brooke House. He knew better, however, than to question such an odd arrangement. No one else knew of it. Not George, to whom the news of the marriage was like a thunderbolt; nor Lady Montagu, who thought the whole thing very shocking, and wondered if her one-time companion had lost her mind.

George had been in an agitated state ever since his encounter with John Catchpole. It had never concerned him in the least that Dagonet had taken all the blame over the Milly Trumble affair. He knew that his cousin maintained some old-fashioned sensibility about his honor, and would never tell George's role to anyone. He had been worried for a while that the girl's sister, Mary, had suspected who had really been Milly's lover, and that was why he had wanted to keep Dagonet from talking to her. It seemed, however, that Mary really knew nothing. As to what had actually happened the day that Millicent was drowned, he had never worried about it before. He was totally in the clear himself, thank God, having been with his mother all day. What was that Catchpole fellow insinuating? The drowning lay at Dagonet's feet, not his! Nevertheless, Catchpole may have known that George was the one who had won the servant girl's favors, and that was dangerous knowledge. If grandfather, or Miss Ponsonby ever found out! And Miss Hunter was somehow involved, and Dagonet had married her. A vicar's daughter without a penny! What gave his cousin such confidence in the future? Did he plan to expose George after all, and claim Lion Court? Sir George found his cravats tended to become uncomfortably tight whenever he thought about it.

Amelia tried only once to gain her sister's confidences, and then gave up. Catherine treated the whole marriage as if it were a great joke, and refused to say anything further. She was not to escape so lightly.

"Cathy! Look at this!" Amelia was going through her correspondence. "It's from old Lady Easthaven. Oh, no! She's going to give a ball the week before Christmas—for you and Dagonet! As grande dame of the family, of course, she would see it as her right."

Catherine leapt up. "Amy, this is dreadful! A formal ball? Whatever shall I do?"

"Put on your prettiest gown and give me the first waltz, of course." Dagonet strolled into the room. "I showed myself in, Lady Brooke. Forgive your footmen, they are no match for me when I am in such a black mood."

His face looked anything but black. In fact he was laughing.

"Oh, how can you laugh, sir?" snapped Catherine.

"To marry you was bad enough, but to have to act the blissful newlyweds in public! It's too much!"

"I'm sorry that you find it beyond your powers, Kate dear, to behave towards me with even a semblance of affection. I shall do my best, however, to look the doting spouse, and perhaps my performance may be enough for both of us?" He raised an eyebrow.

"Can't you persuade her not to do it?"

"What, deny an old lady the honor of celebrating our nuptials? You could not be so cruel, Kate. Besides, if we are to convince the *beau monde* that there was nothing shady about our hurried union, we had better face down the world with panache. What better setting than a ball given by a staunch patroness of the ton?"

"My life seems to be a series of traps these days!" wailed Catherine. "Of course, I can do it, but I shall not pretend that it will give me anything but discomfort."

"Kate! My heart is broken!"

"You don't have a heart to break, Mr. de Dagonet. So do not give me such fustian!"

"We are more in harmony at the piano, aren't we, wife? Let us play a duet, or Lady Brooke will have me thrown from the house."

"My footmen wouldn't dare, sir," said Amelia, as Dagonet sat at the piano. He turned expectantly to Catherine.

"Ne Jupiter quidem omnibus placet, dear Kate."

"Not even Jupiter may please everybody, sir, but at this moment you are pleasing nobody. I don't care for your choice in music and—"

She was not to finish, since Annabella, hearing from one of the maids about the visitor, burst into the room. Thus it was not Catherine, but Annie, her face beaming, who ended up sitting at the piano with Dagonet. Catherine was thoroughly relieved. The mood became as merry as she could possibly wish, the laughter drowning out the insistent message that her heart was trying to give her.

The ball was to be a splendid affair. She had a new gown made up for the occasion in white silk. The bodice was cut lower than she had ever worn before, but the modiste insisted that as a married lady, she must not look like an ingenue. An overdress of finest gauze fell in classic folds past her shoulders and floated over the silk underskirt. The whole was caught up under her breasts with ivory ribbon. Since she had no jewelry of her own, she tied a matching ribbon around her neck. One of her sister's maids dressed her hair high on top of her head, leaving just a handful of ringlets to brush teasingly past her cheek. She could barely recognize herself in the mirror. She went downstairs to join the party, who were to travel together to Lady Easthaven's massive mansion in the Brooke carriage. Since David had been forced to leave again on business, Dagonet was to escort the sisters. He awaited her at the bottom of the stairs.

He swept her an elegant bow. His immaculate evening clothes set off his muscular figure to perfection. As a mark of respect to Lady Easthaven's old-fashioned tastes, he wore silk knee breeches rather than trousers. At least I have that satisfaction, thought Catherine ruefully: he will be the most distinguished-looking gentleman there.

"Sweet Catherine, you are breathtaking!" he said simply, causing a blush to spread over her cheeks. "There is but one thing lacking, my dear." He came over to her.

"What is that, sir?" asked Catherine defiantly. "Do I have mud on my cheek?"

"Hardly mud, my dear; but the bloom of fresh spring roses."

"Please don't act the fool, Mr. de Dagonet! I shall never get through the evening, if you make fun of me with exaggerated compliments."

Taking her by the shoulders, he turned her away from him, so that she could see herself in the hall mirror. As she watched the reflection, he carefully untied the ribbon that she had placed around her neck. The touch of his fingers on her bare skin was a delicious torture.

"I do not exaggerate," he said gently. "Close your eyes."

"Why? May I trust you, if I do?"

"Of course. When have I ever betrayed your trust?"

"Often," she stated, but she closed her eyes.

In the next instant she felt something cool and smooth settling around her neck. Her lids flew open. He was just fastening the catch of his mother's diamond necklace. She had last seen the brilliant jewels slipping into his pocket in the drawing room at Lion Court, after he had taken them from Charlotte.

"Mr. de Dagonet! Whatever are you thinking of? I have no right to wear these!"

"Nonsense, you are my wife. Here are the earrings. Put them on."

She could not read his expression, but there was something in his tone that told her not to remonstrate further. "Now, if you can manage to make it through the evening without falling into a puddle, you will do me proud. Come, we had better make haste. The others are waiting."

*   *   *

The ballroom was a blaze of light. Everywhere a throng of sumptuously dressed ladies and gentlemen milled about, beneath great chandeliers full of candles and a rococo effusion of flowers and greenery. Lady Easthaven greeted them in person and began to immediately introduce Catherine to a succession of fashionable young people. Giving her a slight wink, Dagonet disappeared into the crowd, leaving her dance card to fill up with the names of strangers. In vain, she looked about for him, and was only able once or twice to catch a glimpse of his broad shoulders or dark hair, through the crush. Lord Kendal lead her into dinner and kept her laughing throughout the meal. Whatever story Charlotte Clay and Lady Pander might be spreading among their cronies, this ball was obviously going to be an effective antidote. Not once did she lack for a partner. Not once was an eyebrow raised or a look given her askance. Had Dagonet not insisted on the marriage, she would instead have been an outcast. Even if she didn't care for her own reputation, she must care for Amelia's sake. But her thoughts were interrupted.

"You have been the belle of the evening, my dear. I have watched in an agony of jealousy, as every young blade trips up and down the floor with you. Am I not to have a dance with my own bride?"

"It is hardly the thing, sir, for husbands and wives to squire each other about the ballroom. Besides, I am promised to Lord Kendal for this dance."

"Those may be the rules of the *beau monde*, my dear, but in spite of the glitter that surrounds us this evening, and the fawning flattery of those who mistakenly think Lady Easthaven makes me her protégé, I am still a renegade. Lord Kendal will not dare to challenge me. Come!" He grasped her hand and led her from the ballroom into the quiet hallway. There was a small anteroom where the footmen had waited earlier to greet the guests. It now stood deserted, but the strains of the band could be heard quite clearly.

"Now I have you at my mercy!" declared Dagonet with a grin. "May I have the honor of this dance, ma'am?"

As the lilting notes of the waltz swept into the little room, he pulled her into his embrace and they swirled together into the steps of the dance. Catherine half closed her eyes. If only he meant it! She allowed herself to relax into his arms, as they spun around together. As the music stopped, she opened them again to find him looking down at her. The green eyes were shadowed with an indefinable emotion. He did not release her. Instead, as the diamond necklace rose and fell with her breathing, he took her head gently in both hands and tilted her face up to his.

"The last time I danced alone with you, wife," he murmured against her lips, "we were rudely interrupted. I think it's time to finish what I began then."

His kiss was questioning at first, and gentle; but as she began to respond, he became ever more demanding, until she caught fire in his embrace.

The blood pulsed in her veins, and strange, delicious sensations ran up and down her spine under his skillful fingers. His clever lips searched the sensitive tip of her tongue, before running sweet kisses across her ear and, exquisitely, down her neck. Then he sought her mouth again, until she was quivering in his hands like a bowstring. When he at last released her, she felt her eyes fill with tears. "You cannot help yourself, can you?" she said desperately. "You promised that our marriage would be in name only."

"Damn it, Kate!" He tore away from her, and stalked across the room. "I am only human!"

"And so am I, sir! But we mean nothing to each other, so such behavior is inexcusable."

He had himself under control in an instant, except for the storm that tossed in the depths of his sea-green eyes. "You are right, of course, madam. What more could you expect from me, than that I should break my promise? It is only my idle boast that should I see you in diamonds, I should feel obliged to ravish you."

"Then I had better not wear them!" Catherine reached up unsteady fingers and removed the gems from her neck and ears. "Here, sir!" she said, and laying them on a side table, she turned to leave the room. Amelia stood in the entry.

"Oh, Cathy!" she wailed. "A message has come from Brooke House. It's Annie! She is nowhere to be found."

17

The night of the ball seemed to Annie to be an ideal time to take her turn in the pursuit of the elusive Mr. Catchpole. She had begun by going out and accosting a cab driver.

"Please take me to Lower Hobb Lane, in Whitechapel. I'm from Brooke House. You will be recompensed."

"Now, then, missy! Hobb Lane? What would you want with such a place? Your folks don't know you're out here alone now, do they? I think you had better come with me, and I'll take you back home instead."

The friendly cabby had begun to dismount. The little girl was well dressed, no doubt he would be amply rewarded if he could return her to her undoubtedly privileged home. Seeing his intent, Annie took to her heels and dodged behind a convenient stand of bushes. There was already someone there.

"Here! Look out now! Cor blimey, what have we got here?"

She was looking into the grimy face of a street urchin, who couldn't have been much older than herself. In one hand he held the handle of a homemade broom, with which he could earn a farthing or two by sweeping the street in the path of a lady or gentleman who wished to cross.

"My name is Annabella Hunter," stated Annie, without prejudice. "Who are you?"

"Archibald Piggot, at your service!" The boy gave her an exaggerated bow and a huge grin. "You got pluck, ain't you? Why was you wanting to go to Hobb Lane, then?"

"To find a man called John Catchpole."

"Well, you won't survive there looking like that! Cor, the girls would have the dress off your back in no time."

"Then how am I to go there?"

"You'd have to look like me, see?" He indicated his own tattered rags. "No one notices Archibald Piggot. I goes where I likes."

"Well, you could get me some clothes that would look right and take me there, couldn't you?"

"Well, I could." The boy gave her another saucy grin. "But it wouldn't do you no good. John Catchpole ain't there no more, no how."

"Then where has he gone?"

"That'd be telling, wouldn't it?"

But Archibald Piggot had not run into someone with quite Annie's determination before. He was not sure why he agreed. It would cost him some skin if Catchpole knew that he'd done it, but he found himself offering to escort Annie to the latest den of that highly sought-after ruffian. In ten minutes she had shed her costly woolen frock and the matching pelisse, and pulled an extremely filthy black dress over her petticoat. She shuddered a little at putting it on, but it was worth a great deal to find the proof of Mr. de Dagonet's innocence. Besides, the evening promised to be a great adventure. Young Mr. Piggot was good to his word, though the means of transportation that he adopted were a little unorthodox to his innocent companion. Annie found herself clinging to the back of a swaying carriage, right underneath the feet of a tiger. She and her guide then dropped off and scurried between the hooves of innumerable horses, before catching hold of the undercarriage of a ponderous cart that was apparently going in the right direction.

"You're a game bird for a toff, ain't you?" whispered Archibald.

The carriage was hastily called, polite excuses made, and Dagonet escorted the sisters back to Brooke House.

"A man called at the house, not an hour ago. The driver of a hack! Annie was asking to be taken to a place called Lower Hobb Lane!" wailed Amelia. "Whatever was she thinking? To run off alone into London! She's just a little girl!"

"I will bring her back, Lady Brooke," stated Dagonet firmly. "Pray do not distress yourself. No one would harm Annie. She has too much impudence for anyone to dare."

"I insist on coming," said Catherine. As Dagonet turned to her with a denial on his lips, she glared defiantly at him. "You shall not gainsay me, sir! She is my sister: she may need me when you find her. Besides, it is my fault."

"Very well. If you are determined. How do you propose to keep up with me in your silk dress?"

"I shall borrow some breeches from David's wardrobe. Don't look so shocked, Amy! Lord Brooke wouldn't mind if he were here, and you shan't stop me!"

Dagonet grinned. "We shall need to look inconspicuous, dear Kate, which you, in a pair of your brother-in-law's trousers would not be, however popular a ruse it may be in the pages of romances. If you will come with me, we shall return to my lodgings, and I shall see that we are both suitably attired."

Within half an hour, the glamorous denizens of the ballroom were unrecognizable. Dagonet had changed his silk knee breeches for a pair of dark worsted trousers. A shapeless jacket covered his shirt, and a battered round hat sat jauntily on his dark head. For Catherine the disguise was simple. He had gone to her wardrobe at Brooke House, and taken one of her older afternoon gowns. In a few simple movements, he had torn off the modest and costly lace inset around the neck, and left a neckline that revealed much of her bosom; at his lodging in Jermyn Street, he had produced the scarlet cloak that she had worn on her last escapade in Whitechapel.

"There, my dear. With a little dirt once again smeared onto your cheek, you will pass for an inhabitant."

If it had not been for the fine dueling pistols that he thrust into his pocket and the sword cane that he once again carried, Catherine might have thought him bent on nothing more than an evening's entertainment. He gave her a reassuring grin as they left the house.

"Once more, the game's afoot! We shall find her, Kate, and also, very probably, John Catchpole!"

They had no difficulty whatsoever in returning to the house where John Catchpole had held her captive. Dagonet sauntered casually along Lower Hobb Lane, with Catherine on his arm. They both gave the impression of a rather advanced state of inebriation. In spite of her anxiety about Annie, Catherine was kept smiling by a steady stream of pithy observations and absurd quotes. She played her part with a will. They had just arrived at the shadowed entrance, when Dagonet gave her arm a warning squeeze.

"Look you, wench! The Red Queen!"

The woman with the greasy mobcap was fast approaching the house. She paid the disreputable couple lounging in the doorway no more attention than they had received from any of the other denizens of Lower Hobb Lane, and made as if to rudely shove past them. Without a word, Dagonet had quietly released Catherine's arm, and freed himself for action. As she pushed up against him, the woman stopped and her face paled beneath its network of red veins. The drunken fellow blocking her path had a small knife pressed into the side of her neck. From the perfectly steady feel of the blade, he was not in the least drunk.

"Forgive this rude introduction, mistress," said Dagonet icily. "We want a word."

With no further conversation, they followed the woman into the little room where Catherine had first met her. Dagonet allowed her to sit down in one of the scabby chairs.

"Now, ma'am. John Catchpole."

Catherine expected some remonstration, but there was none. The inhabitants of Lower Hobb Lane understood physical violence, but they also understood implacable determination. The woman knew without the need for any further demonstration that Dagonet would have his way. She looked at Catherine in her scarlet cloak and grinned.

"Well! You led the fellows a merry dance! But no need to act bosky with me, I'll tell you right enough. Catchpole's not here anymore: if you want him tonight, he went to meet a gentleman, out by Hampstead. Business."

"Have you seen a little girl?" asked Catherine.

"We're not in the children racket!" announced the woman with indignation.

Further questioning revealed no more information. Annie had not been seen. Dagonet acquired the address in Hampstead, and they left their informant sitting alone in her filthy room. Catherine was frantic.

"How can we be sure that Annie is not somewhere here? Or hidden in the house? She must be terrified out in these streets alone."

"Annie is a resourceful miss, Kate. If she came to find John Catchpole, then our best bet is to follow the quarry in the hopes of catching the huntsman: or in this case, the younger sister of an extremely headstrong and interfering family." He caught her suddenly by the hand. "Never fear, we'll find her. Now, to Hampstead!"

They rapidly wove their way out of the warren of streets and courts and back to the main thoroughfare. There stood the high-perch phaeton with Dagonet's tiger at the horses' heads. Catherine was handed in, and they cantered out to the village of Hampstead, not far from London. The heath, notorious in earlier days for being a favorite haunt of highwaymen and robbers, still loomed bleakly in the darkness. The air was brittle with frost, and Catherine wished she had her fur-lined pelisse, instead of the thin red cloak. They pulled up some distance from the house to which the woman in the mobcap had directed them, and Dagonet instructed his tiger to walk the horses in the opposite direction. They then crept up to the place on foot. It was a run-down house, little better than a shack, well on the outskirts of the village. They reached the cover of some thick bushes in the garden.

"Stay here," ordered Dagonet.

"If Annie is here, I must know!"

"Kate! What must I do to convince you? I had no

desire to bring you on this hunt tonight. God knows what danger may await us here! You will stay under this tree, until I tell you otherwise!"

Pale moonlight cast shadows across the planes of his face as he carefully extracted a pistol from his pocket, and checked the priming. His face was as cold as the sky, and the expression was as remote. Catherine could see that she must do as he wished. If it came to a fight, she would only be in the way. Silently she nodded her head, and Dagonet disappeared into the shadows. She had no idea how long she stood there, jumping out of her skin every time that some small creature made a rustle in the underbrush. One time she had to bite her lip to keep herself from crying out, when an owl swept by on silent wings. She hugged the thin cloak around her shoulders, and took comfort from the solid, rough bark against her back. There was no sign of activity from the house, only the faint glimmer of a candle shining inside one of the windows.

She almost fainted when something touched her shoulder. She whirled around. It was Dagonet. "Come on," he said quietly. His even teeth shone white as he grinned. "I want you to see this."

She followed him up to the window and peered inside. John Catchpole sat snoring by a roaring fire that cast its flickering light about the tiny parlor, his feet sprawled out in front of him and the wine jug still dangling from his huge hand, its loop caught on one of his sausagelike fingers. His heavy features seemed flattened in the dull light, and the massive chin shuddered like a wet horse with every snore. The sound was enough to rattle the rafters. Catherine's glance rested only a moment on him, however, for her attention was caught by the other occupants of the room. Two ragged children sat across from

Catchpole, side by side on the table, their feet swinging
back and forth in time to the thunderous snoring. They
were tearing with great gusto into a big hunk of bread,
which they took turns in dunking into a very greasy-
looking pot of gravy. From the looks on their faces, they
were having a great time. Both children were dressed in
tattered rags, and the boy had bare feet. Catherine did
not recall ever having seen him before, but she had no
problem recognizing his companion. It was her little sister Annie. She turned in amazement to Dagonet. His face
was alight with laughter.

"God knows by what means your sister has arrived
here, Kate. But she seems to have fallen very firmly on
her feet. Come on."

In moments they were inside. As John Catchpole continued to snore, Annie turned and saw them. She leapt
from the table.

"Cathy! And Mr. de Dagonet! However did you get
here? This is my friend Archibald Piggot, and we've had
the best time. See, we found John Catchpole; only he's
drunk, and we can't get him to wake up and tell us
anything!"

"Annie, for Heaven's sake!" Catherine wanted to
shake and hug her at the same time. "This is unconscionable conduct! We've all been so worried about you!"

"But you were supposed to be at the ball! I told Archibald that he had to get me home before anyone found
out!"

Dagonet was leaning against the door. "And you, Master Archibald, are this young lady's escort?"

Master Piggot had stepped down from the table at the
sight of the fellow who addressed him, who—however
roughly dressed—was unmistakably a gentleman, and, if
Archibald were any judge, also a soldier. Not someone to

treat lightly from the look of those shoulders and the set of that mouth. He shrugged.

"I've took good care of her, guv. Archibald Piggot's not one to get into trouble. At least not too deep anyhow."

"We came out here on the back of a coster wagon, Cathy. The driver never knew we were there the whole time. It was the best fun!"

"But look at your clothes, Annie!"

"I don't think I look any worse than you!" Catherine glanced down at her ragged frock and blushed. It was only too true. They were both covered in dirt, and their clothing was a very far cry from their usual neat habits. Annie gave her a hug. "I am sorry if you worried, but Archibald said I must dress like this, if I was to get through the city unnoticed, and he fetched me the stuff in trade for my pelisse. It's a good thing, too, because I would have torn it all up anyhow clinging to the back of those carts and things."

Catherine didn't know whether to laugh or cry. "Annie, you could have been killed! It's too dangerous to go gallivanting off across London by yourself. Promise me you won't do it again!"

"But I did find Mr. Catchpole! And I wasn't by myself; I was with Archibald."

"Mr. Catchpole was not, however, lost, Miss Annabella, and did not need to be found by you," interrupted Dagonet. "Perhaps you were not aware that Mr. Catchpole is reliably reported to be expecting company tonight, although I admit that at the present moment, he does not seem as if he will be in any fit state to receive anyone. I intend in the next few minutes to remedy that situation, and it may not be a suitable sight for ladies. I would therefore suggest that you allow your sister to escort you home."

"No!" cried Annie. "Not after all I went through to get here. You shan't send me home now! And Cathy doesn't want to go either!"

One glance at Catherine was enough to tell him that she would not willingly leave without hearing what Catchpole was about to say. Dagonet laughed. Two Hunter sisters was more than he wanted to argue with, but they should go. His intent was distracted before he could say more, by the sound of a horse outside.

"We have company already," stated Dagonet. Quickly he motioned Catherine and the children into the darkest corner, and positioned himself behind the door, gun in hand. Heavy footsteps sounded on the gravel path up to the cottage, and someone hammered at the entrance. Catchpole slept on. They heard the creak of the front door hinges as it opened, and someone's labored breathing and solid tread, as he came down the corridor. In the next instant, the door to the little parlor was thrust open and the visitor came into the room. He was arrested in mid-stride by the thrust of Dagonet's pistol in his ribs.

"Why," said Dagonet with a grin. "If it isn't Cousin George. Do take a seat, dear cousin, and join us in our merry party."

George had turned white and then red. "What the devil are you doing here, sir?" he blustered. "Is this all a trap set up by you? Blackmail is just your line, isn't it?"

"Blackmail, cousin? Now, don't tell me that our slumbering friend has taken up that unpleasant trade?"

"It's because Mr. Catchpole knows that you murdered the Milly girl," squeaked Annie, running up and placing herself squarely in front of Sir George. "He wants money or he'll tell everyone!"

"Annie!" Catherine stepped forward and caught her sister by the shoulders. "You will apologize to Sir George this instant. Mr. de Dagonet already told you that Sir George was elsewhere, when Milly was drowned."

George sat down and loosened his cravat, twisting his fat neck as he ran a finger around it. "So that's it, is it? You're the force behind this little caper, Miss Hunter—or Mrs. Charles de Dagonet, I should say."

"I have nothing whatever to do with it, sir!"

Dagonet intervened. "I imagine that Mr. Catchpole was quite able to think up a scheme to blackmail you, dear George, without anybody else's help. However, we shall gain nothing by accusing each other. It would be more constructive, I believe, if we were to attempt to gain the story from the horse's mouth. Master Piggot! A bucket or two of water from the well, if you please!"

"Yes, sir!" The boy ran to obey.

"I had not planned such a spellbound audience for my meeting with our unconscious friend, I must admit," continued Dagonet smoothly. "But *fortuna favet fortibus,* does it not, cousin? Fortune favors the bold."

Archibald struggled in with two leather buckets sloshing over with slightly slimy water. "Here you are, sir," he said, and saluted.

"Well done, Mr. Piggot," replied Dagonet. "Now let us test the wisdom of the old French saying: *Il ne faut pas éveiller le chat qui dort;* or since we English prefer dogs to cats: Let sleeping dogs lie. We may live to regret this action." A bucket of the icy water was dumped unceremoniously over the reverberating head of John Catchpole. He moaned and shook his jowls. Archibald Piggot fled the room.

"I enjoy doing foolish things, George," continued Dagonet. "Or else I should never risk waking this slumbering mountain." The second bucket followed the first, and John Catchpole sat up and bellowed. With a great paw he made as if to wipe away the slime that ran down his face, and only succeeded in thumping himself in the chin with the wine jug that was still attached to his finger. He bellowed again, then his red eyes swept around the room and blinked as they took in its occupants.

"Feeling more the thing, Mr. Catchpole?" asked Dagonet politely. "Or do you require another bucket? Please don't get up. I have the most dreadful itch in my trigger finger."

The bloodshot eyes glared at the powerful figure who had a fine pistol aimed so casually at his waistcoat button. "Well, now," said John Catchpole, with a grin. "If it ain't Devil Dagonet to the life!"

"The very same, dear John."

"You were ever a hand with a pistol, weren't you?" said Catchpole. "Never saw a prettier hand with a horse neither. Still ride like Old Nick was on your tail?"

"If the occasion warrants, sir."

John Catchpole shook his head again. Slime rippled down over his greasy coat.

"Now, what would you be wanting with poor old John after all these years?"

"An accounting, sir. I would prefer more privacy, as perhaps you would also, but this importunate audience dogs our coat tails. What happened on that much regretted day, when simple Millicent Trumble was found floating in Lion Court Lake?"

"Well, maybe I'm not of a mind to recall that. It being such a long time ago and all."

"But you will recall, my friend, and you will recall the truth. I have enough information gathered about your recent activities to string you up at the Old Bailey several times over. Not to mention your clumsy attempt to blackmail my helpless cousin here. You knew that it was Cousin George who had won the fair Milly, didn't you? Unfortunately, the information will not embarrass my cousin, since this fact is well known in the family." The lie was so blatant that Catherine caught her breath. George was gaping at his cousin in open astonishment. "You will see," continued Dagonet, "that everyone in this room is cognizant of that unfortunate fact."

Catchpole looked Annie and Catherine in the face. They did obviously know about George's involvement with the serving wench. "Thus," Dagonet went on, "there is no ground for blackmailing Sir George. You might as well take it like a man, and realize that your dreams of riches from that quarter are now dissolving like smoke."

Catchpole scowled. "What did you want to know?"

"Just the facts, dear sir. The simple facts. What happened when Milly died?"

18

There was a dead silence in the room. Catherine held Annie firmly beside her, her breath seeming to stick in her throat. George sat as if riveted to his chair, his breathing coming fast, and his face a sickly hue in the candle-light. Only Dagonet seemed unmoved. He propped himself casually on the edge of the table, and the sea-green gaze rested without malice or expectation on the hulking form of John Catchpole. It seemed as if he would be content to wait all the rest of the night. It was not long before the silence was broken. Catchpole began to laugh.

"There's nothing to tell!" he exclaimed. "Nothing that ain't already known. I swear it on my mother's grave. I was coming up from the lower pastures past the lake, when I see Milly Trumble a-floating in the reeds. She looked kind of peaceful-like, but her neck was all bruised. She'd been murdered all right. At first I thought it was Sir George did it, like the little girl said. I had kept my eyes open about the place: Sir Henry Montagu liked an ac-counting of what was going on. I knew the girl had been fooling about with his son, and he wasn't too pleased when I told him, neither."

George gulped. "What the deuce! You blackguard! You told father, eh?"

"And he gave me a tidy sum to keep it to myself, too. Of course, I found out later that you'd been in Fernbridge all day with your mother. The kid's wrong; it wasn't you."

"Then who?" breathed Catherine.

"Well, she had another lover, didn't she? I caught her running about one night, when George was away. She tossed her head at me and gave me some cheek, so I never found out who he was, but there was another fellow sharing our Milly with George, right enough. When I came up past the lake and found you in the woods, passed out cold and with a wine bottle in your hand, I figured it was you, Mr. de Dagonet. Sir Henry seemed happy enough to agree. That's all I know, and all I've ever known, God help me."

But Dagonet had burst out laughing. *"Parturiunt montes, nascetur ridiculus mus!* The mountains labor, only to bring forth a ridiculous mouse, indeed. You were cuckolded, George! Simple Milly Trumble was making a cuckold out of you. But it wasn't me, Mr. Catchpole. I was not amongst the number to enjoy the fair Milly. Perhaps some lad in the stable! Anyway, I suppose we shall never know, and I am as guilty of being there and of letting it happen as always! You have led me a merry dance, sir, and caused a great deal of trouble, for such a tiny rodent of information!"

"Isn't there anything else?" cried Annie, her face bleak with disappointment.

"I'm afraid not, Miss Annabella," said Dagonet, suddenly grave. "You must take me as I am, it seems. Anyway, you do accept now that it wasn't Sir George that killed Millicent Trumble, don't you?"

"Yes," said Annie. "But it wasn't you either! I still won't believe it! There was some other fellow. The Catchpole man says so!"

"And it's information that is beyond our reach. You can stop looking green, George. I shall not inherit Lion Court after all, and you may marry the undoubtedly charming Miss Ponsonby—that is the name that rumor is linking so solidly with yours, isn't it?—without threat. Mr. Catchpole knows that if he approaches you again, he will answer to me and the judges at the Old Bailey for it."

Catherine could feel the disappointment turning in her stomach. For all this time they had thought that John Catchpole held some vital piece of information. She was as sure as Dagonet that Catchpole was telling the truth, and so they had nothing to show for all their trouble. Catchpole had become a petty criminal, but he was not a murderer. He had thought to blackmail George over his involvement with Millicent, and Dagonet had effectively scotched that. How could Dagonet be so generous to George, as to protect him from Catchpole's blackmail attempts? Nothing had changed, Dagonet was still thought to be guilty of the seduction of Milly Trumble in the eyes of his grandfather, and he intended to let that stand. She stood up.

"I think I must get Annie back home. Lady Brooke will be worried."

They drove back in silence. Archibald Piggot stood up behind them with the tiger, and Annie sat squeezed in between Dagonet and Catherine, her sister's arm round her shoulders. George had not uttered a word of thanks for being extricated from the clutches of a potential blackmailer, and had ridden off as if he were the hero of the hour. John Catchpole they left to his bottle.

* * *

Dagonet left the sisters at Brooke House and, after a quick bath and change of clothes, went to one of the worst gaming hells that he knew. He was as entertaining and merry as the dandies had come to expect and he stripped the entire table of their wealth, before staggering home in the early morning, considerably the worse for the lack of a night's sleep and a little too much excellent wine. He was not to tumble unmolested into his bed. As he entered the study at his lodging, pulling off his perfectly cut jacket and loosening the folds of his cravat, he stopped short. A gentleman sat in his favorite chair by the fire. It was Lord Blythe, Marquis of Somerdale, his maternal grandfather and owner of Lion Court. The old man rose as he entered and shook his cane. His face was puce with rage, and the white hair stood up around his head like a halo.

"You damned rogue, sir!" he shouted. "The servant girl wasn't enough, eh? You've had to embroil Miss Catherine Hunter in your progress into the sewer!"

Dagonet had gone white. He shrugged his arms back into his jacket, and straightened his cravat. "My lord," he said calmly, and bowed. "It has been some years. To what do I owe the pleasure of this sudden visit?"

"Don't come over cool with me, you insolent devil!" The cane shook dangerously close to Dagonet's set face. "What made you marry her? She's a damned fine girl, sir, and deserves better than a gambler and a libertine!"

"I couldn't agree more, my lord. I assume you have had a visit from dear Mrs. Clay, and heard all about our little encounter at the Rose and Crown."

"Charlotte Clay is a vicious busybody, and I'm

ashamed to admit that she's my granddaughter, sir, but you'll not deny that what she told me is true?"

"That I compromised Miss Hunter at the finest hostel in Marlborough, and was obliged to marry her? It is true, my lord. You would rather I had not married her?"

"Does she care for you?"

"I have no reason to believe that she does."

"Then you can be damned, as far as I'm concerned, sir!"

"Then nothing much has changed, has it, my lord? Perhaps if you have nothing further to offer but insults, we might be better to close this conversation. I have been out all night, and would prefer my regrettably lonely bed at this moment."

"I don't see how you can look me in the eye, sir! You will release Miss Hunter from this marriage in a way that will secure her good name."

"The marriage was in itself an attempt to do so," said Dagonet dryly.

Lord Blythe continued as if he had not spoken. "And if you do it like a gentleman, I'll see that she wants for nothing. I'm fond of the girl, dammit. She'll lack nothing that money can buy, and I'll find her a decent husband."

The Marquis was trembling. It was more difficult than he had thought to face down the man that his once favorite grandson had become. He had been profoundly shocked, all those years ago, when he had learned that after assuring him otherwise, Dagonet had seduced Millicent Trumble, but he had tried to put it out of his mind. Now, however, the results of several years of insinuations and poisonous comments from George and Charlotte were having their effect. Miss Hunter was a decent girl and the daughter of the local vicar. Mrs. Clay had come straight from the Rose and Crown with the tale. It was unforgivable for Dagonet to have compromised her. The marriage made it all the worse, if Catherine had been forced into it. The Marquis felt it his duty to make sure that his grandson could do no more harm. There was only one solution that would finally put it all to rights!

Dagonet dropped into the chair opposite the old man. "A welcome thought, my lord, I admit. Do you suggest that I put a bullet into my head, and thus relieve the world and Mrs. de Dagonet of my unwelcome presence?"

"I suggest that you try to redeem the past by acting with honor for a change; I shall make sure the opportunity comes your way. Can you offer me anything that would change my opinion of you?"

Dagonet laughed aloud. "I wish that I could, my lord. But disappointment is destined to be both our lots to-night. Now if you have nothing further to say, I am going to bed."

Lord Blythe heaved himself to his feet, and, taking up his cane, he thumped from the room. Dagonet heard the door slam behind him; for a moment, he did not move. Then he turned and went into his bedchamber. Catching sight of his own reflection in the mirror, he stopped and smiled ruefully to himself. "Well, now, Devil Dagonet," he said aloud. "Would she be better off a widow, do you think?"

Catherine was amazed a few days later to be similarly honored with a morning visit from the Marquis of Somerdale. Particularly as he was accompanied by both his Montagu grandchildren. Charlotte swept into the drawing room at Brooke House in a rustle of starched satin.

"My dear Mrs. de Dagonet," she effused, as if they

were old friends. "I hope you will forgive me if I have been slow to congratulate you on your wedding. It came as such a shock to us all, as you can imagine, I'm sure. We do not admit your husband as a member of the family, but as the sister of Lady Brooke, you are always beyond reproach. I hope you don't mind if I speak plain. As Mr. Clay always used to say: 'Speak what's on your mind and you will be understood.'"

"I'm sure those were wise words, Mrs. Clay," replied Catherine, trying to suppress a smile.

"It's very odd, of course, that you stay here at Brooke House, but we in the family can understand. You are quite pale! You don't look at all well. Mr. Clay was a man of the greatest propriety and sensibility, and he always noticed when one didn't look altogether the thing. I remember him when we were staying at Lion Court that last time, insisting that I have a room of my own, since I looked unwell, he thought. He was always everything that was considerate."

She was interrupted by the arrival of Lord Blythe, who due to another attack of the gout, had been helped up the stair by Sir George Montagu. The Marquis beamed at Catherine as they entered, but she was not surprised to see George avoid her eye.

"Wouldn't come to London without seeing you, my dear!" barked the old man, as Catherine hurried to supply a padded footstool for his sore leg. "Had George and Charlotte bring me round from Somerdale House."

"Let me ring for some refreshment, my lord," said Catherine, going to the bell. "I am most honored that you would visit."

"Wanted a word, young lady. I'm here to let you know I intend to secure your future, and make sure that grandson of mine doesn't bother you again."

Catherine wasn't sure what the old man meant, but she was unable to pursue the subject since Amelia and David came in to pay their respects to the visitors. Conversation became general, until the guests rose to leave. As Catherine shook hands with the Marquis, he leaned to her and said gruffly, "You're a fine young woman, my dear. I've spoken with Dagonet: I'm going to ensure that he gets the opportunity to do the right thing this time!"

She had no idea what he intended, but she was relieved to see the party leave. Morning visits from the Montagus and the Marquis of Somerdale were not her idea of the most pleasant way to spend one's time. She wanted to have the opportunity to be alone, and think through everything she knew and had learned about Millicent Trumble. There must be something they had all missed.

Hobart's Club was not one of the most famous or fashionable of the gaming establishments of London, but Dagonet could be assured of always finding a suitable crowd of young bloods there, eager to loosen their purses over a game of hazard. He moved through the crowd nodding to his acquaintance, and exchanging slightly barbed witticisms with some of the bolder players. He was known to be a genial companion and a demon player, but there was a certain undercurrent of opinion that he would be a dangerous man to cross. There was a general ripple of apprehension, therefore, when the young Viscount Hammond deliberately stood up, and, blocking Dagonet's path, belligerently demanded that he stop and give an accounting of himself.

"Whatever do you mean?" asked Dagonet quietly.

"You're a very clever fellow at the tables, aren't you, sir?"

"I hope I may give the other gentlemen a good game, sir. They say that next to the pleasure of winning at hazard, the next greatest pleasure is losing."

"But you don't lose often, do you?"

"La critique est aisée, et l'art est difficile." Dagonet bowed insolently, and made as if to move on, but the Viscount, who was by now extremely red in the face, caught him by the lapel.

"Damn your French, sir!"

Lord Kendal had approached the two men and sat nonchalantly on the edge of the nearest table. He took a delicate pinch of snuff from an exquisite gilt box.

"Mr. de Dagonet comments that it is easy to criticize, sir, but art is difficult. Hazard presents the highest opportunity for art. Don't you agree, Viscount?"

"I say that there is more cunning than art in his skill, sir!" insisted the youth. "Lady Luck never smiled so long on one player, without a little assistance from the backs of the cards or a weight in the dice."

"I think you are drunk, sir," said Dagonet calmly. "Perhaps you should cool yourself, before you say more than you mean?"

"I mean you're a cheat, sir!"

A deadly silence had fallen over the room. No other outcome could possibly arise from this exchange than a deadly meeting with their seconds at dawn. Every man in the room unconsciously held his breath, waiting for Dagonet's wrath to flatten the importunate accuser. The reply was made casually, however, and while gently removing the viscount's fingers from his coat, Dagonet's sea-green eyes showed nothing but amusement. "And the liquor agrees, no doubt."

The viscount was stiff with determination. He raised his hand and tried to strike the taller man in the face. Dagonet caught his wrist in an iron grip.

"I am not drinking, sir!" hissed Hammond. "I accuse you in front of your friends. You win their money by base trickery! You are a cheat, sir!"

"You are resolved, aren't you, my friend?" replied Dagonet wearily. "Very well. Since you insist. Lord Kendal and Lord Brooke would be happy to represent me, I'm sure. Your friends may wait upon them at their leisure."

With that he bowed, and left the room.

Viscount Hammond sat down, and the room exploded with conversation. In the hubbub, one of the viscount's friends leaned close and said quietly, "Are you out of your mind, sir? Nobody believes the man a cheat, and I hear that Dagonet is the best swordsman and marksman in the city. He'll kill you!"

"It's a risk I'll have to take," muttered the viscount. "I have also been told by the old Marquis of Somerdale that Dagonet will stand there and allow me to slay him. If he does, and I can dispatch him, the Marquis will pay off my debts, and set me up in the world. If he does not and kills me instead, Lord Blythe will make sure that the authorities are informed, and Dagonet will hang. If I don't get out of debt, I shall go to the devil anyway, so it's a bargain for me; and either way, Devil Dagonet dies."

"Good God!" said the other man. "What on earth does the Marquis of Somerdale have against Charles de Dagonet?"

"I've no idea," said Viscount Hammond, with a bitter laugh. "He's his grandfather, I understand."

* * *

Catherine saw no more of Lord Blythe or his grandchildren. She hoped daily that Dagonet would call, but there was no sign of him. She spent her days escorting her little sister about London to see the sights. The capital city was festive with preparations for Christmas. Not even the Punch and Judy show or the string choirs singing carols, however, seemed able to lift Annie's depressed spirits very much. They did not raise his name, but both sisters found themselves looking about in the streets, without any luck, for a glimpse of Devil Dagonet. Amelia was happy because David was home for the holiday. They all spent a merry enough Christmas day together at Brooke House, even though Lord Brooke seemed to have something on his mind, and was often distracted when the ladies spoke to him. Amy put it down to the press of business. She had no idea that her husband had gone to see Viscount Hammond's friends and arrange a duel with rapiers for one morning early the next week. The duel concerned Morris more than he wanted to admit. No one could best Dagonet with a sword, of course, but dueling was illegal: and there was something else. Ever since the night of the ball at Lady Easthaven's, his friend had been in a very odd mood, drinking deeper and gaming more carelessly than was his wont, and always with a splendid wit. When David had challenged him to discuss whatever was on his mind, Dagonet had laughed. "They say the gallows sharpens the intellect, dear Lord Brooke. Perhaps a duel has the same effect?"

"I refuse to believe you are rattled by the Viscount Hammond, Dagonet," David had replied.

Dagonet had given him one of his most infuriating smiles. "No, I am not. But I am rattled by my grandfather. You will have fast horses on hand, so that you can make your own escape, won't you?" And with that enigmatic statement he had refused to say any more.

Catherine was playing softly at the pianoforte one morning, going over again in her mind, as had become her habit, every conversation, every encounter with Charles de Dagonet. It was no surprise that she had lost her heart. Women had been doing so for many years. How long would it be before he was able to get the marriage annulled and release her? Would she then never see him again? The thought was chilling. She was interrupted by one of the maids.

"There's a person below to see you, ma'am."

She looked up. "I really don't want to see anybody. Please say I am not at home."

"He was most persistent, ma'am. Said he didn't want the reward, but what he knew was a burden to him, and he'd be glad to unload it."

Catherine stopped playing in a jangle of chords. "What? What name did this person give?"

"Peter Higgins, ma'am. He's a sailor. Said he wanted to talk with you about Lion Court."

The color had fled from her face, then returned in a rush. Peter Higgins! She had never given the gardener's boy any more thought. All her efforts had been launched against Catchpole. But the memory of Mary's voice, all those months ago at Lion Court, came rushing back at the sound of the name. "Poor Peter Higgins ran off, too. He was just a lad really, I dare say it broke his heart." Peter Higgins: the gardener's boy that Milly Trumble thought she was too good for. The name that Mary had mentioned in the same breath with Catchpole's, but that Catherine had unconsciously dismissed, and therefore not mentioned to Dagonet when she had told him, in Captain Morris's garden, what she had learned from Mary. Peter Higgins also had disappeared from Lion Court, before Dagonet awoke from his coma. Had he fled because he had some vital piece of information?

"Very well," she said a little unsteadily. "Show him up."

The man that entered the drawing room a few moments later had obviously not long been ashore. He had the sailor's honest, far-seeing gaze and wore the typical reefer jacket with mother-of-pearl buttons of his trade. He looked about nervously at the luxurious room, and at the lovely young woman who rose to greet him.

"Was it you, ma'am, as put in the ad about John Catchpole? My Ma saw it and figured it might involve that business at Lion Court. If it does, I'd be glad to tell what I know; it's been a burden to me these many years."

"Please sit down, Mr. Higgins. My name is Catherine de Dagonet. Charles de Dagonet is my husband." The words gave her a strange thrill to say out loud. "I can reward you well, if you will tell me the truth."

"I don't want no reward, ma'am. The truth is all you'll get from me. I'd be happy to get it off my mind."

"Please," said Catherine. Her throat was dry, and the words felt as if they might choke her. "Just begin at the beginning and tell me the whole." She rang for the maid. "Please bring some ale for Mr. Higgins, Susan, and see that we are undisturbed."

Then, with her heart in her mouth, she turned to her guest, who had once been gardener's boy at Lion Court and in love with Millicent Trumble.

19

"Well, it was this way, see, ma'am," began the sailor, sipping his mug of ale. "Milly was the prettiest girl at Lion Court, and merry and bright with it. Nothing seemed too high for our Milly. I suppose you could say she was a flirt, though she wouldn't look at me that way, and I mooned over her like a calf. I was just the gardener's lad, and hadn't much in the way of prospects. She treated me like a little brother, and would confide in me. It's awful hard, ma'am, to love like that and not have it returned."

"Yes," said Catherine with a wry smile. "I know. Please go on, Mr. Higgins."

"Well, she took up with a gentleman in the house. She was flattered by his attentions. I believe she thought he would marry her, but she ought to have known better. He was a careless, cruel fellow, and didn't really care for her. It's just a casual thing with these gentlemen, ma'am."

"Yes, I believe it often is. And that was Sir George, Mr. Higgins?"

"It was, ma'am. Master George, as he was then. But I believe Mr. de Dagonet found out. And John Catchpole knew about it, and he may have told Sir Henry. Of course, Sir Henry wouldn't have cared, as long as it didn't get known to old Lord Blythe. She thought it was such a secret, but these things tend to get about. George wasn't a subtle fellow, not like the other gentleman."

"The other gentleman?" Catchpole, too, had believed she had taken another lover!

"Well, you see, ma'am. George began to pay her less attention. I believe Devil Dagonet had confronted him, because you could see George trying to avoid his cousin. Master George had given her some gewgaws and baubles; more than any of us working lads could afford, and she liked to feel important, and enjoy fine gentlemen paying her compliments. So when George began to neglect her, and the other gentleman began to notice her, she didn't say no. But this time she got herself in trouble. She told the father, didn't she; and like a silly ninny she thought he'd take care of her, but he laughed in her face. Well, she was desperate. A girl in her position, she'd have been turned off without a reference, and she didn't have no one to help her. Sir Henry Montagu was a hard man, he'd have given her no sympathy at all, and if he did know about her and George, he would have wanted to make sure that no one would spread the tale. The old Marquis was a stickler for his grandsons treating the servants right. He wouldn't have liked it, if he'd known that George had seduced Milly and started her on that kind of a life. She was dead afraid, ma'am, of Sir Henry Montagu, and she wept to me that she'd been a silly fool. And George, for all he'd been willing enough to ruin her, would never have helped her; he was too afraid of his father and the Marquis."

"And the other gentleman?" Her heart was in her mouth. So Millicent Trumble had not been carrying George's child; there had indeed been someone else.

"The fellow had promised to set her up in a house in London, and get her away from Lion Court, but all his promises were worthless. He'd given her ribbons and such frippery, too, and what was more to the point, started her drinking his fine wines and brandy, instead of the honest ale that was right for her station. Let her think she could dine like the gentry the rest of her days; she teased me about it when she saw me in the yard with my tankard. But he left without a thought for her. She was cruelly betrayed, ma'am."

"It was not Mr. de Dagonet?"

The sailor laughed, his brown face open and candid. "Master Charles was kind to her, ma'am, and all the girls worshipped him. Such a fine set-up young man as he was, and always funning and teasing, and so dashing and handsome and all. There wasn't a woman on the place as wouldn't have given her eye teeth for a special look from Devil Dagonet. But there was only kindness there, nothing more; they all understood that. The men liked him, too. He was always fair and caring. Not like Sir Henry, or young George. It was Dagonet as found her crying in the stable, and offered to help her. She wouldn't tell him what her trouble was, though. He figured it was with Master George, I reckon. Anyway, he offered to meet her by the lake, so he could get her story out of her, most like, and figure out a solution. He sent her a note; she showed it to me."

Catherine felt a warm rush of satisfaction. So that was exactly as she had surmised. Dagonet had not been involved with Milly at all, except to try and help her.

"So why did he not meet her as he had offered, Mr. Higgins? Nothing else really has mattered all these years except what actually happened at the lake."

"Well, he set off to meet her, right enough. I had followed her, do you see? I was still right sweet on Milly. I'd have taken her to wife, bastard child and all, if she'd have had me. But I was just a lad. No doubt she knew I didn't know what I was saying. I hid way up on the ridge above the spinney and watched her. She was already waiting by the lake, fretting and wringing her hands. I figured she was crying, though I wasn't in earshot. I had some thought that after she talked with Master Dagonet, I could go down and offer myself, and Dagonet would back me up, and she'd marry me." Peter Higgins shook his head and sighed. "But then a gentleman came up Rye Water from the direction of the high road. He was afoot, but he wore riding clothes, and he was carrying a package. He must have hidden his horse down in the woods. When Milly saw him, she ran across and threw her arms around him, like her savior had arrived. She knew he was coming, right enough. He pushed her off, though, and began to open up the parcel he was carrying. I could see he had presents in there for her. Thought he could buy her off, most like. She had no fear, our Milly. She would've been waiting for Master Dagonet to arrive and take her part, you see. It seemed that she spurned the stuff, and they began to argue. I could see him waving his arms about. Then he took her by the neck and started to shake her. They were right on the edge of the lake, and I saw her lose her footing and fall back into the water. It's the hardest thing I ever did, ma'am, not to try and run down there right then. I know I stood up and shouted like a madman, but the wind carried my words off, and there was no way I could reach her in time to save her. Besides, I saw Devil Dagonet coming down the path from the house. He could swim like an otter. If anyone could save her, he would. I was rooted to my perch, ma'am, with my tongue clove in my mouth. Dagonet came striding down through the birch spinney without a care in the world, but Milly must have already told the other fellow that she was expecting him, because the man in the riding boots had picked up the package and dodged behind a tree, and was waiting. Dagonet was a formidable fellow with his fists and quick as a hawk to react, but the fellow struck him from behind with the butt of a pistol, and he dropped like a felled lamb. It was treacherously done, ma'am. I saw the whole thing like a play laid out before me, and then I ran down as fast as my legs would carry me."

"And it was too late?"

"Worse than too late. I reached Dagonet first. The gentleman had taken a brandy bottle—from the parcel he'd brought for Milly, most like—and was pouring the liquor over Dagonet's mouth and chin. Then he sopped some into his clothes, so he would smell like he'd been drinking, and left the bottle by Dagonet's hand, where he might seem to have dropped it. He took off then into the woods like the hounds of hell was on his heels, taking the rest of the stuff with him. I heard his horse's hooves thundering away. You'll understand, though, that all my thoughts were for Milly."

And Catherine did understand. Peter Higgins's sweetheart had fallen into the lake, and could perhaps have still been saved. No wonder the lad had left Dagonet where he lay.

"But you could not save her, could you?"

The sailor's young face crumpled. "She was drowned, ma'am. I doubt that the fellow had really meant to kill her. He probably just meant to frighten her and make her keep her mouth closed, but she was dead all right. Milly couldn't swim; she'd have sunk like a stone. I pulled her from the water into the reeds, and wept over her, but it was all to no good. Poor Milly. She wasn't the first girl to be blinded by a fine gentleman's sweet words, and she won't be the last."

"Why didn't you tell anyone what you had seen?"

"I was only a gardener's boy, ma'am. Who'd have believed me? Sir Henry might even have thought I'd done it, for jealousy. They all knew what Milly meant to me, though I wouldn't have harmed a hair on her pretty head. Besides, I was that upset I couldn't think straight at all. When I heard someone coming, I ran off and hid. It was John Catchpole, and I was afraid of him. He was a tough customer, and hard on us lads. He'd been stealing, too, from the stables, and selling off feed on the side. I couldn't have him find me there; it would have been made to look black for me. No, all my thoughts were for Milly. I can see it was wrong now, of course, but I didn't even get my things together. I ran off for Bristol, and I was taken up on a ship as cabin boy, and put Lion Court behind me. The sea's my life now. I think about Milly sometimes, and how things might have turned out, if George had never cast his eye on her, but you can't change the past, they say. When my Ma told me, though, when I was between ships this time, that someone had inquired in the newspaper about John Catchpole, I couldn't stay silent. Ma heard that Mr. de Dagonet had taken the blame. It's time things were put right."

"Past time, Mr. Higgins." How could she blame him? He was very possibly younger than herself, and had seen his sweetheart murdered before his eyes. No wonder that he had run away.

"And the gentleman that betrayed Milly and let her fall into the lake. Did you not want justice?"

"The good Lord took his own justice, ma'am. The fellow died within a few months, of the smallpox, I heard."

"And he was someone that you knew?"

"Well, of course," replied Peter Higgins. "I can tell you his name."

20

Lord Blythe, the Marquis of Somerdale, was feeling very old. The pain from his gouty leg was making him roar more than usual at the servants. How could his favorite grandson have become such a profligate? When the servant girl at Lion Court had been found drowned and Dagonet brought up to the house passed out from drink, he still wouldn't have believed the lad guilty, if Sir Henry Montagu had not told him that he knew it was Dagonet who had seduced her. He had thought his heart would break then. Lion Court ought to have been passed to Charles de Dagonet. George neither cared nor was competent to run the place, yet there was no one else left in the family. When he heard that Dagonet was returned from the Peninsula, he had almost hoped that the lad could somehow redeem himself: until he had learned about Miss Hunter, the story fully embellished by Charlotte's vivid tongue. Something had snapped inside him. The world would be better off without such a renegade. The clever, fine daughter of the Reverend Hunter! Dagonet had seduced her! He couldn't bear to have such a man associated anymore with the family. In a moment of passion he had made the arrangement with the young viscount. He set his stubby jaw. He would not rescind it! Let Dagonet die on the dueling field, or the gallows, and Miss Hunter would be free to make a good match. He would see to it. The pain shot once again up to his knee, and he roared aloud.

"May I fetch you anything, grandfather?" It was Charlotte, who sat primly across the room. "You know, it was most unwise to have port after dinner. Mr. Clay was always most abstemious when it came to port. He believed it inflamed the blood."

"Be damned to Mr. Clay, madam! I'll drink what I like!"

"Don't prose on so, Charlotte," said George. "Can't you let a fellow have what he wants, without prosing on?"

"You might be better had you not indulged so deep yourself, George. I never recall you so abusing the bottle, as you have recently. Mr. Clay never drank to excess. He was moderate in all things." She sniffed audibly.

"There is a lady below to see you, my lord." It was the footman, in his powdered wig and livery.

"So late? The Marquis is too ill to see anyone," announced Charlotte.

"I'm not in my grave yet, madam! I still make the decisions in this house. Who is it, Larson?"

Larson bowed and presented a card on a silver tray. Lord Blythe picked it up and peered at it in the firelight. "Miss Hunter! Send her up!"

"There is a person with her, my lord."

"I don't care if the Archbishop of Canterbury is with her. Send her up!"

Within moments Catherine and Peter Higgins had entered the room. Charlotte rose instantly and confronted them. "Who is this person, ma'am?" she said, indicating the sailor. "Could he not wait in the kitchens?

Mr. Clay always made sure that no one from the street ever entered our drawing room."

"I believe Lord Blythe would wish to hear what this man has to say, Mrs. Clay. By all means retire. I'm sure you would be more comfortable."

"What's this? What's this?" The Marquis was waving Catherine over. "Glad to see your pretty face, my dear. Who is this fellow now?"

"Peter Higgins, at your service, my lord. As was gardener's boy at Lion Court seven years ago. I was there when poor Milly Trumble was drowned. I saw it happen, my lord. The lady thought as how you might be of a mind to hear me out."

"It concerns no one but you, Lord Blythe," added Catherine quietly. "I did not know that Sir George and Mrs. Clay were with you."

Catherine sincerely hoped that George and Charlotte would leave the room, but they both insisted on staying. George had gone green around the gills, yet he sat as if planted in his chair. Mrs. Clay would not miss some new piece of gossip for the world. Lady Pander would be all ears to hear the latest about Devil Dagonet and his checkered past. Charlotte settled herself firmly, spreading her skirts, and gave a self-satisfied smile.

"I trust that since we are *en famille,* nothing need be kept from any of us," she announced. "Pray, Mr. Higgins, let us hear the tale."

With a bashful nod of the head, the sailor began to repeat the story he had earlier told Catherine. They heard him start in a dead silence until, with an embarrassed look at George, Peter Higgins was forced to tell the role that gentleman had played. The Marquis turned on his grandson.

"What's this, sir? Was it *you* seduced the girl? Be

damned to you! Why did you not own up like a man? You let your cousin take the blame! Why did Dagonet not tell me at the time?"

George's face was damp with cold sweat. "Because he swore an oath to me that he would not," he mumbled. "We made a bargain. If he was fool enough to keep his side of it, when he knew I had broken mine, more loss to him." Suddenly red color flooded back into his cheeks, and his voice rose to a bellow. "Why shouldn't he have suffered? He always had everything! He could ride better, shoot better, fence better than anyone else. He never studied at his books when we were boys, yet he could do all the lessons and argue rings around me in class. Everything was his! Everything! All the girls were in love with him; even Milly! She came to my bed, but it was Dagonet she was in love with. And you always loved him more than me, grandfather—always! He was the apple of your eye. You never noticed anything I did! It was Dagonet with you, always Dagonet! You even gave him that stallion!"

"Because your father had provided you a stable full of hunters, and Dagonet had no horse of his own, sir!"

"But the stallion was better than any of them!"

"And you could not have handled him! Your behavior is vile, sir, vile! To have allowed your cousin to take the blame for your irresponsibility! To have stood aside and relied on the strength of his honor, at the sacrifice of your own! How could you have lived with yourself all these years?"

But George's large body had crumpled, as if the wind has suddenly gone from a balloon, and burying his face in his hands, he began, in great audible sobs, to weep. The sound echoed into an appalled silence. It was broken by Mrs. Clay.

"I fail to see that this changes anything!" she sniffed. "The girl was murdered; Dagonet was there, and George was not. If it was George who had fallen prey to her wiles in a moment of weakness, who can say that it was not Dagonet who had corrupted her to start with? No one has ever laid the charge of the girl's death at George's door! He was in Fernbridge at the time with Mama. Dagonet was found drunk in the woods. He was at the scene." She turned to Peter Higgins, who stood awkwardly twisting his hat in his hands. "How do you explain that, my man?"

"There was another man, ma'am," replied the sailor, and as George stopped his weeping and dried his eyes, the erstwhile gardener's boy continued the tale. He was listened to in a hushed quiet. As the story unfolded, Catherine could not take her eyes from the old Marquis. His face was beginning to look different, as if years of pain were slowly peeling away. His beloved, favorite grandson had never betrayed his word, had behaved with nothing but the highest honor, in the face of all their misplaced wrath and discord. How could he have ever believed otherwise?

"And this other gentleman? The man who attacked Dagonet and left Millicent Trumble to drown?" said the Marquis in an unsteady voice. "Did you recognize him?"

"Why, yes, indeed, my lord. I knew him well."

"So who was the mystery stranger?" queried Charlotte impatiently. "Really, this is all too sordid. Let us have some plain speaking on this at last. Mr. Clay always recommended plain speaking."

But the sailor would not meet her eye, and stood silent, eyes downcast.

"Well, sir?" demanded the Marquis.

The sailor looked at the old man, avoiding the eyes of

everyone else in the room. His voice when he spoke at last was perfectly steady and true. "It was Mr. Clay, my lord. I couldn't have mistaken him; he had been there earlier that summer for two full months. Mr. Clay was your culprit, my lord."

There was a piercing scream, as Charlotte rose to her feet, then collapsed back onto her chair. "This is calumny of the highest order," she cried. "My dear late husband! How dare you mention his name in connection with this horrid tale?" She pointed wildly at Catherine. "She has paid this fellow to tell you all these lies, Grandfather. Nothing can be proved! She tries to clear Dagonet by putting the blame on dear Mr. Clay, who is not here to defend himself! The man lies! All lies! No one can corroborate such an accusation!"

And that was when Catherine was truly surprised for the first time that evening. She herself had been amazed when Peter Higgins had told her that it was Charlotte's late husband, Mr. Clay, who had attacked Milly at the lake, then knocked out Dagonet, and poured liquor on him, so that he would be left to take the blame. Mr. Clay, who on that summer visit to Lion Court, had seduced the maidservant from George with promises to set her up in a London establishment of her own. And then, when the promise proved empty, and Millicent, desperate, must have threatened to expose him to his wife, had come back secretly and silenced her forever. The same Mr. Clay who had eloped with Charlotte to start with, instead of honorably approaching her father. It was only by Charlotte's account that he was remembered as such a stickler for the proprieties. The evidence was that he had been anything but. Charlotte was right, however. Why should the Marquis believe Peter Higgins? And that was when

Catherine was to witness the most unexpected development of the evening.

"I can corroborate it, Grandfather. Millicent told me herself: she was with child by Mr. Clay. She wanted me to help her! Me! She had made me a damned cuckold, and she wanted me to help her! I told her to go hang! Your husband killed the girl all right, Charlotte. It wasn't me and it wasn't Dagonet. I have guessed it all along, and I think father did, too." It was George.

With a strangled sob, Charlotte fled from the room. Respectfully pulling his forelock at the Marquis, Peter Higgins allowed himself to be shown to the kitchen for a mug of ale.

"I suppose this means that Dagonet gets Lion Court after all," continued George dully. "He always wanted it. Mama won't care. Now that Sir Henry's dead, she said she wouldn't live there anymore. Damned old-fashioned place anyhow, stuck way out in the country; rather live in the city myself." With a heavy sigh, he walked to the door. "Good night, Grandfather."

The Marquis ignored him, and was pounding on the floor with his cane. "Larson! Fetch my man of business! I want to change my will!"

"He may be abed, my lord," replied the manservant gravely.

"Then have him roused from his slumbers, damn you! And I want a message sent round to my grandson, Charles de Dagonet. He's to come here this instant!"

"Yes, my lord."

Lord Blythe turned to Catherine. "You care for him, don't you? I can see it in your face every time his name is mentioned. Damn me if he isn't going to stick by this marriage. I'll see to it!"

"I pray you, my lord, please do not! There was nothing

to our marriage but an attempt to save me and my family embarrassment." Rapidly she outlined to the old man the events at the Rose and Crown, when Dagonet had saved Annie from the fever. "We have agreed to have it annulled."

The Marquis grinned, his round face beaming. "Then he's a dashed fool after all, if he does not fix his interest with you. If I were his age, I'd choose you for myself!"

They were interrupted by the arrival of a slightly disheveled solicitor, who had obeyed with dispatch the peremptory summons from his noble employer.

"I want Lion Court made over to Charles de Dagonet, with all the proceeds from the estates. Do it this instant! And then change my will! He is to be my heir!"

"My lord," asked Catherine hesitantly. "Do you leave George nothing? He has been foolish and selfish, but not truly wicked, surely." Indeed, how could George have revealed what he knew without destroying his sister?

"He can marry Miss Ponsonby! She has enough to set them up in a respectable situation. He'll get nothing from me, but I'll not foul his marriage. There's nothing in this story we've heard tonight that need leave this house. From what I hear, Dagonet has lived it down already! Lady Easthaven had the nerve to tackle me about him, and call me a fool. She's right; I have been, I have been! We can let it be known that Dagonet's innocent without involving George. Bah! The fellow leaves a sick taste in my mouth! Never could stand him, nor Charlotte!" And suddenly he threw back his head and began to laugh.

The man of business was shown to the study, where he could begin to draw up the necessary papers, and Catherine determined to leave. She could not have Dagonet discover her there, when he came to make his peace with his grandfather. She was arrested by the return of the footman.

"Mr. de Dagonet left Jermyn Street some time ago, my lord. He is not at his lodgings, and not expected to return tonight. His manservant commented that he left alone on the gray thoroughbred. He had his rapiers with him."

At which pronouncement, the Marquis turned as pale as his own whiskers. "He's gone to meet the Viscount Hammond," he breathed. "What have I done? What have I done?"

"My lord," cried Catherine. "Whatever is it?"

"I demanded he release you, my dear!" The old man's voice was a hoarse whisper. "I arranged that he should be forced to fight a duel."

"But he could never be bested in a duel with swords, my lord."

"Unless he has determined to die. I thought you would be better off a widow, my dear, and told him so to his face. I thought his death would free us all! I determined that you should have wealth, position, respectability; I thought you tied to a villainous libertine. I didn't know! I told him if he died, I would secure your future, and I fear that Dagonet has enough honor to do it. A last gallant, unselfish gesture! He would do it, I know! Viscount Hammond will kill him!"

The Marquis struggled to his feet, tears running down the wrinkled cheeks, only to be felled by the pain in his gouty foot.

"If he has left for a duel," said Catherine, her face pale, "it will not be fought until dawn. I shall find him, my lord. Lord Brooke will assist me. Never fear!"

21

She arrived back at Brooke House, only to find that Lord Brooke had also left, very late, with Lord Kendal. Amelia was woken from her sleep, but she had no idea where they had gone. Catherine would not worry her sister, so she told her nothing but that there was good news about Dagonet that she wanted to share with his best friend. She left Amy to fall back asleep, while she paced the hallways. Half the night had already worn away. There were only a few hours left. Where were the gentlemen planning to meet? Somewhere outside the city, no doubt, where the chance of discovery was less. They must now be at an inn somewhere, close to the chosen site. Would Dagonet truly plan to die, in order to release her? She couldn't bear it! She must find him in time! Flinging her cloak around her shoulders, she set off for Jermyn Street. After a great deal of pounding at the entry, Dagonet's manservant opened the door, his nightcap still on his head.

"I must know where Mr. de Dagonet has gone," she demanded. "Did he say nothing?"

"My employer does not confide in me, ma'am. If you would forgive me, it is very late."

He tried to close the door, but Catherine pushed inside.

"Did he drop no hint? Pray, sir, please wrack your brains!"

"I am sorry, ma'am."

"I know where they went!" Catherine whirled around. In a smart, almost clean, set of new clothes, Archibald Piggot had appeared beside her. "Mr. de Dagonet took me on to be underfootman, ma'am! But I keeps my eyes and ears open, don't I? Lord Kendal was here, and I heard them talking about it. They're going to meet the Viscount Hammond at Highgate. It'll be a right pretty mill, I'll bet! I'd give my eyeteeth to see it!"

"Are there horses here?" At the boy's nod, Catherine continued, "Saddle up two, Mr. Piggot. You will have your wish sooner than you planned. You and I are going to Highgate, right now."

They were an odd sight as they clattered off through the silent streets, leaving the correct manservant gaping. Archibald's eclectic education had not included much horsemanship, though he hung on gamely enough, and within half an hour was as balanced as a monkey on a branch. Catherine, with her skirts spread around her, was sitting astride on a man's saddle, since the contents of Dagonet's stable did not extend to sidesaddles for ladies. Under a dark, overcast sky they cantered north, until the city streets began to give way to vegetable fields and bare fruit trees. Mud from the road splattered up around the flying hooves in a cold, soaking spray that bespattered her clothes, and speckled Archibald's round face, like extra freckles. There was no one else abroad.

The village of Highgate was beginning to awaken to its morning routine, as they arrived breathless and sore in the main street. Rapidly they went to each of the inns in turn, ignoring the curious looks of the stable boys. At the last, a landlord was able to tell them that a party of three gentlemen had just left in the direction of the woods.

"Gone to Bottom Acre, I shouldn't wonder," he said with a sly wink. "That's where the gentlemen usually meet."

"Please, sir," said Catherine. "The directions!"

Archibald Piggot, with a grand flourish, handed the innkeeper a coin. "For your trouble, my man!" he said grandly.

The innkeeper's affronted pride at being so addressed by a ragamuffin, was not enough to prevent him pocketing the silver as he pointed. "Go down yonder about a mile, and turn left at the five-barred gate. Follow the track, through Rookery Wood, you can't miss it."

They galloped off. "Where did you get the money, Mr. Piggot?" asked Catherine as they rode. In spite of her desperate concern about Dagonet, she could not suppress a smile at the thought of the street urchin playing the lord with the innkeeper.

"Was my month's wages!" shouted Archibald, with a cheeky grin. "Mr. de Dagonet will pay me back!"

It had already begun a freezing drizzle as they entered the woods. A muddy track led down through the trees and emerged into a mown meadow, well sheltered from the road. In the clearing stood six gentlemen: Lord Brooke and Lord Kendal at one end; two strangers at the other; and in the center of the sward, Dagonet faced a nervous young man over the naked blades of their rapiers. Both swordsmen were stripped of their coats, and the increasing rain was making the fabric of their shirts mold onto their bodies. The grass, already icy, was becoming slick. As she watched, they saluted and the blades clashed together.

Catherine slipped from her mount. Dagonet was already giving way before a furious, if uncoordinated, attack from the younger man. He was laughing.

"Come, Viscount. I am ready to die on your blade, sir, but my pride forbids that I fall onto it, without at least an attempt at skill on your part."

Goaded, Hammond flailed wildly, but still Dagonet gave way before him.

"Come, sir! I cannot find a moment when you are steady enough for me to impale myself! Must I just drop to the grass, so that you can run me through?"

"He shall not!" cried Catherine out loud. Picking up her mud-stained skirts, she ran across the clearing towards them. "Pray, stop, sirs!"

Lord Kendal and David Morris turned and made as if to intercept her, but Dagonet had already reacted. The rapiers clashed together. With a rapid turn of the wrist, and a side step, he had overwhelmed the viscount's unsteady arm, and that gentleman's sword flew from his hand into the grass. Catherine raced to them. How it happened, she did not know, but as she arrived at the astonished feet of the viscount, she tripped over some unevenness in the ground, and sprawled headlong. She slid across the wet turf and landed without ceremony at Dagonet's polished boots. Putting up his blade, he reached both hands to hers and helped her to her feet.

"Sweet Kate!" he said and laughed. "Must you always land in the mud, when you attempt to save me from some precipitate action?" He reached up a hand and brushed the hair from her cheek. Her face was flushed from the cold ride; her eyes brilliant with unshed tears. "There was no danger from Rye Combe Bog, and there is none, I assure you, from Viscount Hammond's inexperienced blade."

"But the Marquis thought that you would let him kill you!" she wailed.

"Yes, I am aware that he had some such intention when he arranged this sorry duel. The Marquis is a man of violent emotion. But I am not so selfless, dear Kate; my intention was simply to let the viscount go home a tired and humbled survivor. I have no desire to die just yet. Did you come out here from London just to prevent my gallant demise?"

"I though you meant to free me from the marriage. I could not bear it, if you were to die!"

"Dear Kate, can this mean that you put some value on my worthless life? Please tell me that it does, because I have loved you ever since Exmoor, and though I don't expect you to return it, I would treasure whatever modicum of good feeling you might find it in your heart to offer."

Her heart leapt to her throat. She tried to steady her voice, as the drizzle began to turn into sleet, threatening to freeze them both where they stood. "Please don't tease me, Mr. de Dagonet, I can't bear it! What do you mean?"

"That I love you, fair Kate. Always have, always will. But I assure you, I shall not burden you with unwelcome advances. Let us get this damned marriage dissolved as soon as possible." The sleet settled on his dark hair and over the chiseled planes of his face. His shirt was plastered to his arms and chest.

Catherine looked straight into the sea-green eyes, as ice coated her hair and mud-bedraggled cloak. "If you really love me, sir, I would much rather consummate it," she said boldly. "If you would have me, after all, for your warlike mate."

He caught her again by the hands. "Kate! But I have nothing to offer you, but my worthless self. Sweet Miss

Hunter, it won't do, will it? The Marquis is right, you deserve better."

"I don't see anything in our way, sir. I would gladly live in a ditch with you, if you will only say again that you love me."

"I love you, dear Kate. I loved you at Lion Court, when you tried to call the butler. I loved you in the grotto. I loved you bravely fighting with Westcott's sheep. I loved you in our country dance with the vase and the fire screen. I believe I have always loved you, even in my dreams. 'But love is merely a madness, and, I tell you, deserves as well a dark house and a whip as madmen do.' I'll not keep you to such a rash promise, when being Mrs. Charles de Dagonet means being the wife of an adventurer."

"There is nothing wrong with being Mrs. de Dagonet, when it means being mistress of Lion Court, though, is there?"

His face changed, and he raised one eyebrow. Rapidly she told him of the arrival of Peter Higgins and the truth that they had learned about Millicent Trumble.

"The Marquis was rewriting his will as I left," she explained. "And Lion Court is to be yours as of today."

The emotions raced across his face: disgust, anger, relief. Yet when she finished he was helpless with laughter. "Poor foolish Milly! So it was Mr. Clay! Alas, poor Charlotte! She will never recover. Why did I not guess? To have been felled in the woods by pale Mr. Clay! It doesn't do much for my pride, does it?"

"He didn't do much for George's either, I gather," said Catherine wickedly, "when he replaced him in Milly's affections."

"Poor George. He never cared for Lion Court, but it meant a lot to him to be Lord of the Manor and Member of Parliament. So the Marquis forgives me my rattlepated ways? I trust Miss Ponsonby will still have George, when she learns about this."

"If she loves him, she will have him, whatever. She has plenty for them both to live on," stated Kate. "As I will gladly have you, if you will let me."

"Bold Kate! I don't think you could stop me! It is time to make you Mrs. de Dagonet in truth!" With a wicked laugh, he pulled her into his arms and began to kiss her very thoroughly on the lips.

Viscount Hammond and his seconds had already crept away. Lord Kendal turned to Lord Brooke. "It would seem that our friend no longer needs our assistance, my lord," he drawled. "This rain is uncommonly cold and damp, don't you know? And I believe it will be snow by lunch time. What do you say to breakfast, before we commence our journey back to London?"

With a delighted laugh, David Morris nodded his head. Thus, when Dagonet finally released Catherine, they were alone in the clearing except for Archibald Piggot, who tactfully gazed up into the treetops as he held the horses.

"Come, wife," said Dagonet. "We are wet to the skin. Mr. Piggot! Take those sorry jades back to London. Mrs. de Dagonet rides with me!"

Archibald saluted, mounted one of the horses, took the other by the bridle, and led him away. Dagonet led Catherine over to the gray thoroughbred, who stood nervously under a tree, and tossed her into the saddle. Springing up behind her, he turned his horse's head in the direction of Jermyn Street. Held securely against his chest, she relaxed into his arms, as the powerful horse bounded away.

* * *

They were soaked and half-frozen by the time they entered the simple bedchamber at Dagonet's lodgings. He brought her a towel, and, pulling out the pins, she began to rub at her hair.

"Were there really tons of lovers?"

He laughed and pulled her to him. Through his wet shirt, she could feel the fine fire of his skin. "Whoever said that?"

"Annie. A quote from our maid Polly."

"Enough, I should hope, that I shall know what I'm doing." Catherine felt herself blush, but she could not stop her hands from running up his strong back. His green eyes smiled into hers. "Do you mind? There has been no one since I met you, which strikes me now as extremely odd."

She laughed back up at him. She had no doubt that he was telling the truth, but surely he owed her something for letting her believe him indifferent for so long?

"Then what about the hairpins?" she said.

"What hairpins?" he replied at last, when he lifted his mouth from hers.

It took a great deal of concentration to reply at all, since his beautiful fingers were caressing the side of her face and neck. "When we came back from Whitechapel, there were some here, on the dresser."

His laugh was filled with genuine delight. "I can hardly believe, sweet Kate, that you couldn't recognize your own hairpins! I managed to slip some in my pocket, you see, after relieving your hair of their offending presence in the alley, and I set them in here while you warmed yourself at the fire. The comb, alas, was my own!"

"You deliberately deceived me!"

"How else," he said softly, "could I possibly keep us apart?"

It was clear from her expression that she had long ago forgiven him. "Then you make no plea at all? Can't you even give me a suitable quote from the poets?"

He ran his hands through the long, russet strands of her hair. Though the emerald gaze was alight still with laughter, there was something else there that made her heart sing in her breast. "Dear Kate, I am defenseless before you. I should plead guilty to anything you say. As for the poets, there is no verse in the language that could express what I feel."

Catherine had no idea that what happened between a man and a woman could express love with such an exquisite music of pleasure and delight. She felt herself peeled of her defenses, layer upon layer, until her innermost self was revealed to his care, but he gave back of himself in equal measure: passion tempered with grace; power with subtle restraint; intensity with wit and with poetry. But what else could she expect from Devil Dagonet?

Some hours later, Catherine lazily sat up. The sheets slipped away from her back, and her tumbled hair fell around her breasts and shoulders, but she felt no false modesty. He reached up and pulled her back into his embrace.

"Sweet Kate," he said gently. "Never leave me." She nestled against his firm chest.

"I wish we hadn't waited so long, Charles," she sighed.

He traced her lip with his finger, and kissed her. *"La patience est amère,"* he breathed softly, *"mais son fruit est doux."*

It was an old French saying: "Patience is bitter, but its fruit is sweet."

"If I'd had any idea how sweet," she said shyly, "I could never have been so patient."

Jean Ewing grew up in the English countryside in a Georgian house steeped in the romance of history. There were regular visits to Cornwall and with her father's family in the Highlands of Scotland. After completing her M. A. degree at the University of Edinburgh, she came to America and fell in love. She and her husband live in a mountain valley with a cat who likes to take showers and two horses who are often more full of themselves than they should be. Jean returns to England frequently to visit her family, who generously help research historical details. The Regency period, with its appreciation for honor, gallantry, and wit, is a particular favorite of hers. She sincerely hopes that the reader enjoys the company of Charles de Dagonet as much as she did while creating him.

ZEBRA REGENCIES
ARE
THE TALK OF THE TON!

A REFORMED RAKE (4499, $3.99)
by Jeanne Savery

After governess Harriet Cole helped her young charge flee to France—and the designs of a despicable suitor, more trouble soon arrived in the person of a London rake. Sir Frederick Carrington insisted on providing safe escort back to England. Harriet deemed Carrington more dangerous than any band of brigands, but secretly relished matching wits with him. But after being taken in his arms for a tender kiss, she found herself wondering—*could* a lady find love with an irresistible rogue?

A SCANDALOUS PROPOSAL (4504, $4.99)
by Teresa DesJardien

After only two weeks into the London season, Lady Pamela Premington has already received her first offer of marriage. If only it hadn't come from the *ton's* most notorious rake, Lord Marchmont. Pamela had already set her sights on the distinguished Lieutenant Penford, who had the heroism and honor that made him the ideal match. Now she had to keep from falling under the spell of the seductive Lord so she could pursue the man more worthy of her love. Or was he?

A LADY'S CHAMPION (4535, $3.99)
by Janice Bennett

Miss Daphne, art mistress of the Selwood Academy for Young Ladies, greeted the notion of ghosts haunting the academy with skepticism. However, to avoid rumors frightening off students, she found herself turning to Mr. Adrian Carstairs, sent by her uncle to be her "protector" against the "ghosts." Although, Daphne would accept no interference in her life, she *would* accept aid in exposing any spectral spirits. What she never expected was for Adrian to expose the secret wishes of her hidden heart . . .

CHARITY'S GAMBIT (4537, $3.99)
by Marcy Stewart

Charity Abercrombie reluctantly embarks on a London season in hopes of making a suitable match. However she cannot forget the mysterious Dominic Castille—and the kiss they shared—when he fell from a tree as she strolled through the woods. Charity does not know that the dark and dashing captain harbors a dangerous secret that will ensnare them both in its web—leaving Charity to risk certain ruin and losing the man she so passionately loves . . .